THE CHRISTMAS PROPOSAL

What Reviewers Say About Lisa Moreau's Work

Lovebirds

"Lisa Moreau writes the most appealing characters, with a gentleness and understanding that I've yet to find in another author. Her stories are so romantic, but when things get hot she knows just what buttons to press. I loved seeing how the relationship between Emily and Sydney developed. It was sweet and sexy but also very empowering. I really enjoyed this story, as I have everything I've read by this author. I can highly recommend *Love Birds*."
—*Kitty Kat's Book Review Blog*

"*Lovebirds* by Lisa Moreau is a totally adorable romance that I had a hard time putting down. …This is a very gentle, lovely story. It was super easy to sink into and made for perfect escapism at the end of a couple of long work days. Lisa Moreau's getting stronger from book to book, so I can't wait to see what she has in store for us next."—*Lesbian Review*

"This is a light, funny and entertaining read based on an original idea with the beautiful setting of Ojai valley in California. As she did in The Butterfly Whisperer, Ms. Moreau describes nature skillfully. The dialogues are funny and witty, the main characters are lovable and their chemistry is spot-on."—*Lez Review Books*

"*Lovebirds* by Lisa Moreau is a delightfully fun, syrupy sweet opposites attract romance. …*Lovebirds* is an endearing story that had me captured to the very last page. I loved the spark between the two mains and the dialogue between them was witty and fun. This is a good romance with a little something extra to set it apart."
—*Romantic Reader Blog*

Picture Perfect

"This is a witty, entertaining and thoroughly enjoyable light-hearted romance. It's extremely well written and edited, a wonderful and well developed cast of characters, excellent dialogue, extremely funny at times and with a warmth and humour throughout. It's my first from this author but definitely won't be my last, I thoroughly enjoyed it."—*Lesbian Reading Room*

"*Picture Perfect* has a light, breezy feel to it, making it an excellent beach read. It's sweet, sexy, and a lot of fun with characters I enjoyed and a romance that gave me a happy sigh!"—*Lesbian Review*

"This novel makes me think summer read, lying on the beach, with book in one hand and Mai Tai in the other. Another great novel by Lisa Moreau. Her novels just keep getting better and it leaves me desperate for what comes next. 5 Stars."—*Les Rêveur*

"*Picture Perfect* is a charming romance between two equally yummy main characters. I loved the setting and the wonderful descriptions of Catalina. The family dynamic was compelling and I liked how Olive became a part of it. I was enthralled by this story."
—*Kitty Kat's Book Review Blog*

The Butterfly Whisperer

"This was a beautifully written novel by Lisa Moreau that tells the story of unrequited childhood love. ...When Jordan and Sophie finally got round to expressing their love, you could feel the tension and the genuine love..."—*Les Rêveur*

"*The Butterfly Whisperer* is a lovely heart-warming story of two women who come back into each other's lives after ten years and find that the feelings they once had have not changed. ...The town of Monarch was wonderful and I loved the characters inhabiting it. ...There was a warmth and a feeling of community and I wanted Jordan to see that these things were more important than her Hollywood lifestyle."—*Kitty Kat's Book Review Blog*

"[A] fast and easy read, very lighthearted. …The sex was written with taste and beauty, definitely romantic."—*Artistic Bent*

"*The Butterfly Whisperer* by Lisa Moreau is a lovely romance with a bunch of my favourite themes all in one book. It has friends becoming lovers, an ice queen gets thawed, and it's a second chance love story. It even has the right amount of delicious angst to keep the pages turning. …I had a great time reading it and I'm looking forward to seeing what Lisa Moreau has in store for us next." —*Lesbian Review*

"*The Butterfly Whisperer* was just what I needed after a long week of craziness that just won't quit. A great escape, that didn't overthink what it really was, two girls with a life-long bond that even after ten years of separation, the love was still there." —*Romantic Reader Blog*

Love on the Red Rocks

"This was a lovely read, immersive and beautiful. Thoroughly recommended!"—*Inked Rainbow Reads*

"*Love on the Red Rocks* by Lisa Moreau is a very nice book for the author's first novel. It was engaging and entertained me as a standard romance novel kind of way. The best thing about this book, it is full of likable, fun characters."—*Romantic Reader Blog*

"When I read this book I had no idea it was a debut novel because it was written so well. The story had me hooked from chapter one."—*Les Rêveur*

Visit us at www.boldstrokesbooks.com

By the Author

Love on the Red Rocks

The Butterfly Whisperer

Picture Perfect

Lovebirds

A Moment in Time

The Christmas Proposal

THE CHRISTMAS PROPOSAL

by

Lisa Moreau

2021

THE CHRISTMAS PROPOSAL

ISBN 13: 978-1-63555-648-3

This Trade Paperback Original Is Published By
Bold Strokes Books, Inc.
P.O. Box 249
Valley Falls, NY 12185

First Edition: December 2021

CREDITS
EDITOR: SHELLEY THRASHER
PRODUCTION DESIGN: SUSAN RAMUNDO
COVER DESIGN BY TAMMY SEIDICK

Acknowledgments

Radclyffe, I was a fan of your writing long before I signed a contract with your amazing publishing company, Bold Strokes Books. Thank you for allowing me to continue to reach a large audience with my stories and investing in your authors through education, advertising, and more.

Sandy Lowe, you must have some incredible juggling skills considering everything you do as senior editor. I appreciate all your hard work and particularly your input with my book proposals. You always know the right questions to ask and the suggestions that make it a stronger story.

Shelley Thrasher, my editor, this is the sixth book we've worked on together. I've learned so much from you and appreciate your gentle demeanor. You make the editing process less scary and *almost* pain-free. You're a sharp woman who knows her craft and I trust you implicitly.

Holly Stratimore, you're not only a fellow Bold Strokes Books author but also a great friend. I owe you big time for being a beta reader on this book. You improved it greatly! Thank you for your time and input. You have a generous, kind heart.

Judi, thank you for brainstorming with me and giving me the idea to write about a proposal. You're my favorite biggest fan and I love you.

Dedication

For my mom

Thank you for giving me thirty-one
perfectly magical Christmases.

Chapter One

Endings and Beginnings

Whoever said dating your boss is a rotten idea was wise. Too bad that person wasn't Grace Dawson. In Grace's defense, it wasn't something she'd planned. She certainly didn't think that at age twenty-seven she'd be working as an event director for a video-game company and shagging her boss. She'd had dreams for her life. Big ones. But things don't always work out the way you intend.

It was a typical manic Monday at Worth Entertainment when Grace sat across from Christina Worth's desk and watched her furiously pound on the computer like she was repeatedly punching someone in the nose. Talk about intensity. Surely, Christina had to replace her keyboard every week, considering the beating it was taking. Henrietta would know, but she'd quit, which wasn't a shocker considering she was the third personal assistant who'd abruptly left in just two months. She took a bite of turkey sandwich and sighed. For once, it'd be nice to spend a little quality time with her girlfriend without work interfering. Their dates had been reduced to lunches in Christina's office or a quick latte break at Sacred Grounds, Christina's favorite coffee shop. She couldn't remember the last time they'd gone to dinner, much less slept together. That's what she got for dating someone who owned a successful company.

She wiped a dollop of mustard from the corner of her mouth with a napkin and recalled the first time she and Christina had hooked up at The Interactive Forum trade show in Dallas. After twelve hours of manning the booth, the two of them were having late-night TexMex. Sleeping with the boss was the last thing on her mind, but she'd be lying if she didn't say she'd been smitten. Heck, anyone would be. Christina was soap-opera stunning. You know, one of those gorgeous women with thick, blond hair past her shoulders, amazing blue eyes, and perfect proportions. If Christina was walking down the sidewalk, men—and women—would run headfirst into streetlamps. Seriously. It had happened before. After dinner, Christina, who was acting all suave and protective-like, had escorted Grace to her room. When they reached the door, Christina peered down with those dreamy blue eyes and said, "If kissing you is wrong, I don't wanna be right." Yeah. Corny as hell. Maybe it was the three frozen margaritas she'd had with dinner, but she totally fell for it. One year later and they were still going strong.

She popped the last potato chip into her mouth and glanced around Christina's office, making tsk-tsk sounds under her breath. Not one Christmas decoration in sight. She made a mental note to get a small tree and a few decorations. There'd probably be a lot of hemming and hawing like last year, but it seemed a sin not to have a little festivity. Grace's family would have a collective heart attack if they knew about her girlfriend's lackadaisical attitude toward the holidays. They lived in Mistletoe Mountain, which was a year-round Christmas village that overlooked Los Angeles.

She took a swig of water and glanced at her watch. Darn. She had to get back to work, and they'd barely said two words to each other. "Aren't you hungry?" She looked at Christina's uneaten sandwich.

"I need to finish this email." Christina spoke without even a pause in typing. "You can have it."

She rolled her eyes. Like she could eat two turkey sandwiches. She could, though, eat two cookies. She snatched the chocolate-chip delectable off Christina's plate and took a big bite. It felt so freeing not to have to count calories or worry about getting fat like she had when she was younger. She was at least twenty pounds overweight and couldn't have cared less.

"Is that about *Egyptian Tomb*?" She popped the remaining cookie into her mouth. Personally, she had zero interest in video games—not that she'd ever mention that to Christina, of course. She didn't see the point in living vicariously through made-up characters. "Will it be done in time for The Interactive Forum?"

"It better be." Christina groaned, reading what was probably a scathing dissertation to the developers.

"Speaking of the trade show, do you remember what happened in Big D last year?" She grinned and lowered her voice several octaves to sound seductive. "I'll never forget our first kiss."

She'd read somewhere once that the key to happiness is not having expectations of others. Not having mastered that advice yet, she was disappointed when Christina didn't even give her a sideways glance. Was it too much to ask that her girlfriend jump out of the chair, whisk her off her feet, and deliver a long, passionate kiss? Something between them had to change. Their relationship was great when work didn't get in the way, which, unfortunately, was all the time. They wouldn't have a problem if they lived together. If anything, they'd certainly see each other a lot more.

Christina spun around in her chair. "I'm sorry, Grace. I've totally been ignoring you."

"You have." She frowned, not even trying to hide her irritation. "Maybe there's a solution."

"What do you mean?"

Her heart raced, and her palms were sweaty, like she'd just run a 5K. Obviously, she hadn't learned anything from her last two girlfriends. They'd promptly dumped her like a bag of bricks at the mere mention of shacking up. No U-Haul-loving lesbians in her past. Of course, she'd have to fall for the distant, independent type. Surely Christina would be different, though. They'd been together a year. Most lesbians move in with each other after two months.

She straightened her spine and squared her shoulders in an attempt to look confident. After swallowing hard once, she said, "We could move in together."

"Riiight." Christina snorted.

Grace furrowed her brow. Was that sarcasm?

Christina looked at her cell phone when it dinged with an incoming text and burst out in an uncharacteristic laugh. Grace drew her head back, surprised. Not that Christina wasn't the laughing kind, but she never indulged in a slap-your-knee-tears-running-down-your-cheeks sort of laugh.

"What's so funny?"

After at least a minute of rolling around like a hyena, Christina said, "Beryl is hilarious."

Beryl? The attorney? Granted, she'd had little interaction with Worth Entertainment's newest employee, but nothing about her screamed funny. In fact, just the opposite.

Still giggling, Christina leaned back in her chair. "What were you saying?"

She rested her elbows on the edge of the desk and intertwined her fingers. "We rarely see each other except at work. If we lived in the same house, we could spend more time together. I make the best ugly-Christmas-sweater cookies you've ever tasted. It's my mom's secret recipe."

All the color drained from Christina's face. "What do you mean?"

"They're cookies in the shape of sweaters and—"

"No...no." Christina frantically waved her hands in the air like she was trying to stop a minibus from running over her. "You were serious about moving in together?"

Grace wasn't getting her point across. She stood, walked around the desk, and sat on the edge in front of Christina. This should be a romantic moment, one where she could reach out and stroke her girlfriend's cheek or give her a kiss.

"Think about it," she said. "We can share the rent, expenses, everything." Christina was rich as hell, but she did love a bargain. "And we could share the bed." She leaned in for a kiss and almost toppled over into Christina's lap when her chair rolled back.

"Whoa." Christina gawked at Grace with the same horrified expression she got every April when taxes were due. "Where's all this coming from?"

She righted herself and adjusted her blazer. "Don't you think it's time we take the next step in our relationship?"

Christina bolted out of the chair. "I'm not looking for a long-term commitment, and moving in together definitely falls into that category." She paced back and forth in front of the panoramic window overlooking Hollywood Boulevard.

"Hold on," she said. "You never said anything about not wanting a commitment."

Christina stopped and put her hands on her hips. "Before we slept together, I told you work is my life and marriage and the whole family thing isn't for me. I said I wasn't looking for anything serious."

Had someone turned on a fog machine in Grace's brain? She didn't recall any of that conversation, and why should she? It had been a year ago, and she'd been in a lust-filled haze at the time. Christina could have said she was an ax murderer, and she wouldn't have heard her.

"Did you think we'd just date forever?" She threw her arms into the air.

Christina rubbed her forehead. "Grace, you really need to ask yourself why you ever wanted to hook up with me in the first place. Did you think I'd change?"

She collapsed into Christina's chair as a strange sensation of déjà vu washed over her. This was the exact conversation she'd had with her last two girlfriends right before they'd broken up. Apparently, she was deaf, dumb, and blind when it came to women. Any fool could see Christina didn't want a committed relationship. She hadn't been a priority, and she'd been a first-class, romantic buffoon to think otherwise.

"I didn't mean to hurt you. I thought we were on the same page." Christina spoke in a softer tone than before.

The office door swung open, and Beryl rushed inside, glancing from Grace to Christina. "Oh. Sorry. I didn't mean to interrupt."

Fear flashed across Christina's eyes right before she went to the desk, grabbed a stack of papers, and shuffled them with trembling hands. What was the big deal? Everyone knew Grace and Christina were an item, and it wasn't like Beryl had caught her sitting in Christina's lap. Far from it.

Beryl inched closer, wobbling a bit in ten-inch heels. "Is this about the trade show in Dallas?" Her eyes widened, and her entire size-four body seemed to tense.

"No," Christina said much too quickly.

Beryl and Christina looked at each other as a silent knowingness passed between them. Grace's chest tightened. It was as though all the air had been sucked out of the office, and it grew thick, hot, which made it difficult to breathe. Every second that passed felt more uncomfortable than the last.

After what seemed like an eternity, Beryl pried her eyes away from Christina and focused on Grace. "I hope you don't mind missing The Interactive Forum this year."

Grace turned to Christina, who was tomato-red. "What's she talking about?"

Christina cleared her throat and stared at the space several inches above her head. "I thought it would be a good idea if Beryl went in your place. You know, to give her some exposure."

What? That made absolutely no sense whatsoever. Grace was the event director and never missed a trade show. Beryl was a lawyer, for Christ's sake. She had no reason to attend. She might be a little slow, but it was finally hitting her.

"You slept with her," she said, in a much-too-calm tone, considering the anger rising in her chest.

"I'll leave you two alone to talk." Beryl rushed out of the office and closed the door.

She looked around for the trash can, sure she was about to lose her turkey sandwich.

"I didn't have sex with Beryl." Christina crossed her arms over her chest, feet planted firmly on the floor.

"But you're going to, aren't you? At the same place where you first seduced me."

Christina huffed. "I wouldn't say seduced. You were a willing participant."

Fair enough, but she was in no mood to be fair. She glared up at Christina as she towered over her. "Tell me the truth."

Christina rubbed the back of her neck. "All right. Fine. Beryl and I have gone out a few times."

She bolted out of the chair, rolling it back so far it crashed into the keyboard. Christina peered over her shoulder, seemingly more concerned about the computer than Grace.

"Oh my God! I can't fault you for not wanting what I want in a relationship, but I most certainly did not think you were a cheater. Did you plan to tell me about you and Beryl?"

"Eventually. Yes."

"Unbelievable. I was thinking about us moving in together, and you were going to break up with me. I have to get out of here." She rushed past Christina and stopped when she grabbed her arm.

"I'm sorry. I didn't mean to hurt you."

She shook free and silently prayed to escape before she started crying, not wanting to give Christina the satisfaction of knowing how hurt she felt.

"I'm done with you and this company. I quit."

She bolted out the door, suddenly jobless and single.

It felt like a dream. Bridget Cartwright was about to open the door to Worth Entertainment and meet her idol, Christina Worth. And not just meet, but interview for a position as computer programmer at the best video-game company on the West Coast. The first time she'd heard about Christina was ten years ago when she was fifteen. *DCGamer* had done an article about her favorite video game at the time and mentioned that it was developed by a new and upcoming company. Since then, she'd kept tabs on everything Worth Entertainment had done. Most kids dream of moving to Hollywood to become a movie star. Not Bridget. She'd hoped that one day she'd work for Christina designing video games, which were such a large part of her life. In fact, on more than one occasion, they had saved her life.

She took a deep breath and pushed through the door, feeling uncharacteristically proud of herself. From the moment she was born, life had been a "rough bull ride at the rodeo," as they said in Texas. The fact that she had survived her childhood and was starting a new chapter proved she was a survivor. Strutting to the receptionist desk, she glanced around—not a soul in sight.

Unsure what to do, she sat in a nearby chair and placed her resume, which was in a brown leather portfolio, on her lap. Running her fingers over the soft, worn surface, she hoped Christina wouldn't notice the imperfections. More importantly, though, she hoped the sparse resume wouldn't send her into hysterics. Bridget had certificates in C++, Python, Java, you name it, but she didn't have a bachelor's degree like most computer programmers. She'd designed and developed dozens of video games and was only eight when she'd coded her first one. Unfortunately, she'd done all that in the solace of her bedroom and not at a corporation.

Staring at the nameplate on Christina's door, she tried to keep her right knee from bobbing up and down. She was nervous, like sick-to-her-stomach nervous. This was the chance of a lifetime, and she could potentially blow it with her lack of communication skills. Not that she disliked others, but she felt more comfortable in the companionship of a digital warrior fighting a dragon than she did flesh-and-blood humans. In a video game, she had the power to determine what happened, but with people, you never knew what you were going to get.

Her heart jumped into her throat when the office door opened and out walked a brunette dressed in a power suit and high heels. She should have worn something nicer than black pants, a white button-down shirt, and loafers. But then again, she could barely afford to pay the rent, much less go on a shopping spree at the Beverly Center. She was, after all, unemployed.

"Is anyone helping you?" the brunette asked.

"Yes. I mean…well, no. I was just waiting. I have an interview with Ms. Worth." The inside of her cheek stuck to her teeth, and the back of her throat felt like she'd swallowed a cactus. She really needed to pull it together. If she was this nervous with a stranger, what would she be like with Christina?

"Nice to meet you. I'm Beryl." The woman stuck out her hand.

She stood, wiped sweaty palms on her thigh, and shook. "I'm um…uhh…" *What the hell is my name?* "Bridget Cartwright," she said, much too loud.

Beryl smirked, no doubt finding humor in her uneasiness.

"The receptionist is gone." She pointed over her shoulder at the empty desk.

Beryl nodded. "Henrietta is no longer with the company. I'd get Christina for you, but…" She looked back at the office door with a pained expression. "She's in a meeting right now."

Of course. Another interview. Her confidence plummeted even farther. The competition was probably unbeatable. Every game-obsessed programmer would want a shot at working for Worth Entertainment.

"Why don't you take a seat, and I'm sure Christina will be with you soon. Good luck," Beryl said and walked away.

A chill ran up and down her spine. The way she'd said "good luck" had sounded almost eerie, like she was about to spend the night in a haunted house. She lowered herself back into the chair and chewed on her bottom lip. Only one thing could relax her. She took her cell phone out and opened *OceanFront*, which was a serene game where she could swim with the dolphins and sail across the ocean.

She hadn't gotten very far when a woman, probably no more than five-two, shot out of Christina's office and slammed the door hard. Her face was flushed, her chest heaved, and she was practically seething. Despite her sweet, all-American appearance of blond hair and blue—or maybe it was green—eyes, she looked like she was ready to grab a bull by the horns and wrangle him to the ground. Bridget's money would be on the woman, not the bull. What in the world had happened in the interview to upset her so much?

Bridget's eyebrows shot up when the woman suddenly burst into tears. This was a highly unexpected, and undesirable, turn of events. She shifted in her seat, wanting nothing more than to hide behind the ficus tree in the corner. One of the great things about computer programming is that it's based on logic. You tell the computer a sequence of steps to perform to achieve a desired result. That's pretty much it. No magic, no sorcery. Just logic. This hysterical person standing before her was not logical.

Fear shot through her gut when the bloodshot-eyed woman looked directly at her. She dropped her chin and desperately pressed buttons on her cell phone, pretending to be totally engrossed in getting her sailboat ready for an imaginary trip to Paradise Island. Surely the woman could see how busy she was and take that as a sign she wanted no part of her dramatics.

"Crap!" The woman inhaled sharply and covered her mouth with her hand. She rushed toward Bridget and stood so close that her knees were pressed against the woman's legs. She flinched and shifted sideways in the chair.

"You have to help me." The woman's eyes were the size of big-rig hubcaps.

In a last-ditch effort to avoid what was happening, she looked to the left and right, hoping the woman was speaking to someone other than herself. Of course, no one else was there. Maybe that Beryl-woman would come back and save the day.

"I left my purse in the office. You have to get it for me."

"What? No way." She shook her head.

Oh, God. Here came the tears again. They spilled out from the rims of her eyes like a waterfall. She cursed her heart for melting at the sight. The woman looked so distraught, so desperate. From here she could see that her eyes were indeed green and absolutely stunning, like two turquoise jewels glistening in the sunlight. So much prettier than Bridget's boring brown.

"I can't go back in there. I don't want her to see me crying." She was practically pleading.

She felt bad for the woman. Obviously, her interview had gone terribly wrong, which was concerning . If her meeting had ended in tears, how would Bridget's go?

"I'm not going to burst into Ms. Worth's office and make the worst first impression ever," she said adamantly.

"My purse is in one of the guest chairs." The woman tugged on her sleeve, which was probably wrinkling it. "It'll take two seconds. Pop in and out."

Maybe it was those sad eyes and desperate plea, but she surprised herself by standing and allowing the woman to guide her toward Christina's office.

She stopped and looked down into a pretty, albeit distraught, face. "Why don't you get it?"

"I can't…just…I can't."

She looked at the door, wondering what was so horrible in there. Maybe she was about to walk into a bloody crime scene and become an accomplice.

She jerked her head back to the woman. "How do I know that's your purse and you're not asking me to steal it?"

The woman sighed and glared at Bridget like that was the most ridiculous thing ever. "Have a heart. It's one simple favor."

She gritted her teeth, knowing there was only one way to get rid of her. She lightly tapped on the door with her knuckles.

The woman placed a hand on her left hip. "Seriously?" She made a fist, banged three times hard, and quickly stepped aside to get out of the line of sight.

Fifteen seconds later, the door swung open, and she was face-to-face with her idol. Christina looked exactly like she did on the cover of gaming magazines and TV interviews, except even more impressive.

"What?" she asked, sounding irritated.

"I…umm…someone left their purse in your office."

A mixture of confusion and annoyance crossed Christina's face. "Who are you?"

"Actually, I'm here for an interview." She held up her brown portfolio, like Christina would know her resume was inside.

"Oh. Right. Come on in."

She followed and spotted the infamous missing purse in one of the guest chairs. She should have ignored it, but she couldn't get that crying woman's face out of her mind. So, she snatched it and said, "I'll just hand this to the woman in the reception area."

Understanding filled Christina's eyes when she looked at the handbag. She took that as permission to return the item, so she rushed out and shoved it into the woman's hands.

"Thank you. I owe you one." She clutched the bag under her arm and hurried out the door.

Bridget chuckled to herself, finding the woman's last words odd. They hadn't exchanged phone numbers, or even names, for that matter. How in the world would she ever repay the favor when they'd never see each other again?

CHAPTER TWO

Sacred Grounds

One year later

Driving in elf shoes wasn't easy. The pointy toes kept getting caught on the brake pedal, and they were so tight Grace's feet were numb from lack of circulation. What she wouldn't do to make a client happy. After the breakup with Christina, she was lucky enough to nab a new job within a month. Considering she was sour on the love-thing at the time, it was surprising she'd accepted a position at Tie the Knot, a wedding-proposal-planning company. At first, it was hard to plaster on a smile when it came to romance, but after a while she grew to enjoy helping starry-eyed men and women propose. It was certainly more exciting than video games. She'd done everything from organizing flash mobs to doing treasure hunts. Most of the time the job was fun, except today.

She stopped at a red light and looked at her cell phone when it rang. Normally, she loved talking to Betsy, but rehashing her morning was the last thing she wanted to do. By the fifth ring, though, she felt guilty for dissing her big sister.

"Hi, Betsy."

"Hey. How are you?"

"Great!" She cringed, knowing her response had sounded much too cheerful to be believable.

"Gracie, I know better than that. Tell me what happened."

Betsy would make a great mom. Her tone had been the perfect mixture of censure yet compassion.

"Well, let's see…I'm wearing an itchy red and green elf suit and spent the morning helping a nervous guy dressed as Santa propose to his girlfriend at the coffee shop where they first met. Just another normal day for me." She took a sharp right into the lot of Tie the Knot.

"That's not what I meant, and you know it. What was it like being in Sacred Grounds again?"

Since breaking up with Christina, Grace hadn't entered or even driven past that particular café. It was Christina's favorite coffee shop since it was the only place within a two-hundred-mile radius that served Kopi Luwak, one of the rarest, most expensive coffee beans in the world.

"I'd love to say it didn't bother me, but I wanted to puke the moment I walked in." She circled the lot and frowned at the lack of available parking spaces. December was a busy time for proposals, which was great, except when it came to parking.

"That's understandable," Betsy said. "It was bound to bring up memories."

"I was just surprised when all those feelings of insecurity and not being good enough resurfaced. I thought I had let all that go."

"You have to be gentle with yourself. You've come a long way, and now you have a clearer understanding of who you are and the type of woman you want to be with. You won't allow yourself to settle again."

"You're right." She slammed on her brakes and flipped the blinker when she saw a man getting into his car. "Let's talk about a brighter topic. How's my godchild doing?"

"Kicking up a storm right now."

She pictured her sister placing a hand on her stomach. That kid was damn lucky to have Betsy as a future mom. It still burned her up how some of the old-fashioned codgers in Mistletoe Mountain looked down on Betsy for doing artificial insemination. According to them, it wasn't a family unless the child had a mother *and* father.

"Wish I could feel him…or her…kicking." She immediately regretted the comment, knowing where it would lead.

"Why don't you come this weekend?" Surprisingly, Betsy sounded hopeful. You'd think after all these years she'd give up trying to convince Grace to visit.

She did feel terrible about missing out on her sister's pregnancy, birthdays, holidays, everything, but going home wasn't an option. She loved her family, but she'd been back to Mistletoe Mountain only once since leaving ten years ago, which was one time too many. She was focused on the future, and being in Mistletoe Mountain would be like taking a step back to a time better left forgotten.

She pulled into the available spot and cut off the engine. "Work is insane right now. I can't take off, especially when I'm trying to impress Melanie so I can get that promotion."

"Are you serious about moving to Maui? That's so far away."

She sighed. They'd been over this a gazillion times. "This is a chance to become a manager and run my own office."

"I know," Betsy said, sounding dejected. "I miss you."

Her shoulders sagged. "Me, too. Listen. I just got to work. I'll talk to you later."

Planning proposals hadn't been Grace's first career choice, but since her lifelong dream had gone belly-up, she was determined to be successful at something. Besides, it was an opportunity to get out from underneath her boss's thumb. Penelope was condescending, rude, and seemed to find great pleasure in dismissing every creative idea she had. Whenever possible, she'd overstep Penelope and go straight to Melanie, owner of Tie the Knot, who was much more amenable.

She rested the back of her head against the seat and closed her eyes. She needed a minute to herself to absorb the morning's events. When she'd first found out the proposal would take place at Sacred Grounds, she'd tried to get out of it. Penelope had gone ballistic, since no one else had been available to take over the client, which meant they would have lost a boatload of money. What bothered her most about the whole thing was that she didn't think anything about Christina could still affect her. In fact, before she stepped foot in the coffee shop that morning, she'd felt emotionally healthier than ever before.

Their breakup had spurred Grace on a year-long journey of self-realization about how screwed up she really was. At first, she'd blamed Christina for everything, but after a ton of relationship books and the cheapest therapy she could find, she'd realized that no one was to blame but herself. Christina was a scoundrel, for sure, but she was the one who had settled for something less than what she wanted in a partner.

The real kicker was that she'd subconsciously dated women who couldn't commit because *she* was the one scared of getting close to someone. All those years of blaming ex-girlfriends when it was really her. Well, no more. After a year of being single, she was ready to attract her forever partner, and no way was she going to fall back into old patterns. This morning was nothing but a small setback and even more reason she should look to the future and forget the past.

A tap against the window caused her to open her eyes and see Melanie peering into the car. Immediately, she sprang into action, grabbing her bag and opening the door. All she needed was for the owner of Tie the Knot to think she was sleeping on the job.

"Are you okay?" Concern filled Melanie's eyes.

"Yes. Totally fine." She hoped that sounded genuine.

"How was the proposal this morning?"

She fell into step beside Melanie as they walked down the sidewalk. "Everything went smashingly well. The bride-to-be was shocked and happily accepted."

"And the location didn't cause any issues?" Melanie looked at her out of the corner of her eye. "Penelope said something about you trying to get out of the job."

Her hands tightened into fists. Of course Penelope would tattle on her. "No problems whatsoever. How was your Maui trip?" She not only wanted to change the subject but also get the scoop on the new office.

"Everything is on track to begin operations in March."

"That's great. Any idea when you'll make a decision about the office manager?" That was a legitimate question, considering the person would have to relocate soon, which she was more than happy to do.

"You should know something in the next few days." Melanie stopped several feet from the entrance to Tie the Knot and faced her. "I really value your contributions to the company, Grace, but someone with more seniority also applied."

Her spirits deflated. "Of course. I understand."

"Don't look so defeated." Melanie smiled. "Just keep up the good work, and I'll let you know soon."

Despite not being with the company a full year, she felt like she had a good shot at the promotion. She had double the client load of anyone else, always came up with the most creative proposals, and had the highest ratings. Even though she butted heads with Penelope, Melanie seemed to appreciate her, which was the most important thing.

She slowly smiled. She was no stranger to competition. Winning was in her blood. All she had to do was work her butt off and do anything and everything she could to impress Melanie.

The strong scent of freshly brewed coffee assaulted Bridget's nostrils when she opened the door to Sacred Grounds. Personally, she never touched the stuff, but her boss, Christina, loved it. She frowned when she saw how many customers were waiting to order, sure she'd be late getting back to work. With no other choice, she filed in line and released a loud, exasperated sigh.

The woman in front of her turned. "Long line, huh?"

"No kidding. They're usually not this busy."

"They were closed this morning for an event. It was a proposal." The woman beamed.

"A business proposal? That's weird." She wrinkled her brow.

"No, silly." The woman laughed. "A wedding proposal."

She cringed, embarrassed. Anyone else would have gotten that, but love wasn't really foremost on her mind.

"I heard the man dressed up like Santa. Isn't that romantic?" The woman stared dreamily into space.

She surveyed the café, noting the abundance of holiday decorations. Poinsettias, twinkling lights, an inflatable Santa, and a humongous tree decked out in big red balls and silver tinsel. Talk about going overboard. Funny she hadn't noticed when she'd first walked in, but then again, she had a blind eye to anything Christmas since it was her least favorite time of the year.

"Of course, I wouldn't want a *man* proposing to me. If you know what I mean." The woman winked.

Was she flirting? Bridget wasn't good at detecting these sorts of things, but it certainly seemed that way.

"Do you live around here?" The woman inched forward.

"No, but I work down the street."

"Have you been to the new sushi place on the corner? Maybe we could meet there sometime."

Okay, she was definitely flirting. Not that she minded, but she didn't have time to date. Work took up the majority of the day, and at night she was busy developing video games. At age twenty-six she'd never had a serious relationship. In fact, the longest she'd dated anyone was a few months. As far as she was concerned, though, she was better off being alone.

"Thanks, but I'll have to pass."

"Don't tell me. You're already taken." The woman shook her head, looking disappointed. "Do you mind me asking what nationality you are? You have very striking looks."

Well, that was a loaded question, and one she had no idea how to answer. So, she went with honesty. "I have no idea."

The woman cast her a puzzled look, and she couldn't really blame her. Most everyone in the world knew who they were and where they came from. Not Bridget.

After ordering, the woman gave her a wave and walked out the door with cup in hand. She approached the counter, requested a large coffee, and paid. While the barista poured the drink, a card on the counter caught her eye. She picked it up and read it to herself. *Tie the Knot. Grace Dawson. Executive Wedding Proposal Planner.* That was probably the company that had done the event that morning. Thank goodness she didn't have a job as a love guru. Good to know there were worse things than being Christina's personal assistant. She tossed the card back onto the counter, took the coffee, and rushed back to work.

Things hadn't exactly gone as planned last year in the interview with Christina. There'd been a mix-up, and Christina thought Bridget had applied for the assistant post, considering the computer programmer had already been hired. Call her crazy, but when Christina offered her the job, she jumped at it. Not only was she unemployed, but she couldn't pass up an opportunity to work beside her role model no matter the duties. Not that she regretted her decision, but for the past year she'd been nothing but Christina's gofer. She admired her boss's intellect, creativity, and business sense, but she was beyond ready to do something more than fetch dry cleaning, make Christina's vacation plans, and a host of other tasks.

She breezed into Worth Entertainment and stopped when she saw Christina's closed door, which was a sign she didn't want to be disturbed. She was probably in a meeting or, more than likely, with Beryl. Normally, a boss and employee relationship would be an HR lawsuit just waiting to happen, but they seemed like the perfect couple. Talk around the office was that Christina was quite the player before meeting Beryl, but she had never witnessed that side of her.

She sat at her desk and grumbled under her breath, upset that Christina's coffee was getting cold, which was a surefire way of ticking her off. Logging into her computer, she clicked on an email that had "Going Away Party" as the title. She hated office celebrations. Not only did she have to organize everything, but she always felt out of place. Socializing, particularly in large groups, wasn't her thing. As expected, she was being asked to order the cake and decorate the community room. When she reached the reason for the party, a tingle cascaded down her spine. Guy was leaving the company. He was the person who'd been hired for the computer-programmer position she had interviewed for last year. Or at least the one she'd thought she was interviewing for. Maybe this was her chance to move up in the company.

When Beryl strolled out of Christina's office, leaving the door wide open, Bridget's exhilaration quickly turned to fear. What if Christina didn't want to give her the position? Or, worse, what if she got it and then tanked? Maybe she wasn't good enough to be a successful programmer. Secretly, she'd been relieved to be hired as a personal assistant. At least she knew how to do that.

She retrieved her wallet and slipped a piece of paper out. Carefully, she unfolded the weathered note she'd kept for over twenty years and silently read it, as she'd done a million times before.

Her name is Bridget. It means strength.

As a newborn, she'd been placed on the steps of a church on Christmas Eve with the note pinned to the blanket. Although she had no proof, she'd always imagined her birth mother had written it and left her there. That small item, along with her name, was the only thing her mother had ever given her. She had no idea who the woman was or why she'd abandoned her baby, but at least she'd gotten one thing right. Bridget was indeed strong. With a renewed sense of confidence, she tucked the paper back into the wallet and marched into Christina's office with purpose.

"There you are," Christina said, without looking up from whatever she was writing. A few moments later, she regarded Bridget. "Where's my coffee?"

"It's on my desk. I'll pop it in the microwave and be right back."

"Don't bother." Christina jotted down a few more notes.

Don't bother? But that was her most favorite coffee in the entire world. She had used half her lunch break to stand in line waiting to order it.

"Have a seat. I want to discuss a special project with you." Christina reclined and rested her hands on her stomach.

She lowered herself into the guest chair and studied her boss. She looked different. Maybe a new hairdo or glasses. No. Something else. That's when it hit her. Christina was smiling. And not just any smile, but a big, sappy one that took up her entire face so completely she was almost unrecognizable.

"I have what is probably the most important task I've ever given you." Christina's face lit up even more. "I need you to..." She stopped and peered over the desk. "Where's your pad and pen?"

She looked down at her empty hands. She'd never entered the office without note-taking supplies before.

"Are you okay?" Christina asked. "You seem a little out of it."

Her stomach dropped. It was now or never. Hopefully, she wouldn't regret this. "Actually, there is something I'd like to discuss."

"Sounds serious." Christina rested her chin on her hand.

She shifted in her seat and said, "I want Guy's job." She hadn't planned to blurt it out, but nervousness got the better of her.

Christina's smile fell away. "What was that?"

"If you remember, a year ago when you hired me as your assistant, I was applying for Guy's position. Don't get me wrong," she said when Christina's eyes narrowed. "I was thankful for the opportunity, and I've learned a lot about the company, but I'm a computer programmer."

She felt odd saying that last part. Sitting in her studio apartment developing video games until midnight didn't necessarily make her a professional programmer.

"I see." Christina snatched a pen and tapped it repeatedly on the desk. "And you think you're qualified to be his replacement?"

"Yes, ma'am," she said, hoping that assertion was true. "My whole life has revolved around video games. I've designed and created them since I was a kid, and I'm highly proficient in coding using C++."

Christina raised an eyebrow. She had her now. To create an advanced video game in terms of performance and graphics, writing code from scratch—while more cumbersome and time consuming—resulted in a customized, unique product. Guy knew zilch about writing code, which was probably the reason he was leaving...or maybe being asked to leave.

"Here's an example of a game I created." She pulled out a cell phone, propped her elbow on the desk to keep her hand from shaking, and selected one. "This is geared toward kids," she said, thinking she should have demonstrated something else since Worth Entertainment targeted adults.

Christina snatched the phone out of her hand. "You did that?"

"Yes. I developed the characters, story line, everything."

"Have you done any other games for children?"

"Dozens. But I'm not limited to that area alone."

"I've been thinking about coming out with a line for kids," Christina said, more to herself than Bridget. "Where did you say you worked before?"

"I was in school studying computer programming." She wasn't about to admit that she'd been a checker at Walmart in Needville, Texas.

"You have a bachelor's or master's degree?" Christina asked, never taking her eyes off the screen.

"I have certificates in several programming languages."

"Corporate experience?"

"No, ma'am. After my studies, I moved to Los Angeles specifically to work for your company. I accepted the position as your assistant to get my foot in the door."

Christina slid the cell phone across the desk. "This is a competitive field, Bridget. See this?" She pointed to a stack of papers. "These are resumes from people with degrees and years of experience."

She winced. What made her think she could compete with the big boys? "I'm a reliable, dedicated worker and have always been willing to do anything you required. All I'm asking is for a chance to prove that I can take on a higher role in the company."

After several moments of silence, Christina finally spoke. "Lord knows it's taken me long enough to find an assistant, but I certainly wouldn't want to hold back an employee. Fill out an application online, and I'd like to see more of your work."

A rush of adrenaline coursed through her, and she couldn't contain her smile. She hadn't expected things to go so well. "Thank you," she said and rushed to her feet, ready to submit the application.

"In the meantime, you're still my assistant, and I expect you to act as such." Christina's sharp tone prompted her to sit back down. "As I was saying, I have an important project for you."

"Of course. Whatever you need." She'd happily wash Christina's Lexus, cat-sit for the weekend, do just about anything if she knew a brighter future was on the horizon.

"I want you to plan my proposal to Beryl." A bright smile transformed Christina's face.

She had a flashback to Sacred Grounds, when she'd mistaken "proposal" to mean a business contract instead of marriage, but surely that wasn't the case here.

"You mean…you want me to draft a corporate contract?"

Christina laughed, just like the coffee-shop girl had. "It's a wedding proposal."

She stiffened all over. So many things were wrong with this proposition she didn't know where to start. Considering Christina was her boss, though, she had to tread lightly.

She cleared her throat. "Congratulations. But…umm…isn't that something you'd want to arrange yourself?"

Christina shook her head. "I'm far too busy to plan it by Christmas Eve."

She drew in a sharp breath. That was three weeks away.

"Beryl absolutely loves the holiday." Christina unlocked her desk drawer, took out a box, and opened it. She puffed out her chest as a satisfied smile crossed her face.

Bridget squinted from the glare of the humongous diamond under the fluorescent lights. She didn't know crap about jewelry, but that had to be at least three carats.

"That's gorgeous. I'm sure Beryl will love it." She smiled tightly. "Back to the proposal. This isn't really up my alley. I mean, I'd have no idea where you'd want to do it or—"

"Mistletoe Mountain." Christina snapped the box shut and placed it back in the drawer. "It's the perfect location. Beryl has been begging me to take her there."

Where the hell was Mistletoe Mountain? This was getting way out of hand. Christina had asked her to do some crazy things, but this was out of her league.

"Don't worry," Christina said, probably reading the fear on her face. "I trust you to come up with something amazing. Take Friday off to drive to Mistletoe Mountain and scope out the area. You can let me know the arrangements on Monday."

Bridget's eyes bugged out of her head. She couldn't plan this thing in three days. She had to get out of this, fast.

"It might be hard to get reservations on such short notice." She tried to keep her voice steady but had failed miserably.

Christina gave her a penetrating look. "Do whatever it takes to pull this off, Bridget. Make it classy, romantic, and Christmassy. Spare no expense. I'm counting on you."

The serious look on Christina's face made her throat tighten, so much so that all she could do was nod.

"That's all for now." Christina shooed her away.

She rose from the seat, shuffled toward the door, and stopped when she heard Christina's voice.

"Don't forget to submit that application. If all goes well with this project, I'll consider that promotion in the new year."

That had sounded like a threat. Screw up on the proposal, and she could kiss the computer-programmer position good-bye. When she got back to her desk, she collapsed into the chair and buried her face in her hands. This was the worst assignment ever. Christmas and love were two things she knew absolutely nothing about. She didn't have a clue where to start and only three days to do it. she felt like she was alone on a flimsy inflatable raft in the middle of the Pacific Ocean hundreds of miles from civilization. She had always prided herself on being independent—never one to ask for help—but right now she felt like writing a big SOS in the sky.

Suddenly, she sat upright and smiled. Of course. She didn't have to plan this at all. There were companies that did this sort of thing. But then again, maybe Christina would look down on her for not completing the task herself. Or perhaps Christina didn't need to know. She'd gladly pay for the service herself if it meant getting the promotion, and Lord knows a professional would do a hundred times better than she could.

What was the name of the company that had done the proposal that morning at Sacred Grounds? It was something like…ball and chain or getting hitched. She closed her eyes and visualized the business card. Tie the Knot! That was it. They could rescue her from the flimsy life raft in the big, scary ocean.

CHAPTER THREE

Second Time Around

G race sat in her office at Tie the Knot and stuffed a forkful of salad into her mouth, eyes glued to the computer screen. She'd been working on a marketing plan for a week now, researching data and coming up with a budget. It was a genius idea that even Penelope couldn't reject. Pleased with herself, she smiled and clicked Save.

"Grace, I just emailed you the information on the Roger Johnson proposal," Penelope said, bursting into the office. "Can you handle it?"

"Of course."

Penelope leaned across the desk and motioned to her computer. "What are you working on?"

She had planned to print and bind the presentation, but maybe an informal approach was better. "I've been developing an idea that would be perfect for Tie the Knot. We could drum up a lot of business with some advertis—"

"Print and commercial spots are out of our budget." Penelope's face tightened.

"I know," she said, annoyed by the interruption. "I'm talking about fairs and trade shows. Did you know there are at least twenty romance-related festivals in LA county alone? It would be the ideal place to showcase our business."

"We don't do fairs."

"That's why I'm suggesting it. The cost to participate is nominal compared to the exposure we'd get."

Penelope shook her head. "This isn't for Tie the Knot."

"But if you look at all the information I gathered and the cost analysis, you'd see—"

"Grace…" Penelope let out an exasperated breath. "Just take care of the Johnson proposal and leave running the office to me." And with that she was gone.

Her jaw dropped. It was amazing how Penelope could blacken a good mood in seconds. She was the worst supervisor ever. She hadn't even looked at any of the research or even remotely considered the idea before squashing it like an ant. Penelope had always been obstinate, but for some reason she'd been even more so after finding out Grace had applied for the Maui position. Not that Penelope wanted it, considering she couldn't uproot her husband and kids.

Fuming, she turned to her computer and googled *relocating to Maui*. Melanie hadn't said anything more about her decision, but nothing wrong with planning ahead just in case. Before viewing the more important items like cost and logistics, she clicked through photos of stunning sunsets, the ocean, and waterfalls, each scene more beautiful than the last. Until ten years ago, she had always thought she was destined to stay in Mistletoe Mountain, but living in paradise didn't seem like such a terrible second choice. And the best part about Hawaii? No Penelope.

A few minutes later, she looked at her cell phone when it dinged with a reminder. It was time for everyone to help put up the Christmas tree in the lobby. Most of her coworkers scoffed that it was much too early to decorate, but obviously they had no holiday spirit. Her condo had looked like a festive wonderland well before Thanksgiving. Most people thought she was crazy to erect a live tree so early, but with proper care it could last into the coming year. There was nothing better than the citrus-wood scent of a Fraser fir. She had a petite-sized one in her office and a seven-footer at home. The smell of the pine needles alone made her want to bundle up in a soft blanket, warm her hands around a mug of hot chocolate, and watch a Christmas movie. As much fun as it had been to decorate, her spirits had plummeted when she'd assembled the miniature Christmas village. It brought back childhood memories of when she and Betsy would spend hours admiring the one their mother set up every year. She did miss spending the holiday with her family, but it wasn't worth facing the painful memories in Mistletoe Mountain.

When she reached the lobby, she did a quick visual sweep of the area. "Where is everybody?" she asked Paulina, the receptionist.

"Looks like you're on your own. At least someone brought the tree out." Paulina pointed to several boxes in the corner.

She put a hand on her hip and frowned. Did she work with a bunch of grinches? "How about you, Paulina? Want to help?"

Paulina shook her head. "No can do. I've got a…uhh…bad back."

She'd known Paulina for almost a year and had never heard about a so-called back issue. Well, fine. She didn't need anyone's help. She was more than qualified to do the job herself. First, she tore open the largest box, pulled out the stand, and set it up. Next, she lifted the tree, which had the branches attached, and inserted the pole into the stand. It had been easy to do considering it was only four feet high. Once the branches were fanned out, she could get to the fun part, which was decorating the tree.

"You going to your parents' house for Christmas, Grace?" Paulina asked.

"No. I'm staying in town."

Paulina frowned. "You aren't going to be alone, are you?"

She tugged on a branch and slightly curved it upward. "I'll be fine. What are your plans?"

"Oh, we have the whole family coming down. Kids, grandkids, everyone." Paulina's eyes sparkled.

"That's great." She forced a smile. She was happy for Paulina, but it did make her crave a partner all the more. Her exes had been more concerned about work than celebrating the holiday.

She had finished shaping the tree when a woman walked into the office. She was tall, thin, and professional-looking in dark-blue trousers, matching jacket, and a white, silky-looking shirt. Spotting Paulina, she rushed to her desk.

"I have an appointment with Melanie," the woman said, breathless.

"You must be Bridget Cartwright."

"Yes. I'm Bridget."

Paulina smiled. "Take a seat. I'll let Melanie know you're here."

Bridget paused, as though she were about to say something else, but then turned around. She took a few steps and stood stiff as a statue, wringing her hands. Grace had seen a lot of nervous brides-to-be, but this was possibly the worst case of jitters ever.

"Do you want to hang an ornament?" She held out a silver bell, hoping it'd help Bridget relax. At the very least, it might take her mind off whatever she wanted to see Melanie about.

Bridget's head jerked toward her. She looked startled, as though the bell were a snake about to strike. "What?"

"I'm decorating the tree. Do you want to help until Melanie comes out?"

"No. I'm good right here," she said and stuck her hands in her pockets.

At that moment, Grace was struck by how beautiful Bridget was. Obviously, she hadn't gotten a good look at her when she first walked in. She had shoulder-length dark hair, a warm honey complexion, and eyes the color of espresso beans. If Bridget was here to plan a proposal, her intended was one lucky guy...or gal.

She hung the bell on a branch and watched Bridget pace back and forth, looking like she was about to face a pack of wild lions. She had a feeling this was about more than a proposal. She'd gotten a lot from therapy the past year and learned that worry was nothing more than creating something you don't want.

"This is a Douglas fir," she said, hoping small talk might help lighten Bridget's mood.

Bridget stopped and stared with a blank expression.

"The tree." She swept her arms out. "It's a classic for Christmas. If it were real, it'd smell like sweet pine."

"Good thing it isn't. It'd be dead in a few weeks."

"That's a common misconception. A fresh-cut tree can last well into the new year if it's taken care of." She bent down and picked up another ornament. "I have a live Fraser fir at home and a tabletop one in my office."

Bridget seemed as attentive as a five-year old on the first day of kindergarten. She looked long and hard at Paulina and then finally sat in a chair, her right knee bobbing up and down. She pulled a cell phone out of her pocket and swiped across the screen several times. Suddenly, Grace had a strange feeling that they'd met before.

"Isn't it too early for decorations?" Bridget spoke without taking her eyes off the phone.

"Not at all. When do you put up a tree?" She attached a hook on a glass star.

"I don't."

"I didn't mean to insinuate that you *should* decorate. I respect all religions and even atheists," she said, reminding herself that not everyone celebrates the holiday.

"My reason for disliking Christmas has nothing to do with religion."

The star slipped out of her hand and crashed to the floor, scattering shards of glass everywhere. Why in the world would Bridget not like Christmas?

Bridget turned her attention to Melanie when she appeared in the lobby.

"I'm sorry to keep you waiting. I'm Melanie Moore, owner of Tie the Knot."

Bridget shot out of the chair and shook Melanie's hand. "Thank you for meeting me on such short notice."

Melanie glanced at the mess on the floor and furrowed her brow. "Be careful not to cut yourself," she said to Grace and escorted Bridget to her office.

Grace stood motionless and looked at Paulina. "Did you hear what that woman said? She doesn't like Christmas."

"I heard." Paulina chuckled and rose from her seat. She went into the storeroom and reappeared a few moments later with a broom and dustpan. "Not everyone loves the holiday as much as you do," she said and handed the items to Grace.

"But it's the most wonderful time of the year," she said, not even caring that she was quoting a song. "She's missing out on the lights, trees, and everything that goes along with the holiday."

"Why does this bother you so much?"

She pondered the question. Normally, if someone said they didn't like Christmas, she'd shrug and continue on her way. She did realize that not everyone had been raised in a holiday-obsessed village like Mistletoe Mountain. With Bridget, though, she wanted to know *why* she didn't like it and show her what she was missing.

"I think I know the answer." Paulina grinned. "I saw the way you looked at her. You were infatuated."

"What? That's ridiculous." She hastily swept up the glass, bent down, and pushed it into the dustpan. When she stood, Paulina was still grinning with a knowing twinkle in her eyes.

She blew out a strong puff of air. "Bridget is probably here to plan a proposal. That's hardly dating material. Besides, she's probably not even a lesbian."

"Hmm…interesting."

"What?" She asked.

"I never said anything about dating. Funny how you jumped to that notion." Paulina breezed past her and sat in her desk chair.

She huffed, annoyed at Paulina's cocky attitude. Admittedly, Bridget was gorgeous, and maybe in the back of Grace's mind she'd fantasized a second or two about being with her, but other than that, Paulina was way off. As much as she wanted a partner, hooking up with someone before she found out about Maui would do nothing but complicate things.

A few moments later, Melanie and Bridget came out of the office and walked up to her.

"This is Grace Dawson," Melanie said to Bridget. "One of our best event planners." She looked at the dustpan filled with glass in her hand.

Not realizing she was still holding it, she placed it on the floor. "We sort of already met."

"Great," Melanie said with a bright smile. "Bridget is our newest client, and you're the perfect person for the job."

A twinge of regret gnawed at her insides. So, Bridget was getting married after all.

"There's a bit of a tight timeline, so why don't you take Bridget into your office, and she can give you the details." Melanie turned to Bridget. "You're in capable hands, but don't hesitate to let me know if you need anything or have any questions."

"Thank you. Your company is a lifesaver." Bridget looked relieved.

She led Bridget to her office and closed the door. "Have a seat," she said, motioning toward a round table with two chairs. She snatched a pen and notepad out of her desk drawer and sat across from Bridget.

"Would you like a cookie?" She opened the Santa Claus tin, which sat on the table. The sweet scent of sugar, cinnamon, and brown butter wafted through the air, causing her mouth to water. "My mom sells them at her bakery. They're ugly Christmas sweaters."

"No, thanks." Bridget stared straight ahead with a serious expression.

Obviously, she wanted to get down to business, so she put the lid back on. "Okay, so when would you like to do the proposal?"

"Christmas Eve."

Her eyes widened. Why in the world would Bridget want to propose to someone on a holiday she disliked? No wonder she'd hired Tie the Knot. And Melanie certainly hadn't been kidding when she said it was a tight deadline.

"As in three weeks?" She gulped.

Bridget nodded. "Is that a problem?"

"It depends on what you'd like to do," she said. "Reservations can be difficult to get this time of year."

"It needs to be Christmassy. You know, all that gaudy stuff." Bridget waved her hand towards Grace's tree with red and green twinkling lights. "But definitely classy."

"I see," she said. "So, tell me about your future fiancé. His…or her…likes, dislikes, personality. That sort of thing."

"It's a she," Bridget said.

A tingle crawled up her spine. Bridget was a lesbian. Not that it mattered, considering she was totally unavailable. When Bridget stared at the ceiling, evidently deep in thought, Grace took the opportunity to admire her unnoticed. She believed that the beauty inside a person was more important than the outside, but Bridget was definitely stunning.

Several moments later, Bridget said, "She loves Christmas."

She waited for more words, but none came. That was all she could come up with? Most people couldn't stop gushing about the love of their lives, so much so that she had to stuff a cookie in them just to shut them up.

"Allll right," she said. "What else?"

"She's…um…stylish. You know, dresses nice, likes fancy things."

Was this a joke? She glanced around, sure she'd spot a hidden camera. Any moment now everyone would pile into her office laughing at how she'd been duped.

Bridget leaned across the table and spoke in a low tone. "There's probably something I should tell you. I didn't mention this to Melanie, but I'm not exactly the person doing the proposing."

She furrowed her brow. "I'm not sure what you mean."

Bridget exhaled an exasperated breath. "My boss asked me to plan a proposal to her girlfriend, and I haven't a clue how to do that." The same worried expression Bridget had shown in the lobby was back again.

"Wait a second." She held up a hand. "Seriously?"

Bridget nodded. "I'm her personal assistant, and if I don't do a good job with this assignment, I'm pretty sure I can kiss the chance to move up in the company good-bye."

She melted at the concerned look in Bridget's eyes. She knew all about desperately desiring a promotion, but this was about the weirdest thing she'd ever heard.

"This is a first," she said with a chuckle. "I can't believe someone wants their assistant to plan something so personal and intimate."

"She's a very busy executive," Bridget said, sounding offended. "She doesn't have time for mundane tasks."

A marriage proposal was a mundane task? She wanted to pounce on that comment but needed to remember she was dealing with a client.

"I'm sorry," she said. "I didn't mean to speak badly of your boss. The timing is a challenge, but don't worry. I'll plan something amazing."

Bridget seemed to relax. "Thank you."

"Now what's your boss's name?" She placed the tip of her pen on the notepad, ready to write. When Bridget didn't respond, she looked at her.

"I'd rather not say. Not that I don't trust you, but she owns a well-known company, and I don't want it getting out that she's going to ask her girlfriend to marry her. Plus…" Bridget shifted in her seat. "She doesn't know I'm hiring you. I don't want her to think I'm not doing my job."

Sympathy tugged at her heart. Bridget's boss was probably a tyrant. Grace was no stranger to that type of woman, particularly since she worked for one herself.

"Understood," she said. "We'll call her Madame X."

Bridget's features lightened, and the corners of her full lips quirked upward, which made her look even more beautiful. It was nice to see her relax a bit. Something about her made Grace want to plan a stellar proposal that would appease her bully boss and help her get that promotion.

"Oh. I forgot the most important thing." Bridget held up a finger. "The location needs to be Mistletoe Mountain. Do you think we could drive up there tomorrow to check things out?"

Mistletoe Mountain? Had she heard correctly? Her pulse quickened, and the pen slipped from her fingers and rolled onto the floor. "No," she said forcefully. "I mean, there are so many better places in LA, and I'm sure we'll never get reservations there this late."

"My boss said the location is non-negotiable."

Her head swirled. "That isn't going to work," she said, rubbing her forehead. "The mountain received a record amount of snowfall the past few weeks. The road probably isn't even open." The snow part was true, but she had no idea about driving conditions.

"Could you check that out, because my boss wants me to let her know the plans on Monday."

A trickle of sweat rolled down her back. "Would you excuse me for a minute? I'll be right back." She rushed out of the office.

She hated to do this, especially after Melanie had personally given her the job, but she had to get out of this assignment. On shaky limbs, she went to Melanie's office and knocked once on the halfway-open door.

"Do you have a minute?" She went inside and sat in one of the guest chairs.

Melanie looked surprised at the abrupt interruption but didn't object. "What's up?"

"It's about Bridget Cartwright. First, she's planning the proposal for her boss, not herself, and second, she wants everything to be set by Monday, which is impossible to accomplish." She tried to keep the frantic desperation out of her voice but wasn't sure she'd succeeded.

Melanie sat back in her chair, her expression unreadable. "Are you saying you don't want this assignment?"

"No, of course not." She had learned her lesson about trying to get out of work with the proposal at Sacred Grounds. "I just don't think there's enough time to do the proposal justice."

Melanie leaned forward and folded her hands in front of her on the desk. "Grace, I gave you this job because I thought you could handle the challenge. Don't disappoint me."

She went limp. How was she supposed to argue with that expectation? Objecting further would do nothing but tarnish Melanie's opinion of her and jeopardize her chance for Maui.

She swallowed a bitter taste in her mouth and stood. "You can count on me."

A few moments later, she returned to her office and saw Bridget looking at her cell phone.

"Great news," Bridget said. "The road to Mistletoe Mountain is open. I just looked it up. So, can we leave tomorrow?"

CHAPTER FOUR

Are We There Yet?

Bridget stood outside her apartment building and glanced at her watch for the fifth time. Not that Grace was late, but she had to do something to release nervous energy. She was beyond thankful for the help, even though it'd cost her almost a week's salary, but spending two hours in a car with a stranger didn't appeal to her in the least. What in the world would they talk about? Grace would probably ask questions about Christina and Beryl, and she'd produce nothing but a blank stare. Just because she worked for Christina didn't mean she knew her personally, aside from her favorite coffee and that she required double starch in her pants suits. And all she knew about Beryl was that she was a lawyer and always seemed to be in a rush. Those were hardly useful bits of information.

Grace had seemed shocked when she'd found out Bridget was tasked with planning her boss's proposal. While she could agree it was a bit odd, she also understood. Christina didn't have time to spend on romantic pursuits when she had a corporation to run. If she were in Christina's place, she'd do the same thing. A giggle bubbled in her belly. She'd never get married, much less seriously date anyone. It was fine for other people, but in her experience, relationships never lasted. She'd been tossed around from one foster family to the next until she was eighteen. Just when she would let her guard down and get comfortable, thinking adoption was imminent, she'd be sent back to the Department of Family and Protective Services. Nope. She wasn't going through that rejection again. She was better off being alone.

She placed a hand on her stomach, trying to tame a wave of nausea. She was dreading this trip for more reasons than the proposal. Last night, she'd googled Mistletoe Mountain and learned that it was some kind of holiday hellhole. A remote village high in the mountains, its citizens were apparently unaware that Christmas was only one day a year, not three hundred and sixty-five. Anything to do with that particular holiday reminded her of all the Christmases spent alone with other unwanted kids. Even when she was in a foster home, she always felt like an outsider.

Her heart raced when a white SUV came barreling down the street. The vehicle pulled up to the curb, and the passenger window rolled down.

"Good morning," Grace said, looking like she was holding back a yawn.

"Hey." She opened the door, slid into the seat, and stuffed her backpack on the floorboard.

Grace eyed the bag, which made Bridget wonder if she'd wanted it placed somewhere else.

"Do you have a coat in there?" Grace asked.

"Sure." She unzipped and pulled out a windbreaker.

Grace chewed on her lower lip. "You do know it's like twenty degrees in Mistletoe Mountain, right?"

Jesus Christ! She had never been anywhere colder than fifty. She'd heard it could get down in the forties at night in Los Angeles, but she had yet to experience that type of weather.

"You might want to bring something more like this." Grace pointed behind her.

Her eyebrows rose when she saw that the entire backseat was taken up by a black puffy coat that looked like it had been filled with helium.

"Let me guess," Grace said. "You don't have one. More of a beach bum than snow bunny?"

"Something like that." She shrugged.

"Well…" Grace's frown slowly turned into a smile. "Don't worry. We'll figure something out."

Bridget forced down feelings of insecurity. She felt foolish for not planning ahead and didn't want to make a bad impression. But then again, it would have been crazy to buy a coat for one day when she didn't intend to ever go to Mistletoe Mountain again.

"Buckle up." Grace put the vehicle in drive and screeched the tires as she sped away.

Bridget fell back against the seat, feeling like she'd just taken off in a rocket. Grace pushed down on the clutch and switched gears with vigor as they flew down the road. She was glad Grace had offered to drive, but she wasn't keen on riding shotgun with Speed Racer. At least at this rate, they'd get to the village a lot sooner than two hours. Once they were on the freeway, though, traffic slowed them considerably.

"Are you sure your boss wants the proposal in Mistletoe Mountain?" Grace sighed. "Like I said earlier, there are great places right here in LA."

"Positive."

That wasn't the first time Grace had suggested another location. She had a feeling Grace didn't want to go to Mistletoe Mountain any more than she did, but she couldn't imagine why. Considering all the decorations in her office, she seemed to love Christmas.

Grace reached behind her seat and pulled out a Santa Claus tin. She opened it, keeping her eyes on the road, and inhaled deeply. She glanced at Bridget and displayed a crooked grin. "Road-trip snacks. Help yourself."

"No, thanks. I just had breakfast."

Grace paused, pressed the lid back on, and stuffed the item in the backseat. "I should lay off the sweets. I need to lose weight."

She didn't agree. Grace's figure was perfect and had luscious curves in all the right places.

"I used to be a lot smaller," Grace said. "Most of the women I've dated are hung up on appearance. Must be an LA thing."

A spark went off in her brain. She'd said *women*. So, Grace was a lesbian. Interesting.

"I know what you mean," she said. "My last girlfriend spent eight hours a day in the gym." That was a lie, but she couldn't think of anything fast enough to reveal that she was a lesbian, too, and still have it fit into the conversation. For some reason, she wanted Grace to know.

A wide smile spread across Grace's face. "So, you and your boss are both gay. I love it."

When she gazed into Grace's gorgeous green eyes, they seemed oddly familiar. In fact, the first time she saw Grace she had a feeling they'd met before. As an uncomfortable silence fell between them, she grabbed a phone out of her backpack and booted up a video game that had made Worth Entertainment millions.

"Is that *Moonwalk*?" Grace asked, taking quick peeks at Bridget's screen.

Excitement shot through her. Grace knew video games. That was a topic she could discuss for hours. "Yeah. Is it one of your favorites, too?"

"God, no. I hate video games." Grace's jaw visibly clenched.

She stared at Grace's profile. "Have you ever played one?"

Grace paused and then said, "Well, no. But trust me. I've been around them plenty."

"You really shouldn't say you *hate* something without even trying it first."

"True. Except I know I don't like violence."

Her blood began to boil. Only people who knew nothing about video games thought that. "They're not all violent. Take *Moonwalk*, for instance. It's about a team of astronauts who discover a peaceful civilization on the moon."

"Sorry if I touched a nerve." Grace cringed.

She wanted to say more but decided instead to lose herself in a fictional world where everything was always more pleasant. Grace was nice enough, but it seemed as though they had nothing in common.

An hour later, she looked up from her phone when Grace shifted gears for a steep incline. "Where are we?" she asked and exited the video game.

"Snow Mountain Pass." Grace maneuvered down a curvy road.

A grin creased her face when she spotted patches of snow. At least that was one positive about this trip. She'd get to see some of the white stuff. When the road narrowed, she sat upright. There was barely enough room for a compact car, much less an SUV. She peered over the side of the cliff, noting how far up they'd already traveled.

"Not much room over here." She pressed her nose against the window, trying to see if the tires were as close to the edge as it felt. One wrong turn and they'd go tumbling down thousands of feet.

"We're fine. I could drive this highway blindfolded."

She almost got whiplash turning around to see if Grace had closed her eyes. Thankfully, they were wide open, and her hands firmly clutched the wheel.

"We'll climb for a bit, and then it'll level out before it gets steeper," Grace said.

A chill ran up and down her spine. She didn't know if she could handle steeper. They weren't even halfway up the mountain, and she was already nervous. Most of Texas was flat. She wasn't used to this.

"You've been on this road a lot?" Bridget asked, trying to keep her voice steady.

"More times than I'd like to remember," Grace muttered under her breath. "Relax and enjoy the scenery."

Instead, she rested her head back and closed her eyes. All the curves in the road were making her queasy. Thirty minutes later, her droopy eyelids fluttered open.

"I must have dozed off." She yawned and stretched, as much as one can do so in a vehicle. She blinked several times, amazed at the surrounding scenery. "Oh, wow."

"Beautiful, isn't it?" Grace smiled.

She couldn't see anything but pure white everywhere. It looked like millions of cotton balls had been placed on the ground. A frozen lake to the right was surrounded by a smattering of pine trees with icicles hanging from the branches. To the left towered a mountain covered in smooth, pristine snow. From this vantage point it looked like not a soul had disturbed the landscape, and who could blame them? It was far too steep for skiing, and no animal in their right mind would traverse the area.

Grace's knuckles turned white when she tightened her grip on the steering wheel and stole quick glances at the mountain. Her serious expression caused Bridget's stomach to churn.

"Is anything wrong?" She asked.

"It freaks me out to pass by here. The area up there is called Savage Slope." Grace's voice trembled.

She scooched down in her seat to get a better look. "I hate to ask, but why Savage Slope?"

"It's an unstable area prone to avalanches."

"Avalanches!" Her eyes bugged out. "Has that ever happened before?"

All the color drained from Grace's face. "The last one was a long time ago. Nothing for you to worry about."

Hopefully, that was true. Getting buried in snow wasn't the way she wanted to exit this life. Once they were several miles down the road, Grace seemed to relax, which was reassuring to see.

"Do you think it'll snow in Mistletoe Mountain today?" Bridget asked, excited about the possibility.

"It's not in the forecast."

"Too bad. I've never seen snowfall before."

"Are you from LA?"

She wasn't one to easily open up to others, specifically when it came to her past. In fact, no one she'd dated or worked with even knew she'd been an orphan. It was humiliating to admit that her own parents didn't want her, not to mention the boatload of foster families.

"I grew up in a small town south of Houston," she said, figuring there was nothing wrong with sharing that information.

"How'd you end up here?" Grace glanced at her.

"I wanted to work for my boss's company. She's really brilliant. In fact, she was my idol growing up. I applied for a computer-programmer position," she said, wanting Grace to know she had higher aspirations than being a gofer. "But I had to settle for working as her assistant the past year."

"Do you have family in LA?"

Her temples throbbed. This was why she never talked about herself. The subject always came around to family. "No. How about you?" The best way to deflect a person was to put the focus on them. She'd learned that trick long ago.

"Well…actually…my parents and sister live in Mistletoe Mountain." Grace shifted in her seat.

"Really? Is that where you grew up?"

"Yes," Grace said and snapped her mouth shut.

Maybe she didn't want to talk about her past any more than Bridget did.

Bridget's cell phone rang, and she swiped across the screen. "Hello?"

"Where are you?" Christina asked in an angry-sounding voice.

"On my way to Mistletoe Mountain."

"Oh. Right. I need you to come into the office tomorrow. I have some letters that need to be typed and mailed, and the board-meeting presentations copied and bound before Monday."

Her stomach knotted. She'd planned to work on a new video game this weekend. She was thankful for her job, but it left little time for personal pursuits.

"Can you get here at nine?" Christina asked.

"Sure. I'll be there." she said, knowing she had no choice.

"I'll see you tomorrow, and good luck today."

"Everything okay?" Grace asked after Bridget hung up.

"That was my boss asking if I could work tomorrow."

"Does she always make you go to the office on the weekend?"

"Sometimes." Actually, it was more like all the time. "She owns the company. It's not a nine-to-five job, and I am her assistant."

Grace grunted. "Sounds like my ex. Christina ran her own company, too, and was a total workaholic."

Bridget froze. No. It couldn't be the same Christina. That would be too much of a coincidence, but she needed to be sure. "What's the company?"

"Worth Entertainment."

Every muscle in her tensed, and she could feel the blood rushing through her veins. Frantically, she tried to recall if there was another Christina at Worth Entertainment, but came up empty-handed.

"They produce video games. Maybe you've heard of them?"

"Um…no…I don't think so." Her head spun and she felt flush. "Are you and she still friends?" she asked, praying the answer was yes. That was the lesbian way, after all. Maybe Grace and Christina were BFFs, and Grace would be overjoyed to plan her best friend's proposal. They'd have a laugh about the freak coincidence and sing "It's a Small World After All" until they reached Mistletoe Mountain.

"God, no." Grace looked like she wanted to barf. "Let's just say it didn't end well, and I hope never to have anything to do with that woman ever again."

Bridget sank into the car seat. What was she supposed to do now? She couldn't very well tell Grace that the proposal was for her ex, whom she seemed to despise. She'd never do the job under those circumstances. She didn't have time to find another company, and they were already more than halfway to Mistletoe Mountain. If Grace didn't find out who the proposal was for, what was the harm? Ignorance was bliss, right?

CHAPTER FIVE

Quaking in Your Boots

Grace's stomach knotted with each passing mile. Before long they'd cross the Mistletoe Mountain city limits. Betsy had practically squealed when she had called her last night. She'd hardly given Grace a chance to explain that this trip was for work and she wouldn't be staying. It'd be wonderful to see her sister and parents, but Grace planned to get in and out as quickly as possible.

She stole a quick glance at Bridget, who was silently staring straight ahead. She was an odd person to figure out. From appearances, she seemed put-together—beautiful, killer body, nice dresser—but underneath the surface, she suspected things weren't quite so perfect. Call it intuition or the fact that Bridget had been noticeably vague when talking about herself. Before the day was over, she was determined to understand her better.

"Whatcha thinking about?" Grace asked.

Silence.

She lightly poked Bridget's leg. "You okay?"

"What? Oh yeah. Fine."

"You're not worried about the proposal, are you?"

"No. I trust you." Bridget's jaw muscles visibly tensed.

She wanted to know what was troubling her but decided to leave it alone. She had her own problems, considering they'd just passed a sign stating they were a measly ten miles from town. If she had been standing, her weak knees probably would have buckled beneath her. She needed to get it together. What had happened was ten years ago, and she'd moved on with her life. It was a different one than planned, but a good one, and with some luck she'd soon be living in Maui.

What sounded like a fast-moving train caused Grace to look in her rearview mirror, panic gripping her. It took a few moments to comprehend what she was seeing. It looked as though a giant bowling ball was beneath the road traveling right toward them. The SUV swerved sharply to the right and left. Knowing they couldn't outrun it, she slammed on the brakes, turned off the engine, and put on the emergency brake.

"What's going on?" Bridget asked, fear in her voice.

"Earthquake! Get down!"

She covered Bridget with her own body and held on tightly. If her hands had been free, she would have plugged her ears, the rattling of windows and steel deafening. The SUV shook so violently she was sure it'd roll over. She prayed that one of the pine trees wouldn't topple over and crash into the car, crushing them both. She winced and felt a sharp pain when something hit above her right eye. The tremors seemed to last forever as they were tossed around in the vehicle like ice cubes in a cocktail shaker.

After almost a minute, the jolts subsided. Her heart pounded, and she heard Bridget's rapid breaths. Slowly, they untangled arms and legs. The inside of the vehicle looked like it had been ransacked. Bridget's hair was in disarray, and her clothes appeared to have been slept in. Grace could only imagine what she looked like.

"Are you okay?" Grace asked, her voice trembling.

"I think so. You?"

She nodded even though her head was pounding, and she felt queasy.

"That was insane," Bridget said, wide-eyed. "I'm moving back to Texas."

She inched back across the console and into her seat. "That felt like a 6.0. There could be aftershocks."

Bridget looked alarmed. "But not as strong as that one, right?"

She didn't want to scare her, but she needed to be honest. "I'm not sure. Maybe."

A strong jolt, followed by a rolling wave, made Bridget grab Grace's arm. It lasted only a few seconds, but it was enough to raise her blood pressure. She was no stranger to earthquakes, but she'd never get used to the frightening sensation of the ground moving beneath her.

"I think my heart is going to jump out of my chest." Bridget raked her fingers through her hair. "Shouldn't we, you know…go?" She'd said that like they could actually escape an earthquake.

"It's not safe right now." She flipped on the hazard blinkers and clutched her coat from the backseat. "You stay in here."

"Where are you going?"

In that moment, Bridget looked like a frightened, lost toddler. She wanted to scoop her into her arms and reassure her. "I need to check the gas tank for damage." They didn't want the car to catch on fire, but she thought it best not to mention that possibility.

"Do you need help?" Bridget shivered, goose bumps appearing on her arms.

"No. I'll be right back."

A rush of frigid wind stung her face when she opened the door. She'd almost forgotten how cold it could get on the mountain. She pulled gloves out of her coat pocket and put them on. Normally, she'd jack up the car to inspect the gas tank, but no way would she take time to do that in this weather. Instead, she dropped to the ground and scooted underneath the SUV. She inhaled deeply, glad she didn't catch a scent of gasoline in the air. After removing a glove, she ran her hand along the tank but didn't feel anything. When the ground shook beneath her, she shot out from under the car and hung onto the bumper.

A minute later, she heard Bridget's voice. "Are you okay?"

She got up and saw Bridget standing by the open passenger door, trembling. "Holy Dooley. You're going to freeze to death," she said and guided her back into the vehicle.

She was touched by the concern, but Bridget was in short sleeves, not that her windbreaker would have helped. Once back in the driver's seat, she took off her coat and covered Bridget, who was furiously rubbing her palms together.

"I can't take that from you," Bridget said through chattering teeth.

"We'll both be warm once I get the heater going."

She turned the key, relieved that the vehicle started, and practically melted at the rush of heat. Visions of tropical Maui beaches filled her head. That promotion couldn't come soon enough.

Bridget studied her and frowned. "You have a big bump over your eye, and it's turning purple."

"I got hit with something." She checked her reflection in the rearview mirror, shocked at how bad it looked. Her head hurt and she felt sick to her stomach, but she figured it was from the adrenaline rush.

"You might have a concussion. Let me see if your eyes are dilated." Bridget turned in her seat.

Grace had always thought you could tell a lot about a person by looking deep into their eyes. Bridget's were a soulful, earthy brown and radiated a gentleness that made her heart ache. This was the type of woman she wanted to be with—someone with depth and compassion. Suddenly, Bridget drew in a sharp breath and backed away, her complexion pasty white.

"What's wrong?" Grace tensed all over.

"You…uhh…you might have a mild concussion."

That was a relief. At least she'd said mild. From Bridget's reaction, she was sure she had a major head injury.

"Man, this road trip sucks." She lightly touched the bump on her head.

"Totally." Bridget released a nervous chuckle. "What do we do now?"

She opened the glove compartment and took out an all-hazards weather radio, glad she'd listened to her dad and kept it after moving away. "Maybe we can get some information about road conditions." She turned the radio dial and heard nothing but static. "Reception is terrible out here."

"We should leave. I mean, we are sitting in the middle of the road."

She wasn't so sure about that. There could be downed trees, cracks in the pavement, or worse. But then again, it wasn't like they had much of a choice. Before she stepped on the gas, Bridget grabbed her arm.

"Wait. You should let me drive."

"Why?"

Bridget cocked her head. "Possible concussion."

Oh. Right. She did have a terrible headache, but she could keep an eye out for any road damage if Bridget drove.

"Okay, but if we have another tremor, stop, put it in neutral, and pull up on the emergency brake."

"Got it." Bridget nodded.

For a moment, she considered crawling over Bridget to get into the passenger seat so neither one of them would have to go outside but decided against it. Instead, she took a deep breath, opened the door, and ran around the car. Bridget had already situated herself in the driver's seat, so she jumped in and slammed the door shut.

"Holy Dooley, it's cold out there." She held her hands up to the heater.

"I thought you grew up in Mistletoe Mountain. Wouldn't you be used to this?"

"I left ten years ago and have only been back once since."

Bridget rested her hands on the steering wheel. "You don't get along with your folks?"

"Oh, no. They're awesome. We're really close."

"So why wouldn't—"

"We better get going. Like you said, we're in the middle of the road." Not that it mattered, considering Snow Mountain Pass was as barren as the tundra.

Bridget clutched the steering wheel, racking her brain to remember if the correct position was ten and two or nine and three. She wanted to get it right for optimal vehicle control in case they had another earthquake. Deciding on ten and two, she shifted into first gear and lightly pressed the gas pedal.

Several minutes later, Grace said, "I'm glad you're being careful, but you can go faster than twenty miles an hour."

She looked at the gauge, surprised. It felt like she was going at least forty. She increased the speed a bit and tightened her grip on the steering wheel.

"I'm going to call my folks and see if they're okay." Grace fished a cell phone out of her purse and pressed a button. A few beats later she said, "Yes, it's me. Are you and Dad all right?"

Bridget concentrated on the winding road and tuned Grace out. This had been one hell of a morning. She'd felt her first earthquake and found out that she'd hired Christina's ex-girlfriend. And to top it all off, when she was checking Grace for a concussion, she realized that they'd actually met a year ago. She was sure Grace was the crying woman who'd left her purse in Christina's office. That was probably when they'd broken up. How she hadn't recognized those beautiful green eyes before, she'd never know. Thankfully, Grace didn't seem to have a clue as to who she was, and hopefully it would stay that way.

"My parents and sister are fine," Grace said and stuffed the phone back into her bag. "My mom said The Cookie Jar—that's their bakery—is a wreck, and my sister's bed and breakfast has a little damage, but at least no one was hurt." She covered her mouth and yawned. "She said the earthquake was a 6.5."

"Is that big? It certainly felt big."

"It was a strong one. You're a real Californian now."

Grace yawned again, her eyelids halfway closed. Bridget stole glances at her, concerned about the head injury. A doctor really needed to check it out. As much as she wanted to get the proposal plans in place and head back to LA, a possible concussion shouldn't be ignored. She recalled how Grace had flung herself on top of her when the earthquake hit. She could have stayed in her seat and protected herself, but instead she'd shielded Bridget from harm. No one had ever done that for her before. She could be the one with the big knot on her forehead instead of Grace.

She looked at Grace, alarmed that her eyes were closed. "Hey!" When she didn't respond, she poked her thigh hard.

"Ouch." Grace's eyelids fluttered open, and she rubbed her leg. "What'd you do that for?"

"You're not supposed to sleep when you have a concussion."

"That's a myth."

"Google it."

Grace sighed and got out her phone. A minute later she said, "Ah-ha. See? It says that sleep is actually healing because it helps the brain recover." Long pause, which probably meant she was reading to herself. "Oh. Only if there are no other symptoms such as dilated pupils." She placed the phone on the dashboard and crossed her arms.

"Is there a hospital in Mistletoe Mountain?" She asked, and slowed down to take a curve in the road.

"Yes. Why?" Grace narrowed her eyes.

"Because I think we should get you checked out."

"I'm fine. We just need to keep talking so I don't fall asleep."

"Okay. So…tell me about your ideas for the proposal."

Grace's face lit up. "First, I was thinking the couple should stay at the Candy Cane Cottage, my sister's bed and breakfast. It's the sweetest place you'll ever see. There's a gazebo in the back that would be a perfect location, or if you think your boss wants something fancier, we could always go the horse-and-carriage route. Actually, have you ever seen the movie *Love Actually*?" She giggled, probably at the over-use of the word "actually." "She could do pre-written signs. But maybe that's too cutesy." She bit her lower lip, looking deep in thought.

"You're certainly not short on ideas." She peeked at Grace, who was awfully cute when she got excited.

"Holiday proposals are the most romantic." Grace stared blissfully into space. "If I ever get proposed to, I'd want it to be on Christmas Eve."

"If?"

"Well, I have to meet Ms. Right first."

So, Grace was single. It wasn't a shocker that she and Christina hadn't worked out. Not that anything was wrong with either one of them, but together they were a head-scratcher. Grace seemed like a romantic at heart, and Christina only cared about hard work. She bit her tongue to stop herself from saying anything. She wasn't supposed to know Christina, much less work for her. Keeping the lies straight was going to be a challenge.

"What would be your ideal proposal?" she asked, surprised she wanted to know.

Grace leaned her elbow on the armrest and rested her chin in her hand. A few moments later she said, "It'd be beside a Fraser fir decorated in twinkling white lights. My favorite Christmas song would be playing, and definitely mistletoe overhead."

"Is the mistletoe to ensure you get kissed?"

"Haven't you heard of the mistletoe legend?"

"Nope, but I have a feeling you're going to tell me." She carefully maneuvered around a tree branch in the road.

"When a couple kisses underneath mistletoe, it ensures that they'll have a long, happy life together. And when an unmarried woman isn't kissed, she'll remain single for another year."

She snorted. "You don't actually believe that, do you?"

"I'm not taking any chances."

"So what's your favorite song?"

"'Kissin' by the Mistletoe.'"

"Of course." She chuckled.

Grace's head jerked toward her. "Hey. Why don't you like Christmas?"

"How'd you know that?"

"You told me in the lobby at Tie the Knot."

She inwardly cringed. She'd forgotten about that. It wasn't something that could be explained without revealing her life story. "It's just not my thing. Too commercialized." She mentally patted herself on the back. That sounded like a good-enough reason.

"Don't let anyone in town hear you say that. Especially my dad. He's the mayor and probably loves it more than anyone." Grace clicked on the radio, "Rockin' Around the Christmas Tree" blaring over the speakers. "Maybe Mistletoe Mountain will change your mind about the holiday." She yelled over the music.

"Doubtful," she muttered through gritted teeth.

CHAPTER SIX

Welcome to Christmas Town

The last thing Grace wanted to do was sit in a cramped ER waiting room for God knows how long. The place was packed due to injuries from the earthquake, which—thankfully—all appeared to be minor. She hunkered down in the chair, hoping no townspeople would recognize her. Reliving the past and facing a barrage of questions about what she was doing with her life wouldn't be enjoyable in the least. If her head hadn't been pounding, she would have insisted they leave.

As much as she wanted to fast-track the Mistletoe Mountain trip and hightail it back to LA, it was doubtful they'd get much done today. Maybe they could come back Sunday so Bridget's boss could get an update on Monday. Not ideal, but spending another day with Bridget wasn't the worst thing in the world. She was a sweetheart for caring enough to take her to the hospital, not to mention the fact that she was gorgeous.

Three hours later, they were back on the road heading toward The Cookie Jar. She didn't have a concussion, but she was sporting a killer headache, so Bridget drove again, since the pain killers the doctor gave her made her loopy. She gazed out of the window and watched her hometown pass before her eyes. A mixture of excitement and sadness swirled in the pit of her stomach. She adored Mistletoe Mountain, and the people she loved most lived here, but at every turn she was reminded of painful memories.

"Isn't this place a little overdone?" Bridget asked and stopped at a red light.

"What do you mean?"

"Look around." She shook her head in apparent disgust.

"First, there's no such thing as overdone when it comes to Christmas, and second, it's adorable. I'm glad to see the earthquake didn't do any visible damage."

The town looked even more charming than she remembered. All the stores were constructed to look like gingerbread houses, balsam fir trees with big red balls stood on every street corner, colorful wreaths adorned the lamp posts, and kids were building snowmen in the town square. It was a picture-perfect Christmas card. Nothing like Los Angeles with fake snow, eighty-degree temperatures, and Santa on a surfboard.

Bridget grumbled something unintelligible and pressed on the gas when the light turned green. It was a mystery as to why she was such a Scrooge. The commercialism excuse sounded fishy. Maybe something bad had happened to her around the holiday, like a painful breakup or a death. That was usually why a person in Hallmark Christmas movies didn't like the yuletide, and Grace should know because she'd watched just about all of them.

"Turn right on Evergreen Way," she said. "It's here on the left."

Her heart leapt when she saw the bakery. Her parents had opened it before she and Betsy were born. She and her sister grew up watching their mom concoct all sorts of sugary sensations and had worked in the shop when they got older. Bridget parked, turned off the ignition, and held onto the keys. Grace had a feeling she wouldn't be allowed to drive the rest of the day, which was fine by her.

"Thanks for stopping here so I can check on my family. I know we have a tight schedule today." She decided not to mention the idea of coming back Sunday until she saw how much they'd accomplished. "Wear this," she said and laid her coat across Bridget's lap.

"I'm not taking that," Bridget said, adamantly. "I have a windbreaker."

"That won't help you in this weather." She grabbed a sweater from the backseat. "I'm used to these temperatures."

Bridget snatched the item out of her hands before she could object and pulled it over her head. She looked a hundred times cuter in the garment than Grace ever did. It was at least one size too small, which stretched the dancing reindeer nicely across her chest. Grace had met a lot of flawless-looking women, but Bridget was a natural beauty, someone who didn't need a lot of prep work to look stunning. Unlike some women, Bridget didn't seem to have any idea how gorgeous she was. She had a down-to-earth quality about her and seemed devoid of pretentiousness.

"Before we go in, I have to warn you about something." She looked Bridget dead straight in the eye. "My mom is a hugger."

A worried expression crossed Bridget's face. "Like…what do you mean?"

"You know. A hug." She resisted the temptation to wrap her arms around Bridget to demonstrate. She did wonder, though, what it would feel like. Was she soft, or did she have one of those hard bodies?

"Maybe I should wait for you here." Bridget rolled the keys over in her hand.

"You'll be fine. Just remember to go limp and not fight it." She opened the door, and before she stepped onto the curb, she heard a voice.

"Grace Dawson, is that you?"

A tall, spindly woman with white hair, deep wrinkles, and a scowl was standing two feet away. She inwardly groaned. It was none other than Mitsi Purnell, ringleader of a group of gossiping busybodies. According to Grace's mom, these were the women who'd talked nasty about Betsy for getting pregnant out of wedlock.

"Oh, my. I haven't seen you in years." Mitsi peered over her bifocals. "My heavens. What did you do to your forehead?"

She touched the spot above her eye. "It's just a bump."

"You should cover that with some Mary Kay concealer. It looks awful." Mitsi grimaced. "Your daddy said you're living in Los Angles. What in the world are you doing there?"

"Oh, this and that. Keeping busy."

Mitsi focused on Bridget, who was standing next to Grace, shivering.

"This is Bridget. We should get inside." She tugged Bridget's sleeve and pulled her toward The Cookie Jar.

"Don't be a stranger." Mitsi's voice echoed behind them.

Grace stood motionless at the entrance of the bakery, seeing chairs overturned and broken cookies and candy scattered everywhere. When she spotted her mother and Betsy, all three released ear-splitting yelps. She dove into a soft, safe place when her mother's plump arms wrapped around her. She hadn't realized how much she'd missed her family. They saw each other only once or twice a year, considering it was hard for them to get away to visit her.

"It's so good to see you." Grace's mother tightened her grip.

Ordinarily, she would resist an embrace that practically squeezed the life out of her, but in this case, it was the best thing she'd felt in a long time.

"My turn." Betsy wiggled her way between them.

Grace bumped into her sister's stomach when she put an arm around her neck and gave her a peck on the cheek. "You're huge!"

"Don't remind me." Betsy groaned. "Oh my gosh, what happened to you?"

Both women looked at her with fear in their eyes.

"I bumped my head in the car during the earthquake. It's okay. Bridget took me to the emergency room to get it checked out."

She had forgotten all about Bridget. She looked around and spotted her standing by the front door looking like she wanted to dart outside.

"Bridget, this is my mom, Carol, and my sister, Betsy."

"Hi." Bridget gave a half-hearted wave.

Carol rushed toward Bridget and pulled her into a hug. "Thank you for taking care of our girl."

Grace bit her lower lip to keep from laughing, the expression on Bridget's face priceless. You'd think a boa constrictor was wrapped around her instead of a plump, middle-aged woman. She had a feeling Bridget's mother wasn't quite that affectionate. Maybe she'd been raised in one of those cold, distant homes.

"That's enough, Mom. You're going to smother her." She pulled on her mother's arm.

Betsy held her hand out. "Nice to meet you."

"Likewise." Bridget shook, appearing relieved for the handshake instead of a squeeze.

Grace glanced at the area. "What a mess. But you two are okay?"

"Shaken up, but fine." Betsy hoisted herself up on a nearby stool.

Carol released a sigh. "I do have a lot of cleanup before we can reopen."

Grace wished she could help, but that wasn't why she was in town. "How's Dad?

"I'm better now that you're here."

She turned at the sound of her father's voice and broke out in a wide smile. "Hey, Pop."

"What'd you do to yourself?" He examined the knot on her head.

"It's just a bump."

Grace noticed that Bridget had inched closer to the door. She motioned for her to come forward and said, "Bridget, this is my dad, Drew."

"Thank you for getting our Gracie to visit," he said and placed an arm around Grace's shoulder. "It's been far too long."

"Congratulations on your upcoming engagement," Carol said to Bridget.

"Well, actually…it's not my engagement," Bridget said. "It's for my boss."

Confusion crossed Drew's face moments before he said, "Well, you can't find a better location than Mistletoe Mountain."

"Spoken like a true mayor." Grace patted his shoulder, realizing it was bonier than usual. She looked him up and down and saw that he was practically drowning in his suit. "Dad, you're so thin."

"Stomach ulcer." Carol sat on a barstool next to Betsy.

"He's working too hard and worrying too much," Betsy said through a mouthful. Apparently, she'd found a chunk of fudge that'd survived the earthquake.

Why hadn't Betsy told her about this before? She was supposed to keep Grace apprised of all the news.

"What are you worried about?" Grace asked her father.

"Nothing I can't handle." Drew kissed the top of her head. "I do, though, have some bad news. The earthquake caused an avalanche out by Savage Slope."

Carol gasped and pressed her palm against her chest. "Thank God Grace and Bridget weren't in it."

A wave of nausea hit her, and she found it difficult to breathe. Not again. Silently, she prayed that no one had been injured...or worse.

Carol hopped off the stool and put an arm around her shoulders. "How bad is it?"

"Not sure yet. Crews are on the way there right now to check it out." Drew looked at her. "Honey, you okay?"

"I just hope no one was hurt." She swallowed a hard lump in her throat.

"Me, too." Drew's eyes softened. "I have to get back to the office, but I'll know more after I get an update."

"I hate to ask this right now," Bridget said. "But can we still drive to LA tonight?"

Drew shook his head. "Snow Mountain Pass is the only road into town."

Bridget looked like she was about to hurl. "How quickly is something like this usually cleared?"

"I can't really say until we find out how bad it is."

"You two can stay at the inn," Betsy said, obviously excited. "I have plenty of room."

Grace felt like an eagle was dive-bombing in her stomach, and from the look on Bridget's face, she felt the same way.

❖

"I don't see how in the world there could be only one road into town." Bridget drove down Noel Lane on the way to the Candy Cane Cottage.

Grace examined the bag of necessities they'd bought at Santa's Village, the one and only market in town. "Toothbrushes, toothpaste, deodorant, shampoo, and conditioner. Betsy said she'd have anything else we need. Except clothes."

"Isn't there a trail or something that would lead to the main road on the other side of the avalanche?"

Grace stuffed the bag on the floorboard by her feet. "Trust me. I don't want to be stuck here anymore than you do."

From Grace's exasperated tone, she had no reason to doubt her. With all that hugging and sugary niceness with her family, Grace was clearly happy to see them, so she must have some other reason for not wanting to be here.

"I can't believe this is happening. I have to go to work tomorrow." She was on the verge of whining.

"Surely your boss will understand."

Grace didn't know Christina. No…wait…she did know her, even better than Bridget did. She was totally going to screw up this fib. She could fake it for a day and no more.

She brightened and held up a finger. "Hey, what about a helicopter?"

"Mistletoe Mountain is a no-fly zone except in case of a medical emergency. Besides, the vibrations from the aircraft could set off another avalanche."

"Why would anyone build a town in such a remote area?" She let out a loud, exasperated sigh.

"Mistletoe."

"What?"

"KissMe Mistletoe Farm is about a mile on the other side of town. Turn here." Grace pointed to the right. "They're the largest distributor on the West Coast. Chances are you've bought mistletoe from that very farm."

She snorted. "That isn't something I've ever purchased."

"Ms. Cartwright, you are a true dichotomy," Grace said with a sigh. "On one hand, you're sweet as pie, and on the other, you're a curmudgeon."

"Is that how you talk to all your paying clients?"

"Sorry. Guess I forgot our association for a minute." Grace flushed.

"It's okay." She didn't want Grace to feel bad. She liked her. A lot. Usually, it took months, if ever, for her to feel comfortable with someone, not a few hours.

"I know you're upset, but the priority right now should be search-and-rescue," Grace said in a sharp tone. "Not how fast we can get back home."

"You're right." She sighed. "Remember when you told me there'd been an avalanche before? Were you in it?"

"Why would you think that?" Grace asked.

"When we passed by Savage Slope, you were really nervous, and then when your dad told us about the avalanche, everyone seemed concerned about you." She tensed, wondering if she'd overstepped. Maybe the question was too personal, but curiosity had gotten the better of her.

After what seemed like an eternity, Grace finally spoke. "I wasn't in the avalanche, but my girlfriend, Meghan, was."

"Oh. Wow. Was she injured?" She glanced at Grace before focusing on the road again.

Grace drew in a shaky-sounding breath. "She was killed. It was ten years ago, when we were eighteen. Meghan was skiing and must have gotten lost, because she knew better than to go near Savage Slope. She was in the wrong place at the wrong time."

Her heart plummeted. "I'm so sorry. That's horrible." She fought the urge to reach out and grab Grace's hand.

"We'd known each other since we were kids. We had our whole lives planned out together." Grace gave a one-shoulder shrug. "Like I said, it was a long time ago."

She wasn't buying the nonchalant attitude. Clearly the loss was still heartbreaking. Was that why Grace had stayed away from Mistletoe Mountain?

"It's here on the left." Grace pointed, which wasn't necessary since it would have been impossible to miss.

The inn looked like a giant candy cane stuck in the snow. The two-story building was painted bright red, trimmed in white, and couldn't have looked more Christmassy if it tried. Wreaths were displayed in every window and…she squinted…was that a tree on the porch? By gosh, it was. A gigantic decorated tree stood next to several rocking chairs. That wouldn't last two seconds in LA. Maybe the tree was bolted down, but all the decorations would be pilfered in no time.

"Adorable, isn't it?" Grace hopped out of the vehicle.

There were a lot of words she would use to describe the place, but adorable wasn't one of them. She opened the door and stiffened. Good God. It felt like a million sharp icicles had been hurled at her. Who in their right mind would choose to live in this environment? If they were stuck here more than a day, she'd have to break down and buy a coat.

They rushed down a path lined with small lanterns that had plush red-velvet bows. When they reached the porch, Betsy flung the door open and stepped aside for them to enter. The room reeked of sweet cinnamon, which might have been coming from the umpteen lighted candles.

"Where's your coat?" Betsy asked her and closed the door.

"This jacket is all I have," she said, briskly running her hands up and down her arms.

"I probably have something you can borrow. It's not like anything fits me anymore." Betsy looked at her belly.

"I love what you've done to the place," Grace said, making her way around the room.

Bridget had never been in a bed-and-breakfast before, but this looked like someone's house rather than a hotel. They were standing in a living room that had a fireplace built into a brick wall, big-screen TV, and comfortable-looking leather sofas and recliners. Without the gaudy Christmas decorations, it would have been nice. Was it really necessary to have four wreaths and ten poinsettias in one room? Not to mention hundreds of snow globes and little knickknacks everywhere. If she didn't know better, she'd think Betsy was a holiday hoarder.

"Your tree is gorgeous." Grace stood before what must have been a twelve-foot pine tree. She reached out and touched something. "Is that what I think it is?"

Betsy smiled and joined Grace. Bridget shuffled her feet and crossed her arms, feeling like a third wheel. The sisters probably wanted to reminisce, and she was sorely in the way. She glanced at the stairs, wishing she could escape to her room.

"Bridget, look at this." Grace held up two ornaments.

She took a few steps closer, trying to make out what they were.

"It's Shrinky Dinks. Betsy and I were obsessed with making these when we were kids." Grace looked at her sister. "Remember when mom let us set up a table at The Cookie Jar to sell them?"

Betsy laughed. "I sold zero and you three because you were younger and cuter than me."

She had no doubt Grace had been adorable. Who could have resisted those big, beautiful eyes? After all, those eyes had convinced her to barge into Christina's office and fetch her purse.

"Do you remember making Shrinky Dinks?" Grace asked her and hung the ornaments back on the tree.

Shrinky what? She'd never heard of such a thing. "Um. No. I don't think so. What is it?"

"It's plastic sheets you draw on that get rigid and thick after heating," Grace said.

"Which we'd do in your Easy Bake Oven." Betsy grinned.

Grace chuckled and placed a hand on her sister's arm. "Mom would tell us she could bake ten in the big oven, but we had to do it our way. One at a time."

Her heart ached, imagining what it must have been like to grow up with a sister. Someone you could play with, share experiences, and be best friends with when you got older. Normally, she didn't harp on what she'd missed in her childhood, but watching Grace and Betsy made her crave the sibling she'd never had.

"Do you mind telling me where my room is?" she asked. "I'd like to get cleaned up. It's been quite a day so far."

Betsy clasped her hands together. "Of course. I'll show you both."

They made their way through the living room, past an enormous snow-village display, and ascended the stairs, Betsy leading the way.

"How many guests do you have staying here?" Grace asked.

It took Betsy so long to respond Bridget wasn't sure she'd heard the question. Finally, she said, "Just one couple."

"That's all!?"

Grace sounded alarmed, which wasn't surprising. It was a big place to only have two guests.

"Things have been slow," Betsy said, sounding out of breath.

"It'll pick up in a few weeks with Christmas, right?" Grace asked.

When Betsy reached the top of the stairs, she took a deep breath and let it out slowly. "Not if it's anything like the past few years."

"What do you mean?" Grace asked.

"It's not just the inn. The whole town is suffering. It's almost like everyone has forgotten we're here. Kinda like the island of misfit toys." Betsy's face tightened.

"Bets, why didn't you tell me? Is that why dad has an ulcer?"

"I didn't think you'd want to hear anything about the town," Betsy said, softly.

"I'm still part of this family." Grace frowned.

Bridget cleared her throat. She hated to interrupt, but she didn't want to intrude on their private conversation.

"Your room." Betsy pointed at her. "Follow me."

Midway down the hall, Betsy unlocked a pink door and opened it. "Bridget can stay in here, and right across the hall is Grace's room." She handed her a snowman keychain and gave Grace a reindeer one.

She glanced into the room. It was small but looked nice enough. There was a fireplace with a wreath above it, a wooden desk and chair, and a festive quilt covering a queen-size bed.

"How much do you charge a night?" She asked. The inn looked fancy, and money was tight after paying for the proposal. Maybe there was a cheap motel in town. Anything with heat would suffice.

"Nothing." Betsy held up a hand when Grace opened her mouth. "You're my guests. The bathroom is down the hall on your right."

"There isn't one in the room?" She couldn't have heard that right.

"No, but don't worry. It's only you and Grace since the couple is on the other side. When you're in there, just remember to hang the Rudolf sign outside the door so she knows it's occupied."

Betsy's phone rang, and she fished it out of her pocket. "It's Mom. Maybe she has news about the avalanche." She walked down the hall out of earshot.

Bridget leaned against the door frame. "Do your sister and her husband live here, too?"

"Betsy is single." Grace narrowed her eyes.

"Oh. I just thought…because…you know."

"It's possible to have a baby without a partner, you know," Grace said in a sharp tone.

"Did I say something wrong?" She felt like she'd just had her hand slapped.

"I didn't mean to jump down your throat." Grace's features softened. She glanced at Betsy and whispered, "Some people in town trash-talk Betsy for having a baby and not being married. You know that woman we ran into? Mitsi Purnell? Well, she's the worst of them all."

She shook her head, disgusted. "Your sister is having a baby because she wants one. Some people throw their kids away and just leave them on doorsteps. Now that's something to bad-mouth."

She mentally chastised herself. That had sounded a little too specific. Luckily, Betsy reappeared before Grace had a chance to respond.

"I have good news and bad news," Betsy said.

"What's the good news?" Grace asked warily.

"We'll get to spend more than one night together." Betsy's face brightened.

Goose bumps ran up and down her arms. "What's the bad news?"

"The avalanche is worse than they thought. It's not only snow, but boulders as well."

"Holy Dooley." Grace placed a hand on the banister as though to steady herself. "How long before the road is clear?"

"They'll have a better estimate tomorrow, but it might be days."

Grace's complexion looked like waxed paper. Bridget knew how she felt. This was the worse timing ever. Christina was going to have a conniption fit, considering they had projects up the wazoo. She would have a boatload of assignments when she got back.

She rubbed her face. "This is bad. I don't even have my laptop with me." She felt more naked without her computer than without clothes.

"I have one you can borrow," Betsy said.

She perked up a bit. "Really? Do you have Wi-Fi?"

"The inn is actually one of the few places in Mistletoe Mountain that does. Password is candy cane."

She couldn't get into the Worth Entertainment network, but at least she could access her personal computer through the cloud. She could hide out in the room, work on her video game, and avoid anything Christmas-related until the road reopened.

CHAPTER SEVEN

Candy Cane Cottage

Bridget yawned, stretched her arms wide, and heard something crash to the floor. She looked down, and a plump, red-cheeked, ceramic Santa stared back at her. She sat up, unsure where she was. As memories flooded back, she plopped into the bed again. She wasn't home, safe and sound. Not even close. She was freezing her ass off, stranded in a town filled with elves.

It was amazing everything that had happened since yesterday. They'd been in Mistletoe Mountain only one day, yet it felt like a week. Her thoughts drifted to Grace and the death of her girlfriend, Meghan. At the time, she didn't have a clue how to respond aside from "oh, wow" or whatever she'd uttered. She couldn't imagine what it would be like to lose a loved one. All the more reason to keep her distance. One way or the other, relationships just end up breaking your heart.

The clock on the wall, which had snowflakes in the place of numbers, indicated it was nine a.m. She had put off calling Christina yesterday but had no choice now. No doubt she'd freak out to hear Bridget wouldn't be in the office today. It was hard enough to take a planned vacation, much less an impromptu one, not that this would be a vacation.

Considering the avalanche, maybe she could convince Christina to declare her undying love to Beryl somewhere else. It felt wrong to ask Grace to arrange her ex's marriage proposal in her hometown. It also seemed odd that Christina would want to do it in Mistletoe Mountain anyway, since Grace's father was the mayor and her sister owned the best B&B in town. But then again, maybe Christina didn't know, and she couldn't tell her because she wasn't even supposed to know Grace. This was getting way too confusing.

She pulled back the covers and swung her feet onto the wooden floor. She picked up the Santa, opened the nightstand drawer, and stuffed him inside. The less festivity she was exposed to this week the better. Standing upright, she examined the pajamas Betsy had loaned her. She was grateful, but the red Ho-Ho-Ho shirt and neon-green reindeer leggings weren't exactly her style.

She shuffled to the door, opened it, and peeked outside. She'd wanted to change before parading around looking like she belonged at the North Pole, but she really needed the bathroom. Since the coast was clear, she padded down the hall, glad not to see an occupied sign outside the door. Just to be safe, though, she knocked. A few seconds later, she bolted inside. It seemed odd—and highly inconvenient— to have a shared bathroom. She couldn't really complain, though, since Betsy was letting them stay for free.

Once back in the room, she sat at the desk and dialed Christina's number. She answered on the first ring.

"I'm on my way into the office. Do you have questions about the letters I left?"

"Not exactly. I…uhh…I have some bad news." She gripped the arm of the chair. "I'm stuck in Mistletoe Mountain."

"What do you mean *stuck*?"

It was all over the news, but it wasn't surprising Christina hadn't heard about the avalanche. The woman had a one-track mind when it came to her company.

"The earthquake yesterday caused an avalanche. The only road into town is closed, and it could take days to clear. I'm not even sure I'll be back Monday."

Silence. Lots of uncomfortable silence.

"I asked about a helicopter," she said. "But that's a no-go. Something about a no-fly zone."

After what seemed like an hour, Christina finally said, "I'm sure the California department of whatever is on it. They have equipment to do these sorts of things. They'll have it cleared up in no time."

"Really?" She felt hopeful for the first time.

"It's not ideal, though." Christina sighed into the receiver. "Where are you staying?"

She tensed. Would Christina know Betsy's inn? If so, she could just play dumb. After all, she wasn't supposed to know anything about Grace or her family.

"Bridget? You still there?"

"Candy Cane Cottage. It's a B&B."

"Sounds Christmassy. Beryl would love it. If it's nice, book a room for two nights."

Christina hadn't missed a beat. Obviously, she was clueless about Grace's sister.

"Considering the road is closed, Mistletoe Mountain may not the best location for the proposal," she said.

"Christmas is three weeks away. It'll be clear by then. Besides, I already told Beryl we're driving up there for the holiday." The sound of typing echoed through the phone. "I didn't say anything about the proposal, of course. That's a surprise."

"What if there's another avalanche? There's unstable area all around." As far as she knew, Savage Slope was the only danger.

"I just googled it," Christina said. "The last avalanche was ten years ago. A local girl died. What an awful way to go."

Didn't Christina realize that was Grace's girlfriend? It was like she didn't even know who Grace was. Maybe she'd gotten it wrong, and Christina wasn't the ex. No. Grace had clearly said Christina from Worth Entertainment.

"I have another call," Christina said. "Keep me updated on your return to the office."

She heard a click. That had gone a lot better than she thought it would. And on the bright side, Christina seemed certain the road would be open soon. She lifted the lid of the laptop Betsy had loaned her, connected to the cloud, and booted up *Shipwreck*, her newest video-game creation. She'd gotten a lot done yesterday since she'd stayed in her room all evening. If Grace hadn't brought her a sandwich and slice of pie, she probably would have forgotten to eat. She sat back in the chair, guilt gnawing her insides. She hated lying to Grace. It would be a lot easier if she wasn't so darn likable.

❖

"Tell your cook this is the best thing I've ever had." Grace closed her eyes and moaned when she stuffed another piece of blueberry muffin into her mouth.

Betsy poured two cups of coffee and sat at the kitchen table across from her. "I'm lucky to have her." She placed one of the mugs in front of her.

"Who's going to run the inn when you have the baby?" She took a sip, relishing the fact that her sister knew the perfect amount of sugar and cream to add.

"Mrs. Irving said she'd oversee things while I'm gone. I also have an assistant, housecleaner, and a handyman." Betsy bowed her head. "If things don't pick up, I'll have to let some of them go."

"Are things that bad?" She hated seeing her so upset.

"Like I was saying last night, it's the whole town. The Cookie Jar is in jeopardy, too."

"There's gotta be something we can do." Her chest ached. What would her family do if they went out of business? They'd always lived in Mistletoe Mountain, and until ten years ago she had intended to reside here as well, with Meghan by her side.

"Dad said the city council is working on some ideas, but everything takes money they don't have."

"The mistletoe farm is still thriving, right?"

Betsy frowned. "We've had some harsh winters, which have cut crops in half. Harlan said if things don't improve this year, he's planning to stop growing mistletoe and just have apple trees."

That was awful news. Mistletoe was not only the lifeblood of the town, but its namesake as well.

"What about The Ice Palace?" Her heart raced. She'd be crushed if Gus's skating rink ever closed down.

"It's bad, too. Gus asks about you every time I see him. You should look him up while you're here."

"I don't think so." She felt an uneasy churning in the pit of her stomach and pushed her plate with a half-eaten muffin aside. "By the way, Bridget doesn't know who I am, and I want to keep it that way."

Betsy snorted. "That'll be awfully hard to do in this town. You're like a legend around here." She got up and poured herself another cup of coffee. After sitting back down, she asked, "So, what's the deal with Bridget? Is she single?"

Grace scrutinized her, knowing exactly where this was going. "I have no idea."

"Well, is she a lesbian?"

"Yes, *and* a client."

Betsy batted her hand in the air like that fact was inconsequential. "She's certainly a looker. If I were a lesbian, watch out."

She snorted. "You're so transparent." Yes, Bridget was gorgeous and had kind eyes that could melt steel, but she didn't know much else about her.

"I'm not saying you have to marry the woman," Betsy said. "But it's been a year since you've dated anyone."

She had a sudden urge to bolt from the room. She wanted nothing more than to find her perfect match, but she couldn't shake the feeling that she'd repeat old patterns, ignore red flags, and pick the wrong woman again. That would be disastrous.

"I'm not ready," she said, adamantly. "I need to read a few more self-help books."

Betsy huffed. "You have enough literature to start your own library."

"Do you realize you're trying to set me up with someone who doesn't like Christmas?" That was practically a jail-sentence-worthy crime.

"Maybe she's Jewish." Betsy popped a piece of muffin into her mouth.

"She said it had nothing to do with religion. She just hates it. For no apparent reason."

"Well, I like her. I thought…good morning!" Betsy straightened and focused over Grace's shoulder.

She swung around to see Bridget looking stunningly perfect in yesterday's clothes. She raked her fingers through her hair, suddenly aware that she hadn't even looked in the mirror this morning.

Betsy put a hand on the table and forced herself upright. "How about some coffee?"

"I'll get it. You sit." Bridget rushed to the coffee cart in the corner of the kitchen and poured herself a cup.

Grace pulled out a chair. "Did you sleep well?"

"I did. Thanks." Bridget sat.

"You missed breakfast," Betsy said. "But help yourself to these." She motioned to a plate with apple, blueberry, and banana-nut muffins.

Bridget selected one and placed it on a saucer.

"Did you talk to your boss?" Grace asked.

"Yes. She took the news pretty well. How about yours?" Bridget took a bite.

"Melanie was understanding." She didn't mention that Penelope hadn't been quite as supportive. It had sounded as though she'd expected Grace to shovel a tunnel through the snow herself.

"So, Bridget. Tell me about yourself." Betsy folded her hands on the table. "Are you from Los Angeles?"

Grace glowered at her sister, sending telepathic messages not to grill her client.

Bridget dabbed her mouth with a napkin. "No. Until a year ago I lived in Texas."

"What brought you to California? A boyfriend? Girlfriend?"

Grace groaned and rubbed her forehead. She'd forgotten about the bump over her eye when pain shot to the center of her brain. At least Betsy had played dumb about knowing Bridget was a lesbian. Otherwise, she probably would have known they'd been talking about her.

"No. I'm not seeing anyone." Bridget raised the mug to her lips and drank.

"Single and looking?"

"You don't have to answer that," Grace said, even though she secretly wanted to know.

"It's okay," Bridget said. "I don't have time to date. Work is my focus."

"That doesn't sound like any fun at all." Betsy frowned.

"I like it that way. In fact, I've never been with anyone longer than a few months."

A few months? It sounded like Bridget had never had a serious relationship. Disappointment flooded over her. Bridget was no different than Christina, or anyone else she'd dated. A workaholic with commitment issues or, worse, a player who flitted from one woman to the next.

Bridget swallowed a mouthful, wiped her hands on a napkin, and turned to Grace. "What time do you want to get together to work on the proposal?"

"Well, first we need to go shopping. We can't wear the same clothes every day."

Bridget wrinkled her nose. "My least favorite thing to do."

"That reminds me," Betsy said. "I put some of my coats in the living room, if you want to try them on."

"Thank you. That'll save me some money." Bridget rose from her seat and put her dishes in the sink.

"How about we drive into town in about an hour?" she asked.

"Perfect. I'll get some work done and meet you downstairs later." Bridget walked out.

"Well, that answers that." She stood and went to the coffee pot, needing another jolt of caffeine.

"Answers what?" Betsy asked.

She filled her cup to the brim. "Bridget is exactly what I'm *not* looking for in a relationship." She took a sip and leaned her hip against the counter. "It's for the best really. I don't want an entanglement before I find out about Maui anyway."

What she'd said was true, so why then did she feel so disappointed?

CHAPTER EIGHT

Ugly Cookies and Clothes

Maybe being trapped in Mistletoe Mountain wasn't such a bad thing after all. Bridget had already made more progress on *Shipwreck* than she ever would have back home. She sat at the desk in her room, clicked Save, and smiled. This was by far her best video game yet. A knock prompted her to look at the wall clock. She sprang to her feet and swung the door open, not surprised to see Grace looking miffed, considering they were supposed to meet downstairs almost an hour ago.

"I'm sorry," she said. "I totally lost track of time."

Despite Grace's sour expression, she couldn't have looked more adorable. She wore a red knit hat with a huge, fluffy pom-pom on top, a green scarf, and her puffy coat. Her cheeks were rosy red, either from being overheated in all the garb or maybe irritation.

"What are you doing?" Grace balanced on her toes and looked over her shoulder.

Not wanting her to see anything to do with video games, she rushed to the desk and closed the laptop. It was unlikely Grace would make the connection between her and Christina, but she didn't want to take any chances.

Grace placed a hand on her hip. "I've been waiting downstairs, and you were playing games?"

Obviously she hadn't been quick enough to hide the evidence. She couldn't tell Grace she'd been working on a project to impress Christina. Hurriedly, she put on one of Betsy's coats. She hadn't had much to choose from, so she'd gone with the least holidayish one available, a rust-and-brown plaid. The sleeves were three inches too short, and the buttons were nowhere close to being fastened, but at least it was warm.

"Should I just wear my windbreaker?" she asked, knowing she probably looked ridiculous in a coat two sizes too small.

"You're fine." Grace looked her up and down, a slight smile on her lips. Even though Grace was obviously finding joy in her predicament, she looked awfully pretty with mischievous eyes and a bright, shining face.

She examined the spot over Grace's eye. "Your head looks a little better today. Does it hurt?"

"Only when I touch it." Grace placed her fingertips on the bruise.

"I'd suggest not doing that then."

She pulled Grace's arm down, and their fingers naturally intertwined as though they'd been holding hands every day of their lives. It should have felt strange to lock eyes with a stranger and stand close enough to feel their breath on your skin, but it didn't. Maybe it was everything they'd been through yesterday, but Grace didn't feel like a stranger anymore.

"It's a good thing there isn't mistletoe over the door. Otherwise…" Grace released a nervous laugh.

She dropped her gaze to Grace's mouth. She couldn't remember the last time she'd kissed a woman. It wasn't high on her priority list, which made her desire to kiss Grace right now all the more strange.

She let go of Grace's hand and stepped back. "I guess we should get going."

"Right," Grace blushed in the cutest way possible and darted down the hall.

Once they were on the road, with Grace driving, she asked, "Do you think we could stop by your dad's office and see if there's any news about the avalanche?"

Grace looked at her watch. "It's almost lunch time, so he'll probably be at The Cookie Jar. We can go by there first and then hit some stores."

Main Street looked even more Christmassy than it had yesterday, if that was possible. Had they hung up even more decorations? She resisted the urge to comment, not wanting a speech about the wonders of the holiday. When they stopped at a red light, she spotted a picture-perfect family of a mother, father, and toddler. The father had the kid balanced on his shoulders as they all gazed, wide-eyed, in the window of a toy store. A melancholy mood washed over her. What would her life have been like if she'd had parents who loved her? Or even one parent? Maybe someone like Betsy, who apparently wanted a baby so much she wasn't willing to wait to get married first.

"Hey. Is anything wrong?" Grace asked softly.

Grace's kind, friendly face tempted her to express what she was thinking and feeling. Undoubtedly, she'd be understanding, but Bridget wasn't used to opening up. It'd be humiliating to tell someone that the people who were supposed to love you the most in life didn't even want you.

"I'm fine. The light's green." She pointed straight ahead.

Thankfully, Grace didn't press the issue. Instead, they drove in silence to The Cookie Jar. When they got inside, it was apparent a lot of cleanup had been done. If she hadn't seen the mess yesterday, she would have thought the bakery had been untouched.

Carol, who was tending to a customer, wore a frilly red apron with an embroidered snow scene and had her hair up in a bun. Grace looked a lot like her mother. They had the same green eyes, amiable, trusting face, and welcoming aura that made you want to confess all your sins. Grace and Betsy probably hadn't gotten away with anything when they were kids. Drew was sitting at the bar. He seemed like a genuinely nice fellow, and not that he was a pushover, but she suspected that the three women in his life pretty much orchestrated everything in the family.

When Carol saw Grace, she flew from behind the counter and hugged her. "It's so wonderful to see you walking through that door."

Bridget tensed when Carol turned to her, knowing what was coming next. Luckily, the embrace was quicker and not as suffocating as the one yesterday.

"Betsy tells me you're from Texas," Carol said.

"Yes, ma'am."

Either Carol had the inn bugged or Betsy was a blabbermouth. They'd just had that conversation a few hours ago.

"So you're way out here in California on your own?"

Grace released a frustrated-sounding breath. "Give Bridget a break, Mom. Betsy already grilled her this morning."

From the look on Carol's face, it didn't take a genius to know what she was thinking: possible girlfriend material. Not that Bridget wasn't attracted to Grace. After all, she'd had to practically pinch herself to keep from kissing her, but women like Grace were in it for the long haul. She'd probably been dreaming about her wedding day since she was six and had her dress picked out before she even found a fiancée.

"Hey, Dad," Grace said, and approached Drew. "Good to see you're eating something." She motioned to the grilled cheese and tomato soup.

"If I didn't make him come in here for lunch every day, he wouldn't put anything in his stomach." Carol went back behind the counter.

"Betsy was telling me that the town's in trouble." Grace sat on a stool beside her father. "Does the city council have any ideas of how to revive it?"

Drew dabbed his mouth with a napkin. "Mitsi Purnell is heading an ad campaign. I'm sure they'll come up with something."

Grace and Carol both dramatically rolled their eyes, probably at the mention of Mitsi.

"That woman couldn't save her soul, much less an entire town." Carol scooped up cookies with a spatula and placed them on a platter.

Bridget leaned against the counter beside Grace. "Does Mistletoe Mountain have a website?"

Drew nodded. "Sure do. Mitsi designed it herself."

"Hey. Didn't you say you're up for a computer-programmer job?" Grace asked her. "Maybe you could take a look at it and give us some pointers."

Funny how Grace had said "us" like she was still a resident. It was apparent that she loved the town, and Bridget would be happy to help as long as they were stranded here.

"Sure," she said. "I've taken a few classes in web design."

"Much appreciated," Drew said and jabbed a spoonful of soup into his mouth.

"Are those what I think they are?" Grace asked her mother.

"Indeed, and ready for decorating." Carol placed the last cookie on the plate. "I could use some help, if you and Bridget have time."

Grace looked at her with a pleading, hopeful expression. Was there anything those eyes couldn't make her do? Obviously not, since she said, "Okay, but just one." Besides, it'd give her time to ask Drew about the avalanche.

Grace flew behind the counter and got to work with her mother.

"Any news about the road opening?" Bridget asked, and sat beside Drew.

The bleak look on his face made her stomach tighten. Grace and Carol must have noticed it as well, because they stilled and gave him their full attention.

"It's worse than we thought." He put his spoon down. "There's at least sixty feet of snow and rocks on the pass."

"Oh, my." Carol wrung her hands.

"Was anyone hurt?" Grace asked.

"We don't think so. There aren't any missing-persons reports."

"That's one good thing at least." Grace let out a sigh of relief.

"How long before the road is open again?" she asked.

"We've got men working twelve-hour shifts with excavators, bulldozers, and dump trucks. I'd say at least a week, if not more."

"A week?!" She rested her elbows on the counter and buried her face in her hands.

"Look on the bright side," Carol said, waving a cookie in the air. "You're in the best Christmas town in the West. You can get your holiday shopping done and partake in all our festivities."

She forced a smile, glad Grace hadn't told her parents she disliked Christmas. They probably wouldn't understand.

"I better get back to work." Drew stood.

"You didn't finish eating." Carol narrowed her gaze.

Drew leaned across the counter and kissed his wife's cheek. "I gots lots of mayoring to do, woman," he said with a smile and was out the door.

Stewing about the recent news, Bridget didn't realize for a full minute that Carol had placed a cookie in front of her, along with several squirt-things of frosting. "What's this for?"

"You said we could decorate one," Grace said.

She was tempted to reach out and wipe a smudge of pink frosting from Grace's cheek. "When I said *we*, I meant you. I wouldn't know what to do."

"Didn't you ever decorate cookies with your mother?" Carol forced white frosting from a tube.

"No." She looked down, wanting to avoid the two sets of emerald eyes burning into her skin.

Grace walked around the counter and sat beside her. "It's easy. You can't mess up because, you know, they're ugly sweaters. Give it a try."

A pleasant warmth spread across her chest at the encouraging look on Grace's face. She hadn't ridiculed her or made a big to-do about it. Nor did she force her to participate. Instead, Grace quietly went back to squirting frosting.

Bridget picked up a container and squeezed until a dollop of red plopped onto the cookie. That wasn't so hard. She paused and considered what would make a distasteful sweater. It didn't take long before she made an outline of a tree decorated with multi-colored balls. For an extra touch, she added dots of white for snowfall. She sat back and examined her creation, quite pleased with herself. She glanced at Grace, who was staring right at her with a lopsided grin.

"What?" She asked, unsure of what was so amusing.

"I don't think I've ever seen anyone concentrate so hard before."

"I should hire you two." Carol wiped her hands on a towel and admired their work. "How about doing another one?"

She considered the notion and shrugged. Why not? Besides, she had a great idea for that creepy Elf on a Shelf character.

Since Main Street was one block from the bakery, Grace suggested they walk. She wanted to protest, considering it felt like negative-five degrees outside, but it did seem ridiculous to drive such a short distance. Within minutes they were in the hubbub of town, zigzagging around people lugging handfuls of shopping bags.

"So, is there a Target around here?" she asked.

A slight smile played on Grace's lips. "Mistletoe Mountain doesn't have chain stores."

She blew into her hands and rubbed them together. "Where are we supposed to buy clothes?"

"So many shops have closed. That used to be Fashion Depot." Grace pointed to a boarded-up building. "And over there was Shei's Originals. Guess she went out of business, too."

She shuffled her feet, hoping it'd get some blood flowing through her veins. "How about that place?" She motioned to what looked like a vintage shop. With the exception of underwear, she wasn't beyond buying used, especially since she hadn't planned to purchase a week's worth of outfits.

Grace sighed. "I really wanted to take you to Shei's."

"We're in no position to be picky. As long as they have heat and something in my size, I'll be happy." She tugged on Grace's sleeve and practically pushed her through the door.

They had been in the store all of three minutes before she was regretting her words. The place had heat and her size, but she was most certainly not happy. It was filled with nothing but sweaters more horrendous than the ones they'd just decorated at The Cookie Jar. She held one up that had a gigantic snowman on it with hundreds of fluffy white balls attached. She twisted her face. Did someone seriously wear that? Hopefully it had been a gift that'd gone straight to this store the day after Christmas.

"That's your color." Grace laughed.

She scowled, unsure of what was so funny. "Where are the normal clothes?"

Grace pointed to a sign on the wall that read Nearly New Holiday Happenings. Bridget groaned. Obviously, she hadn't paid close enough attention to the name. She stuffed the item back on the rack.

"We can get undergarments at the lingerie shop on the corner," Grace said, looking through a display of sweatshirts.

The word lingerie conjured an image of Grace in something frilly, red, and see-through. She was lounging on a bed in a seductive pose, beautifully lit by hundreds of candles. Bridget shook her head to rid herself of the sight, but not before she felt a rush of heat. It wasn't like her to have sexy visions of women she hardly knew. Flustered, she removed her coat and draped it across her arm, hoping Grace hadn't noticed how red her face probably was.

"You never did tell me why you don't like Christmas." Grace picked up a shirt and examined it.

"Yes, I did. It's too commercial," she said without making eye contact.

"Everyone says that. You must have some other reason."

"It's…it's sentimental hogwash."

Grace stilled and gaped at her. "That's part of what makes it so wonderful." She shook her head and mumbled something to herself.

A minute later, Grace clutched the front of a green sweater against her stomach and smiled. "I found the perfect thing for you."

"I'm almost afraid to see it." She grinned at Grace's animated, giddy expression.

Grace whipped the item around in one fast swoop. "Ta-da!"

She tilted her head. Actually, that wasn't half bad. An image of The Grinch sneering wickedly looked back at her. If this shop was her only choice, maybe she could at least find something anti-Christmas. With several outfits in tow, they headed to the checkout. Grace snatched the items out of her hands and placed them on the counter.

"What are you doing?" Bridget asked.

"This is on Tie the Knot." Grace handed a credit card to the cashier.

"I can't let you do that."

"Melanie told me to expense anything we need. You're our client, remember?"

Actually, Grace felt more like a friend than hired help. Guilt gnawed at her insides. At first, keeping her mouth shut about Christina had felt like a harmless fib, but now it was more like a deception. She liked Grace too much to continue lying. No matter the consequences, she needed to tell Grace the truth.

CHAPTER NINE

Confessions

Grace stood at the end of her bed and faced Betsy, who was sitting upright with her legs stretched out. She looked huge, uncomfortable, and beyond ready to deliver the baby. She didn't tell her sister this, but she'd thought about coming back in a couple of weeks when Betsy was due. At first, she had dreaded being stuck in Mistletoe Mountain, but so far it had been pleasant. Granted, it'd been only two days, but it was wonderful to see her family again and spend time with Bridget. As long as she avoided one particular place in town, being here wasn't so bad after all.

"Let's see what you bought." Betsy crossed her ankles.

Grace took the items she'd purchased at the thrift store out of a bag and piled them on the bed. "Just a couple pairs of jeans and some sweaters. I was hoping you might have a few things I could borrow. All they had was holiday stuff."

"You love Christmas."

"Yes, but how many of these can I wear?" Grace held up a red sweatshirt with a gigantic drawing of Santa stuck upside down in a chimney.

Betsy grimaced. "I see what you mean."

Grace tossed the item down and sat beside her sister. "You should have seen Bridget's face. It was hilarious." She laughed. It was the kind of laugh that reached deep inside her soul, releasing joy she hadn't felt in a really long time.

"Did she buy anything?" Betsy asked.

"Yes. In the end she was a good sport," she said, still chuckling.

"What else did you do?" Betsy adjusted her position in the bed.

"Bridget actually decorated two cookies at the bakery. I don't think she's as much of a Scrooge as she claims to be." She grinned, recalling how cute Bridget had looked when she hunched down and got to work.

"It sounds like you two had a good time." A smirk crossed Betsy's lips as she studied her.

"What?" she asked, not sure what her sister's odd expression meant.

"You practically glow when you talk about Bridget."

She rolled her eyes skyward. "I do not." She hopped out of bed, opened the closet, and took out a hanger.

"It's not a bad thing. I haven't seen you this happy in a long time." Betsy rested her hands on her stomach.

She put a sweater on the hanger and contemplated her sister's comment. Ever since Meghan's death, she'd felt a heaviness in the center of her chest, and years of dating the wrong women certainly hadn't helped alleviate it. In the past few days, she had felt ten times lighter, but that didn't mean it had anything to do with Bridget. Maybe she just enjoyed being back home again.

"I like Bridget. But we can't be anything more than friends." She pushed down feelings of disappointment. She'd never admit this to Betsy, but Bridget was the first woman she'd met in a long time that had piqued her interest. When they were standing in the doorway earlier, she had to fight the desire to kiss her.

"I don't think you should write Bridget off." Betsy swung her feet onto the floor and stood.

"You heard what she said this morning. She obviously has commitment issues and puts work over relationships. No way am I doing that again."

"You never know. Sometimes it takes meeting someone special to turn a person's whole life around." Betsy waddled to the door, put a hand on the knob, and looked back at her. "Think about giving

Bridget a chance. I have a feeling about you two," she said and left the room.

What in the world was Betsy thinking? She knew about her dating disasters, and the fact that Bridget had never been with anyone longer than a few months made her totally off limits.

She finished hanging the clothes and stood in front of the dresser mirror. Ugh. She looked awful. The winter cap had flattened her hair, and she didn't have any makeup on. She grabbed her purse and rummaged through it, searching for anything that might brighten her pale complexion. Unfortunately, all she found was Chapstick. For a moment, she considered asking Betsy for some blush and lipstick, but she'd just accuse her of getting dolled up for Bridget, which, of course, wasn't true. With no other choice, she fluffed her hair, straightened her clothes, and walked across the hall to knock on Bridget's door. When there was no answer, she went downstairs and found Bridget pacing in front of the fireplace, looking as nervous as she had the first time she'd seen her at Tie the Knot.

She walked into the living room and went right up to Bridget. "I know what you're thinking," she said.

"I don't think you do." Bridget sounded as though her vocal cords were partially frozen.

She placed her hands on Bridget's shoulders and looked directly into her eyes. "Don't worry. I've done hundreds of proposals, none of which have flopped. Your boss will love it, and you'll get that promotion."

A fragrant rose scent wafted through the air, which most likely came from Bridget. Not only did she smell intoxicating, but she looked beautiful. Inhaling deeply, Grace was tempted to lean closer, but instead she dropped her arms and stepped back. When it came to Bridget, she needed to keep her distance.

"Let's go outside, and I'll show you my ideas for the gazebo." She fetched their coats off the rack by the door.

Bridget hesitated but thrust her arms into the sleeves and followed her through the back door. The gazebo, which was behind the inn, was even prettier than she remembered. It was decorated with wreaths and endless strands of garland covered with red-velvet bows. In the center was a tree sparkling with white lights and candy canes, and snowflakes hung from the ceiling.

"Isn't it beautiful?" Grace trekked through the snow. When she reached the gazebo, she looked back at Bridget, who was still on the porch. "Aren't you coming?"

Bridget raised her collar and made her way across the yard. She stood in front of Grace and said, "I need to tell you something."

"What is it?" she asked, concerned about Bridget's somber expression.

Bridget inhaled a shaky breath and let it out slowly. "I had no idea who you were when I hired Tie the Knot. My boss…the person who is wanting the proposal…is Christina Worth."

A giggle escaped her throat, and she playfully slapped Bridget's arm. "She is not. What a lousy joke."

"It's true. I'm her assistant."

"There's no way Christina would get married. She was morally against commitment. In fact, we broke up partially because moving in together was too big of a step for her."

"I swear that this proposal is for Christina Worth of Worth Entertainment." All the blood drained from Bridget's face, leaving her as pale as a vampire.

A shiver went up and down her spine, and she took a step back. Bridget looked dead serious. "You're not kidding."

"I wish I were, but it's true." Bridget winced.

This was insane. What were the odds that someone would hire Grace to plan her ex's wedding proposal? And even crazier was the fact that Christina was getting married!

"Wait a minute," she said. "I told you about Christina yesterday before the earthquake. Why didn't you say something then? I could have turned around, and we wouldn't be stuck in this predicament."

Bridget's eyes shifted back and forth, and she pursed her lips.

She gasped. "You didn't intend to tell me, did you?"

"Not at first, but after I got to know you, I couldn't go through with it. I'm sorry I didn't say something sooner." Bridget's eyes softened, so much so they looked like two melted chocolates. She seemed sincere, but that didn't excuse the fact that she'd lied.

"Hold on," she said. "Who's Christina marrying?"

"Someone named Beryl. Why?"

"Oh my God! She's the woman Christina was having an affair with when I broke up with her."

Bridget's face fell. "Oh. Wow. I'm sorry. I had no idea."

She placed a hand on her stomach, attempting to ease the asteroid-sized knot in her gut. "Obviously I can't help you anymore."

"What do you mean?"

"I'm most certainly *not* planning a proposal for my ex-girlfriend and her mistress." She couldn't believe Bridget would even think that was a possibility.

"But we signed a contract, and I paid."

"Not my problem. You should have told me the truth yesterday." She turned and stomped through the snow.

"You owe me," Bridget yelled, which prompted her to stop and swing around. "I'm the one who got your purse out of Christina's office a year ago, and you said you owed me one."

What in the world was Bridget talking about? Eventually, the memory of that awful day came rushing back. She pointed and asked, "That was you?"

Bridget nodded and inched forward.

"I thought you looked familiar," she said more to herself than Bridget. "This doesn't change anything."

"What would your boss say about you quitting?" Bridget crossed her arms, the sleeves of Betsy's coat inching farther up her arms.

"Are you threatening me?" she screeched.

"It's your job. We all have to do things we don't like to do."

She gritted her teeth, reached down, clutched a handful of snow, and hurled it at Bridget. Thankfully, Bridget had slow reflexes, and it hit her right in the center of the chest. Grace spun around, marched to the inn, and charged up to her room. She slammed the door and threw herself on the bed, staring up at the ceiling.

How could Bridget trick her like that? She'd seen firsthand how distraught she'd been when she'd walked out of Christina's office. Didn't it occur to her that she might have an issue with this assignment? And to think she'd actually been attracted to Bridget.

When she'd looked into her eyes after the earthquake, she was sure she'd seen a good person. Someone filled with compassion. Someone very different from anyone she'd ever dated. How wrong she'd been.

She reached over and pulled a blanket up to her neck, needing to disappear. Christina wanted to get married? She'd been so against any sort of allegiance to their relationship. But then again, maybe she just hadn't wanted to marry her. How many of her other so-called commitment-phobic exes were also getting married?

A hard knock prompted her to bury her face in a pillow, not wanting to deal with Bridget right now. When the door swung open, she threw the blanket off and bolted upright, relieved to see Betsy.

"What in the world is going on?" Betsy came into the room. "You flew right past me in the living room like a maniac."

She didn't even remember seeing Betsy. "You aren't going to believe this." She clutched a pillow tight against her chest. "The proposal that Bridget wants me to plan is for Christina."

"Aguilera?" Betsy's expression brightened. She was a huge fan of the pop singer.

"Nooo. My ex Christina!"

Betsy's mouth opened and then snapped shut. A few moments later, she said, "Wait a minute. How does Bridget know Christina?"

"She's her assistant." Grace scooched over to make room for Betsy to sit beside her. "Bridget didn't know that Christina is my ex when she hired Tie the Knot. Just my lousy luck."

"Damn. What are you going to do?"

"I'm certainly *not* doing the job. No matter what Bridget says. I'll call Melanie and explain." Grace's stomach dropped. "Oh, crap. I just thought of something."

"What now?"

"I asked to get out of doing two jobs recently, which didn't go over well. I'm sure Melanie won't appreciate me trying it again."

"She can't expect you to plan your ex's proposal. I mean, that's a bit much."

"You think?"

"Totally. You have to at least tell her about it and see what she says."

Grace nodded. If Melanie could put herself in her position, surely she'd let her off the hook. She got her phone off the nightstand, took a deep breath, and dialed. Melanie answered on the second ring.

"Hi, Grace. How are things in Mistletoe Mountain?"

"Actually, there's a bit of a problem."

Betsy spread her arms wide and silently mouthed something that looked like *big problem*. Right. She shouldn't underestimate the enormity of the situation.

"Actually," she said. "It's a really huge hurdle."

"What's going on? Was there another avalanche?" Melanie sounded concerned.

"No. It has to do with the proposal. I just found out that Bridget's boss is…well…my ex-girlfriend, Christina. And not only that, but she's marrying the woman Christina was cheating on me with."

Betsy's jaw dropped. Grace couldn't believe she'd forgotten to tell her sister about that part.

"Melanie? Are you still there?"

"I am," Melanie said, curtly. "That's unfortunate, but what exactly are you saying?"

Wasn't it obvious?

"Surely you can't expect me to proceed with this job. Perhaps someone else could take over for me."

"No one else is available. They have their own workload to deal with."

"I understand, but put yourself in my place. What if you were asked to plan your ex-boyfriend's proposal?"

Betsy poked her arm and nodded. Anyone in their right mind would refuse the task. Well, anyone except Melanie.

"I'm not unsympathetic to your plight, Grace…" Funny, because she didn't sound a bit understanding. "I'm sorry this happened, but I expect you to rise above your emotions and do the same stellar job you always have, no matter who it's for."

She squeezed her eyes shut. "You can count on me." If she wanted any chance of getting the promotion, she had to suck it up and plan Christina's wedding proposal.

CHAPTER TEN

Making Up is Hard to Do

A week?!"
    Bridget held the phone away from her ear. She hated to give Christina the bad news, but her boss needed to know how long she'd be gone.

"What an ass-backward town." Christina huffed. "It shouldn't take that long to reopen a highway."

Bridget's temper flared at the derogatory description of Mistletoe Mountain. The last thing she wanted was to be stranded here, but no one seemed incompetent or disorderly. From the sound of it, Drew and all the workers were doing everything they could.

"It's not just massive amounts of snow, but boulders as well," she said in a sharper tone than she'd intended. "They have men working around the clock."

Christina sighed loudly. "How are the proposal plans going?"

"Good." She lied. "I know you wanted details tomorrow, but all the drama around here has slowed progress a little. I'll email you something soon." She hoped Christina would think that "drama" meant the avalanche.

"Keep me updated," Christina said and abruptly disconnected.

She sat on the bed, noting that someone had placed the ceramic Santa Claus back on the nightstand. She picked it up, opened the drawer, and stuffed him inside. She pursed her lips and stared at the bedroom door, tempted to seek out Grace, considering it was almost noon. They hadn't seen each other since yesterday, when she had dropped the bomb. From the looks of it, Grace had stayed in her room, no doubt to avoid her.

She couldn't really blame Grace since it was her fault they were stuck here. If she'd been upfront, they would have driven back to Tie the Knot, and Melanie could have assigned the job to someone else. But then again, she wouldn't have had the opportunity to spend time with Grace, and that was something she enjoyed more than she'd like to admit.

What upset her most about the whole thing was the hurt look in Grace's eyes, as though her lie of omission had been a slap across the face. She needed to ask Grace to forgive her. Not so she'd plan the proposal—although there was that—but so things would be right with the world again. It bothered her immensely that someone she cared about was angry with her. She went rigid, surprised that she felt affection for Grace after such a short time.

She went to the desk, picked up her wallet, took out the crumpled note, and read it.

Her name is Bridget. It means strength.

She lowered herself into the chair and stared at the handwriting. It was moments like this—when she felt most alone in the world—that she needed a reminder of how strong she was. Somehow this simple message gave her a boost, made her feel like she could get through any difficulty. She put the paper back in her wallet, knowing that everything would work out with the proposal, the promotion, and especially with Grace.

She opened the laptop on the desk and did a search for Mistletoe Mountain. Vaguely, she recalled looking at the town's website the night before they left but hadn't examined it with a critical eye.

"Eww," she said to herself when the home page appeared. Talk about an eyesore. This was supposed to be the Christmas capital of the world, or at least the state. Where were the cutesy graphics and photos? Where was the pizazz? This was about as boring as

The Wall Street Journal. She clicked around, each view worse than the last. Mitsi what's-her-name didn't know crap about designing a website. This wouldn't attract Santa himself, much less tourists.

She went to the shopping section, scrolled down, and clicked on a link to The Cookie Jar. This was horrible, too. She exited and visited several of the other stores' websites, shaking her head at each one. No wonder the town was going down the drain. She reached for a pen and mindlessly tapped it on the desk, deep in thought. Moments later, she jotted down ideas on a nearby notepad. Before long, she had several pages worth. Returning her attention to the laptop, she accessed a free website builder. It wasn't ideal due to limitations, but at least she could do a fairly good mock-up of what was possible.

Three hours had flown by when she heard a light knock on the door. She opened it, happy to see Grace. Her fingertips were tucked into her back pockets, and she gnawed on the corner of her mouth, appearing nervous.

"Hi." Bridget crossed her arms and then immediately uncrossed them, not wanting to seem standoffish. Not sure what to do with her hands, she rested one on the doorknob.

Following an uncomfortable silence, Grace said, "So here's the thing. I spoke to Melanie and no one else is available, so I'm stuck…" She cleared her throat. "I mean, I'll help you with the… you know…proposal."

"That's great. I really want you to know how sorry I am. You were totally right that—"

"It's fine." Grace held up both hands like she'd just pointed a gun at her. "Let's just get this…thing…done and go our separate ways."

Her heart plummeted. Grace didn't intend to keep in contact with her, and from the sound of it, she wanted nothing more than a strictly business relationship. While she was happy to have help, she'd miss the friendship they'd forged. Or maybe she was the only one that felt like they'd become friends.

"Under the circumstances," Grace said, "having the couple stay at Betsy's inn isn't feasible. So I'll show you a few other options in town."

"Right. I'm sure the last thing your sister wants is to host Christina." Bridget cringed at the sour look on Grace's face. Apparently, it was best not to utter that particular name again.

"I'll meet you by the front door in half an hour." Grace displayed what was probably supposed to be a smile but looked more like a painful grimace from stepping on a thorn barefoot.

Getting Grace to forgive her was going to take a lot of work.

The silence was deafening as they drove through town, but Grace was in no mood to be chatty. She was still sore at Bridget for not telling the truth sooner. No doubt she was the type who only looked out for herself—just like Christina. Bridget had said her boss was her idol and had even used the word brilliant. Little did she know that she'd been referring to Christina. She gripped the wheel tighter. Anyone who would have a cheating workaholic as her idol was surely off her rocker. Thank goodness Grace hadn't acted on her attraction and asked her out, like Betsy had suggested.

"How many other hotels are in town?" Bridget asked.

"They're called inns." She regretted the snarky remark the moment it was out of her mouth, reminding herself that Bridget was a client. "There's two," she said in a softer tone. "Mitsi Purnell owns one, so we'll leave it as a last resort."

She hadn't been in either lodging and had no idea what they were like, but Bridget was in no place to be picky. Grace reached over and turned on the radio, but not before getting a whiff of how good Bridget smelled. It was the same rose scent she'd detected yesterday.

"Hey, isn't this your favorite song? 'Kissin' by the Mistletoe'?" Bridget turned the volume up a notch.

She stopped at a red light and stole a glance at Bridget, shocked she'd remembered. It'd been a fleeting comment when she had described her ideal proposal.

"That sounds like Aretha Franklin," Bridget said with a smile that made her look prettier than Grace wanted to admit.

"I thought you hated Christmas music."

"Aretha can make anything sound amazing."

Christina had also been an Aretha fan, she disliked Christmas, *and* she always smelled good, too. The similarities between them were uncanny.

About a mile out of town, they pulled up to the Evergreen Inn. Grace worked hard to keep her expression neutral considering the building looked like a rundown shack in need of a fresh coat of paint and shutter repairs. A large part of her would love to stick Christina and Beryl in a place like this, but it'd probably get Bridget fired, and she didn't want that to happen, no matter how angry she was.

Noting Bridget's frown, she said, "I'm sure it looks better on the inside."

They got out of the car and walked along the sidewalk, which required a good snow-shoveling. Once on the porch, they stomped their feet on the rug to shake off excess snow and opened the door. She watched as Bridget did a quick sweep of the room. She couldn't fault the concerned look on her face, considering the shabby surroundings.

Bridget approached her from behind and whispered in her ear. "There aren't any Christmas decorations. Normally that'd be a plus with me, but this *is* a holiday proposal."

A tingle ran up and down her spine when Bridget's breath caressed her skin. For a moment, she was tempted to lean back and feel the length of Bridget's body. She swallowed hard and rubbed the spot on her neck, wanting to rid herself of the pleasant sensation. They made their way to the lobby and approached the desk. A girl, who looked all of twelve years old, appeared startled and pulled earbuds out when she saw them. The way she hurriedly stuffed her phone under the desk made Grace think whatever she was doing wasn't allowed.

"How can I help you?" she asked.

"I'm Grace and this is Bridget. We were wondering if you have an availability for Christmas Eve."

"I'm sure we do." The girl consulted the computer. A few moments later she said, "Yep. No problem. How long are you two staying?"

With the town's lack of tourists, they'd probably have no problem finding a room, but that didn't mean it'd be up to standards.

"Actually, could you show us your nicest suite first?" Grace asked.

"Cool." The girl grabbed a set of keys.

"Do you decorate for the holiday?" Bridget asked as they followed her down a long, dark hallway.

"I'm not sure. My parents own the joint, and they're out of town right now. Not able to get back because of the avalanche." She stopped, unlocked a door, and opened it.

A strong odor of bleach and cigarette smoke almost knocked Grace over when she walked inside. Immediately, she noticed the stained carpet and the atrocious color scheme. Plus, it was smaller than her kitchen. She looked over her shoulder at Bridget, who was still standing in the entrance. She gave a disgruntled look and silently mouthed "no." Clearly, she'd already made up her mind.

After they went back to the car, Grace started the engine and turned on the heater. "Mistletoe Mountain has limited lodging options. You barely glanced in the suite."

Bridget briskly rubbed her palms together. "I wouldn't call that a suite."

"B&Bs are known for charm, not size."

Bridget stilled and looked her square in the eyes. "Can you seriously see Christina and Beryl staying there?"

"No. I suppose not." She sighed. "But you only have one more choice, so at least give Mitsi's place a chance, or else the lovebirds will be sleeping on a park bench."

"Fine." Bridget held up her hands to the vents. "Can we get some coffee? I need something to warm me up."

"What you need is a pair of mittens." She reached into the backseat and felt around the floorboard. Locating what she wanted, she tossed a pair of gloves at Bridget, one hitting her in the face.

Bridget looked at the items that had fallen into her lap. "Thanks," she said and put them on. "But can we still get coffee?"

"You're the boss." Frustrated, she shifted into reverse with vigor, hoping Bridget got the message that coffee had absolutely nothing to do with planning the proposal.

Fifteen minutes later, she parked on Main Street, not far from where they'd shopped for clothes yesterday.

Bridget stared straight ahead at the restaurant in front of them. "The Christmas Carol Café? Isn't there anything in this town that isn't Christmas-fied?"

"Nope. Well, except maybe for the Evergreen Inn." Grace hopped out and went into the café, not waiting for Bridget. Admittedly, she could use a shot of caffeine as well.

Bridget stood in line beside her and studied the menu behind the counter. "How are their lattes?"

"Excellent. They have a special way of roasting the beans."

"My boss is obsessed with a particular kind of coffee." Bridget chuckled. "Every day I have to…" Her eyes popped open and her jaw dropped. "I'm sorry. I forgot…I mean…"

Grace wished she could be lucky enough to forget about Christina. She put a hand on her hip and said, "Kopi Luwak from Sacred Grounds."

"That's right. Actually, that's where I saw your business card and got the idea to call Tie the Knot."

The Santa proposal. She closed her eyes and inwardly groaned. If she hadn't done that job, she probably wouldn't be stuck in this predicament.

Bridget insisted on paying when they stepped up to the counter to order. Grace didn't argue, considering Bridget owed her for not telling the truth sooner. Bridget did seem genuinely sorry, but that didn't change the fact that Grace had to plan her ex's proposal. She still couldn't believe Christina wanted to get married. She had tossed and turned half the night stewing about it. It wasn't that she still loved Christina—in fact, she probably hadn't ever been in love— but what did Beryl have that she didn't? Was it her personality? Slim figure? Status? At one particularly low point, she even questioned if anyone would ever want to marry her. She and Meghan had planned to spend their lives together, but even then they hadn't discussed marriage.

They ordered their drinks and stepped aside.

"Grace?"

She turned around at the sound of a familiar voice and was face-to-face with Gus. A rush of emotions overcame her, elation mixed with pure panic. She wasn't sure whether to hug him or bolt out the door.

"It is you." Excitement filled Gus's clear blue eyes, the exact same color as Meghan's. "How long has it been?"

"About ten years." Her voice trembled, which wasn't surprising considering how her insides quivered.

Gus's smile faded. "Right after the US National Championship."

Her heart leapt into her throat. Wanting to change the subject, she said, "This is Bridget."

He looked at Bridget as though seeing her for the first time.

"Hi." Bridget raised a hand. "What's the national championship?"

"An ice-skating competition," he said. "It's what determines who'll qualify for the Olympics. I take it you're not a skater?"

"Nooo. Not even close." Bridget laughed quietly. "Are you two ice-skating fans?"

He tipped his head and wore a confused expression. "Grace performed in the competition."

Bridget looked at her. "I didn't know you were an ice skater."

"*Were* is the operative word," she said.

"Grace is being modest," Gus said. "She was a US figure-skating champion."

"That was a long time ago." She glanced at the barista. Where the hell were their drinks?

"You and Meghan would have made it to the Olympics if… well, you know." He turned to Bridget. "I was Meghan's father and their coach. I own The Ice Palace, the skating rink in town."

"I can't believe you didn't tell me you're famous." Bridget looked shocked.

"Hey!" Gus said, looking Grace dead straight in the eye. "I'm having a fund-raiser on Christmas Eve. Would you consider doing a performance? I know you'd bring a big crowd."

"I…uh…I actually don't skate anymore."

Gus's eyes softened, and he lightly placed a hand on her arm. "Because of what happened?"

She vehemently shook her head and swallowed a lump in her throat. "No. Of course not. I'm just too busy with work and life."

Out of the corner of her eye, she saw Bridget intently staring at her. The dawdling barista finally put their drinks on the counter. Relieved, she reached over and grabbed them, handing one to Bridget.

"I wish we could visit more, but we really should get going." Grace took a sip, burning her tongue on the steaming liquid.

"Oh. All right." Gus looked terribly disappointed. "Do think about coming to the rink while you're in town."

"I will." *When hell freezes over.* "It was great to see you, Gus. Really."

Once outside, she faced Bridget head-on. "Before you say anything, my life as a professional ice skater is in the past, and that's where I'd like to keep it. I would appreciate you keeping your questions and comments to yourself."

"Okay."

"That's it?" She was shocked it'd been that easy.

"I understand," Bridget said in a quiet voice. "There are things about my past I'd rather not talk about, too."

Although she was glad Bridget hadn't pushed for information, she did wonder what she was referring to. She couldn't ask, though, and not give Bridget the same courtesy she'd just demanded.

"I appreciate that," she said. "Do you mind if we see Mitsi's inn tomorrow? I have a splitting headache." She rubbed her temples.

Seeing Gus again had thrown her off kilter, and she needed some time to herself. On one hand, it was like being reunited with a cherished, long-lost relative. On the other, it dredged up painful memories that made it difficult to breathe.

Since the age of five, she had spent more time with Gus than she did her own father. At first, she'd been interested in skating only to copy her best friend, Meghan. It didn't take long before he realized what a natural talent they both had and began training them for competitions. They'd spent every day after school and the weekends on the ice. She hadn't loved anything more than skating beside Meghan. After her girlfriend's death and bombing in the nationals, she hadn't strapped on a pair of skates again.

CHAPTER ELEVEN

Labor Day

B ridget rubbed her eyes and trudged down the hall. She came to an abrupt stop when Grace barreled out of the bathroom looking absolutely radiant in jeans and a pink sweater. Inwardly, she groaned. Grace would have to catch her in pajamas with little elves frolicking in the snow.

"Betsy loaned these to me," she said, when Grace leisurely ran her gaze up and down her. "Apparently she doesn't have anything that isn't Christmassy."

"Sure, she does, but I told her you needed to get in the holiday spirit."

"This is because of you?" She narrowed her eyes.

"Is it working?" Grace smirked.

"No." Despite her firm tone, she was happy Grace was talking to her again.

"Are you just getting up?" Grace looked at her watch. "It's almost eleven."

She covered her mouth and yawned. "I was up all night working on something."

"That's what happens when your employer is a slave driver."

"It's not anything for Christina." She'd been designing the town's website but wanted to surprise Grace after she finished it. "I can be ready in a jiffy if you want to show me the other inn."

"Actually, I'm having lunch with my mom, and then we're doing some Christmas shopping. Is it okay if we go later this afternoon?"

"Sure," she said and suppressed another yawn.

"All right. I'll see you later."

She watched Grace bound down the stairs. Did she still have feelings for Christina? Maybe part of Grace's upset was the fact that Christina was proposing to someone other than herself. She pushed down an irrational twinge of jealousy at the thought of Grace with another woman. It wasn't like they were dating and probably not even friends anymore.

After showering, she went back to her room and stood in front of the closet. She frowned at the choice of outfits and pulled out the Grinch sweatshirt. Once dressed, she sat at the desk and booted up the laptop, dying to google Grace. After typing *Grace Dawson figure skater*, her mouth fell open. Grace was a big, frigging deal. She felt stupid for not recognizing her, but then again, she'd never followed the sport.

After visiting several sites, she discovered that Grace had started training, along with Meghan, at a young age. They'd both won state, regional, and national titles and were expected to make the Olympic team. Sadly, Meghan had died a month before the US National Championship. She stared into space. Why had Grace stopped skating? It seemed to have been her whole world from age five to eighteen. Returning her attention to the laptop, she opened YouTube and found the video of Grace's last performance.

From the moment the music began, she was captivated. Dressed in a sequined white outfit, Grace looked like an angel gliding effortlessly across the ice. She made it look so easy, and although Bridget had never donned a pair of skates, she was fairly certain it'd be difficult. At one point, Grace spun around in a sitting position and didn't even appear dizzy when she came out of it. She had the beauty and gracefulness of a ballet dancer.

About two minutes into the program, the tip of Grace's blade caught on the ice, sending her skidding across the surface. The crowd gasped. Grace pushed herself up and tried to stand, but fell again. She curled into a fetal position and looked completely helpless. Bridget's heart ached, not knowing if she was injured or just mortified. She wanted to jump into the screen, pick Grace up, and carry her to safety. She wanted to shield her from the audience and flashing cameras and let her know everything would be okay. The commentator announced that Grace had just blown her chance to qualify for the Olympics. Grace must have been devastated. As horrible as that was, though, her decision to never skate again was even worse.

Bridget closed the laptop and put a hand on her stomach when it rumbled. In her haste to research Grace, she'd forgotten to eat breakfast. She went downstairs and into the kitchen, stopping when she saw Betsy braced against the counter clutching her stomach, her face contorted.

She rushed to Betsy's side. "Are you okay?"

Following a lengthy pause, Betsy said, "Phew! That was a strong one."

"You're having contractions?" Bridget's heartbeat quickened.

"Braxton Hicks. It's false labor pains."

"That didn't look false to me."

"I know. Right?" Betsy lowered herself into a chair and sighed. "I hate to think what the real thing will feel like."

"So, you're okay?"

Betsy met her eyes. "I'm fine. I called the doctor this morning, and she said it's normal."

"That's good." Relief washed over her. She had no idea how to take care of a pregnant woman about to deliver.

"Have a seat and keep me company." Betsy motioned to an empty chair.

"Actually, I was wondering if any muffins were left."

"The cook made a fresh batch this morning. Help yourself." Betsy pointed to a Tupperware platter on the counter.

She lifted the cover and inhaled deeply, basking in the sweet aroma. She took a banana-nut muffin and placed it on a saucer, telling herself she'd eat healthier once she was back home. Her high metabolism kept her weight down, but sooner or later all the carbs would catch up with her.

"There's some coffee as well," Betsy said, as though reading her mind.

Loaded with caffeine and sugar, she sat at the table across from Betsy. "Do you know the sex of the baby?" she asked and took a bite.

"No. I want to be surprised." Betsy smiled. "Do you have any brothers or sisters?"

She shook her head and swallowed. "You and Grace seem close."

"We are. I wish we got to see each other more often."

This would be the perfect opportunity to ask Betsy about Grace's skating career and hear firsthand what had happened. She wiped her hands on a napkin and said, "I was surprised to learn that Grace was a professional figure skater."

Betsy drew in a sharp breath. "Where'd you hear that?"

"We ran into Gus yesterday."

A deep crease formed across Betsy's forehead. "Grace didn't mention that."

"Gus told me that she almost made it to the Olympics. He also invited her to perform at a fund-raiser, but she said she doesn't skate anymore. Is that because of Meghan and what happened at the nationals?" She studied Betsy, looking for any clues in her expression.

"You'd have to ask Grace that question, although I doubt she'll talk about it." Betsy got up and put her dishes in the sink. After she turned around, she said, "It's funny, but you know more about Grace than anyone she's ever dated. Particularly Christina."

"I guess you know who I work for." She felt bad for not only deceiving Grace, but her family as well. "I'm sorry I lied. Guess I was just thinking about myself."

"Don't beat yourself up about it. You told the truth…eventually. Besides, maybe it'll be good for Grace."

She snorted. "How is planning her ex's proposal a good thing?"

"Grace tends to sweep her past under the rug. It's time she face things head-on." Betsy held her gaze. "Actually, I think you're just what she needs right now."

She pointed at her chest, surprised. "Me? Why?"

"You challenge her. And besides, Grace likes you."

Betsy's cell phone rang, and she pulled it out of her pocket and answered it. Her voice faded into the background as Bridget puzzled over the last thing Betsy had said. Even though she didn't know what she'd meant by "like," the notion that Grace might be interested in her sent a tingle up her spine.

Betsy hung up and frowned. "It never ends."

"Something wrong?"

"That was the plumber. The water heater needs replacing."

She wished she could do something to help, feeling the need to repay Betsy for the free room and board.

"I'll figure it out. Help yourself to more coffee," Betsy said and left.

After downing the last bite of her muffin, Bridget had a strange desire to go outside. Since arriving in Mistletoe Mountain, she'd balked at the arctic temperatures, but she actually felt like walking in the snow. Bundled in a coat, scarf, and gloves, she stepped out onto the porch. The sky had a deep-cobalt color, and the air was crisp and fresh. She bounded down the steps and placed one foot firmly on the ground, hearing the crunch underneath her shoes. She reached down, got a fistful of snow, and packed it into a ball. Winding up her arm like an all-star pitcher, she flung the snowball into the air and watched it crash into a tree trunk.

When she heard the creak of the screen door, she looked over her shoulder. Betsy, paler than the snow, stood in the doorway clutching her purse and looking faint.

"My water just broke," she said, sounding terrified.

CHAPTER TWELVE

Impatiently Waiting

B ridget dropped her gaze to the ground, halfway expecting to see a puddle. She'd seen enough medical shows to know what it meant when a woman's water breaks.

"Labor," Betsy said through jagged breaths. "Real labor."

Holy crap. Betsy was going to have the baby right here on the porch. Bridget's heart beat in triple time.

"We need boiled water and clean towels," she said in a rush of breath and went to Betsy's side. "Where do you keep the pots?"

Betsy took a deep breath, let it out slowly, and glared at her like she was insane. "Take me to the hospital."

She conked herself over the head with the palm of her hand. "Right. Of course. Hospital."

Betsy fished keys out of her purse and thrust them into her hands. In record time, they made their way through the inn, down the sidewalk, and to Betsy's car. That was the quickest Bridget had ever seen her move. Once Betsy was situated in the passenger seat, she rushed around and got behind the wheel. Just as she closed the door, Betsy doubled over in what looked like intense pain. Bridget turned the key and lightly patted Betsy's back, hoping the baby wasn't on the floorboard when she sat up. As she backed out, she realized she had no idea where she was going. She'd taken Grace to the ER but didn't know how to get there from here.

"Which way?" Cold sweat trickled down her back.

A few moments later, Betsy motioned with her hand. "Forward. Right at the stop sign."

The tires screeched when she floored it.

Slowly, Betsy straightened and appeared to be in less distress than moments ago. "I'm not due for two more weeks."

She turned her head just long enough to see the fear in Betsy's eyes before refocusing on the road. "Don't worry. The little tyke has had plenty of time to grow." She had no idea if that was true, but she did know that Betsy needed to remain calm.

"You think so?"

"Sure. He…or she…will be fine."

Betsy grasped her hand and didn't let go until they pulled into the emergency entrance. Once they were inside, nurses whisked Betsy away in a wheelchair, leaving Bridget feeling helpless in the waiting room. She took a deep breath in an attempt to slow her beating heart. Everything was going to be okay. Betsy was in the right place and under the care of people who knew what they were doing.

Grace. She needed to call Grace. Relieved that she'd had the sense to bring her phone, she found the number in her contacts, dialed, and was immediately connected to voice mail. She tapped her foot. This was the longest greeting ever. After what felt like a gazillion minutes, she finally heard a beep.

"It's me. Bridget. I'm at the hospital with Betsy. She went into labor. Don't worry. I'm sure she'll be fine. Okay. I'll try again if I don't hear from you."

She disconnected and paced. Five minutes later, she dialed again, with the same results. Frowning, she googled the number for the mayor's office and asked for Drew, but he was at the avalanche site and had no cell reception. Next, she called The Cookie Jar, but whoever answered said Carol wasn't there. With a big knot in her stomach, she sat for twenty long minutes before a nurse came out.

"Are you Bridget?" she asked.

"Yes." She shot out of the chair.

"Betsy is asking for you. Follow me."

She fell into step beside the nurse, unsure how much help she'd be in this particular situation. A few moments later, she entered the room and saw Betsy sitting in bed.

"Are you okay?" she asked and held onto the cold, steel, bed railing.

"I will be after this is over." Betsy displayed a weak smile. "Can you call Grace?"

Her shoulders slumped. "I tried several times, but all I get is her voice mail. I also called your dad, but they said he's out of cell-phone range, and your mom wasn't at the bakery."

"Could you keep trying?" Betsy's face tightened, either because of disappointment or another oncoming contraction.

"Absolutely."

Betsy locked eyes with her. "I'm scared. I've never done this before."

"Hey. Everything is going to be all right." She grasped Betsy's hand. Normally, she preferred a hefty amount of personal space, but this wasn't a normal circumstance.

"Would you stay with me until they take me into the delivery room?"

"Of course," she said with a smile.

It felt nice to be wanted. Maybe, if even for a few moments, she could pretend like Betsy was her sister and that the baby would be her niece or nephew. For the next twenty minutes, she helped Betsy breathe through contractions and talked to her about anything and everything, trying to keep her calm. The time went by quickly before Carol and Grace burst into the room.

"What happened?" they asked in unison and rushed to Betsy's side.

While Betsy filled them in on the details, Bridget inched toward the door, not wanting to encroach on their time together. While she was happy they had arrived, she also felt disappointed that she was no longer needed. Without them noticing, she quietly slipped out of the room. When she reached the waiting room, she contemplated driving back to the inn but didn't want to leave until she knew Betsy and the baby were okay. Fifteen minutes later, Grace appeared and sat beside her.

"How's Betsy?" She put aside the magazine she'd mindlessly been thumbing through.

"The doctor said she and the baby are fine. Now it's just a matter of waiting for the delivery." Grace turned and looked her in the eye. "Thank you for taking care of her."

She shrugged. "It was no big deal."

"Yes, it was." Grace placed her hand on her arm. Even through the sweatshirt, she felt the gentleness of Grace's touch. "Betsy told us how sweet you were and that you calmed and reassured her."

At this close distance, she was dumbstruck at how stunning Grace looked. Her face lit up with a beautiful smile, and her eyes gleamed. Drew rushed into the waiting room, and Grace sprang to her feet.

"What's going on?" he asked, breathless.

"Everything is okay…Grandpa." Grace smirked.

Drew's eyes widened. "Betsy had the baby?"

"No, but she will. Going into labor a few weeks early is totally normal," Grace said, probably reading her father's concerned expression. "I know Betsy would love to see you before they take her to delivery. She's in room seven."

"You're not coming?" Drew asked.

"No. They allow only one person with her at a time, but I'm sure you could sneak in."

Drew nodded and looked at Bridget. "Thank you for the message you left with my secretary. I wouldn't want to miss this."

She smiled, his excitement contagious. "My pleasure."

Grace sat back down as they watched Drew hurry down the hall.

"How about I get us some coffee?" She stretched her arms high overhead. When Grace didn't respond, she noticed her sad expression. "Hey. Is something wrong?"

"I just realized this is the first time I've been back in this waiting room since Meghan's accident," Grace said, staring straight ahead. "She was in a coma in ICU for a week before she died. Visiting hours were limited, so I spent most of the time right here in this chair."

"I'm so sorry. That must have been incredibly difficult. How do you even get over a loss like that?"

Grace huffed. "Not very well. I've spent the last ten years making terrible choices."

"What do you mean?"

"You don't want to hear this," Grace said with a dismissive wave.

"Sure, I do." Bridget turned in her seat and faced Grace. "Plus, we certainly have the time. Betsy could be in labor for hours."

Grace wrapped her arms around herself. Several beats later she said, "After I broke up with Christina, I spent a year working on myself and realized that since Meghan's death, I had dated only women who were afraid of commitment."

Bridget's heart lurched when Grace held her gaze for a long moment. She had the distinct impression that Grace would put her in the "afraid of commitment" category, too. It wasn't that she was scared. She just had other priorities aside from romantic relationships…or so she told herself.

"After years of blaming my girlfriends," Grace said, "I accepted that I was the one sabotaging my own chance at happiness. I was attracting the same type of woman because I was afraid of getting close to someone, only to have her leave unexpectedly like Meghan did."

Bridget stiffened. For some reason, this conversation was making her terribly uncomfortable. She needed to defend herself and tell Grace that she was nothing like the women she'd dated.

"I know what you're thinking," she said. "You think I have a fear of commitment, too."

"Do you?"

"No. I just put establishing a stable career over romantic relationships. Nothing's wrong with that."

"Not if that's what makes you happy."

"Well, I am. Happy, that is. I'm really, really happy."

"Okay," Grace said with a chuckle. "I'm glad you're so happy. I just know that I want to find my forever partner. I love my job, and my friends and family, but I feel like something is missing."

Bridget sprang to her feet. "I'm going to the cafeteria to get some coffee. Do you want anything?"

"Did I say something to upset you?"

"No. I just want something to drink."

"Okay," Grace said softly. "Coffee would be great."

Bridget fled and punched the down button on the elevator, not sure why she was so agitated. What she'd told Grace was true. She was happy. Wasn't she?

Half-asleep, Grace draped her arm across something soft and rested her head on a strong, stable surface. A rose scent wafted into her nostrils, making her sigh contentedly. Slowly, she opened her eyes and lifted her head, heat rushing through her when she realized she was intertwined in Bridget's arms. Considering the crooked position of Bridget's neck against the back of the chair, she should have woken her up so she could adjust her position. Instead, she carefully laid her head back on Bridget's shoulder, tightened her hold, and melted into Bridget's body. Undoubtably, this was as close as they'd ever get.

Why did she have to be attracted to someone who had different relationship goals? As proud as she was not to repeat old patterns, it was still disappointing. She felt more of a connection with Bridget than she had with anyone in the past ten years. The slow rise and fall of Bridget's chest and the faint sound of her breath lulled her back to sleep.

"Wake up, everyone!"

She jumped at the sound of her mother's voice and extricated herself from Bridget's arms. Bridget's eyes fluttered open, and she rubbed the back of her neck, seemingly unaware she'd been hugging her.

Drew, who was sitting across from them, yawned and asked, "What's going on?"

"We're grandparents to a healthy baby boy!" Carol beamed, despite looking like she'd just endured a brutal twelve-hour nursing shift.

They all rose and let out yelps of joy. It was official. She was an aunt and couldn't have been more excited. She looked at her watch, noting that it was five a.m. Poor Betsy. She must be exhausted.

"So everyone's okay?" Drew bounced up and down.

"Betsy's resting, and Oliver Drew is awake, ready to take life by the horns." Carol smiled widely. "If you're all quiet, you can see him in the nursery." She locked arms with Drew and led the way.

Grace felt a surge of joy, excited to meet her nephew. She noticed Bridget walking toward the exit. "Where are you going?"

Bridget stopped and turned. "I'll drive Betsy's car back to the inn."

"Don't you want to see the baby?"

An unreadable expression crossed Bridget's face. "I don't want to be in the way."

"What are you talking about? You won't be in the way." She extended her hand, hoping Bridget would accept it.

Bridget hesitated, swayed on her feet, but then grasped her hand, and they walked side by side down the corridor.

When they reached the nursery, she asked, "Which one is he?"

Carol pointed. "Right there."

Her insides melted at the sight of the most adorable bald-headed bundle she'd ever seen. She vowed right then to get past her aversion to Mistletoe Mountain and visit more often. This little guy was going to grow up knowing his aunt firsthand.

She looked at Bridget, glad she was there to share the moment, and was struck by her sad expression. "Hey, what's wrong?" she whispered.

"I should go." Bridget turned and bolted down the hallway.

What had happened to upset Bridget so much? Grace chased her down the hall and into the waiting room. "Bridget, talk to me."

"You should go back to your family."

"Betsy's asleep, and I have a lifetime to spend with Oliver. Now please tell me what's wrong."

Bridget gazed at her for a long moment with sorrowful brown eyes and then sat. Grace lowered herself into the chair beside her.

"I'm not actually sure why I'm so upset." Bridget let out a humorless laugh. "Guess I'm feeling sorry for myself."

"Can you tell me why?"

Bridget reached into her pocket and pulled out a billfold. She opened it, took out a piece of paper, and handed it to her.

She silently read it.

Her name is Bridget. It means strength.

"What's this?" she asked.

"I think my mother wrote it."

"What do you mean you think?"

Bridget took the note out of her hand and stared at it. "Twenty-five years ago on Christmas Eve, I was left on the doorstep of a church in Needville, Texas with this note pinned to the blanket. It's the only link I have to my family."

Grace's gut twisted into a knot. She had a million questions, but all she could utter was, "I had no idea."

"No one does. I've never shared that with anyone. Until now."

"What happened? Were you adopted?" She hoped Bridget would say that she'd been raised by a nice family and that, despite her rocky start in life, she'd been loved and cared for.

Bridget's face tightened. "I spent the next eighteen years getting tossed from one foster family to another. Some of them were great, but for whatever reason it never lasted."

She wished she could do something to erase the pain in Bridget's eyes. She placed her hand on Bridget's arm and gently squeezed. "I'm so sorry you had to go through that."

Bridget ran fingers through her hair. "I guess being around your family, seeing how close you all are, and how excited everyone is about the baby reminded me of what I never had." She smiled weakly. "See. Told you I was feeling sorry for myself."

"It's natural that being here would bring up emotions. I can't imagine what you went through, but it made you into the amazing person you are today."

Bridget looked at her like she didn't know what she meant.

"You're an independent, strong, ambitious, kind woman," she said. "I've relied on my family so much over the years, but you've done it all by yourself."

Bridget sank into the chair, looking embarrassed by the compliment.

"Thank you for showing me the note and sharing what happened," she said.

Bridget buried her face in her hands. "I'm so going to regret this in the morning."

"Hate to tell you, but it *is* morning."

She rubbed gentle circles on Bridget's back. Even though her mind raced with questions, Bridget looked too exhausted to divulge anything further. What she needed now was comfort, and Grace was glad she was the one to offer it.

CHAPTER THIRTEEN

Disappointments and Discoveries

Oliver was the cutest baby Grace had ever seen. He wasn't wrinkly and fussy like most newborns. Instead, he had an angelic face and calm demeanor. She sat in Betsy's hospital room and cradled her nephew in her arms, enjoying the time alone with him as Betsy walked the halls and their mother rested at home.

"You are so loved, and you'll have the best life ever." She gently stroked Oliver's pudgy, soft hand.

Her throat tightened as tears swelled in her eyes, a mixture of happiness for the new addition to the family and sadness for Bridget overwhelmed her. Bridget had been a baby like this once, but instead of being adored and taken care of, she'd had no stability, support, and maybe not even any love. No wonder she'd never dated anyone longer than a few months. She was probably afraid of being rejected, since that's all she'd known. Grace had thought she had Bridget figured out, but you can't really know someone until you understand how their past shapes their present decisions.

"What's wrong?" Betsy asked, shuffling into the room.

"Oh, I'm just getting all sentimental over this little guy." She wiped her wet cheek on her shoulder. She wanted to tell Betsy what she'd learned about Bridget, but it wasn't her story to share.

When Betsy crawled into bed, Grace placed Oliver in her arms.

Betsy smiled and looked with adoring eyes at her son. A few minutes later she asked, "Where's Bridget? I wanted to thank her."

"Still asleep, I imagine. We didn't get back to the inn until six this morning." She yawned.

"You should get some rest, too." Betsy chuckled as though she'd thought of something funny. "I just remembered how Bridget wanted to know where I keep the pots so she could boil water. She must have thought she'd have to deliver the baby herself."

Grace giggled. "Seriously? I'll have to give her a hard time about that."

"Be nice. She was probably freaking out."

"Speaking of Bridget, I should get going. I'm showing her Mitsi's inn today."

"How are the proposal plans going?" Betsy watched Oliver wrap his fingers around her pinkie.

"Between the avalanche and everything else, we haven't gotten anything done." She sighed. "It's only Tuesday, though, and looks like we'll be here all week."

Her cell phone rang. *Melanie.* They hadn't spoken since Saturday, when she had tried to get out of doing the proposal.

"Hi, Melanie." She walked to the window overlooking the parking lot.

"Hello, Grace. How's everything going ?"

"Okay, considering. Did you get the email I sent you and Penelope?"

"I did. I'm sorry to hear it's taking so long to reopen the highway. Listen. I wanted to do this in person but didn't want you to hear it from anyone else. I offered the Maui position to Lynn."

She slammed her eyes shut. "I see."

"It was a tough decision, and I want you to know how highly you're regarded here. You're one of my best employees."

"Thank you and I'm sure Lynn will do a great job."

"Take care, Grace, and we'll talk soon."

Her heart sank. In less than a minute, Melanie had squashed her hopes and dreams. She wasn't going to be a manager, she wasn't moving to Maui, and she wasn't escaping Penelope. She felt utterly and totally disheartened. She'd grown up believing that figure skating was her destiny. Until ten years ago, it had never occurred to her that she'd have to find another profession. After the national competition, she'd floundered for years, in and out of meaningless jobs, until she landed at Tie the Knot. It was something she enjoyed and the first time she felt like she'd found her place in the world. Getting the promotion would have cemented the notion that maybe she hadn't totally screwed up her life by turning her back on her skating career.

"Grace? You okay?"

She turned and exhaled an exasperated breath. "I didn't get the promotion."

"I'm sorry." Betsy looked genuinely disappointed, which she appreciated, considering her sister didn't want her to move. "Maybe something else will open up."

"I doubt Melanie will open another office anytime soon." She slung her bag over her shoulder. "I better get going. Do you need me to do anything at the inn?"

"No. Mrs. Irving is already there. Luckily she was available a couple of weeks early."

"Okay. I'll see you later." She kissed Oliver's forehead and left.

Twenty minutes later, she stood in front of Bridget's door at the Candy Cane Cottage. Hopefully, Bridget wouldn't feel uncomfortable about having shared her past. Grace felt honored that she'd opened up to her.

She knocked and felt a flutter in her stomach when Bridget opened the door and flashed a heart-stopping smile. Her eyes were bright, her entire being seemed to be filled with fresh energy, and she didn't appear to mind that she was wearing a reindeer sweater. This was the happiest Grace had ever seen her. So much for being worried that she'd feel uncomfortable.

"Good morning." Bridget stepped aside.

"Good morning to you, too." She walked into the room. "You're awfully chipper to say you got only a few hours' sleep."

Bridget closed the door. "I know. It's weird, but I feel great."

"Well, you look beautiful." She wasn't embarrassed by the admission. She'd spoken the truth and didn't mind Bridget knowing what she thought.

Bridget locked eyes with her, and the weird flutter she'd felt before returned. Why did being near Bridget make her nervous and excited all at the same time? She'd never felt that way with anyone before, not even Meghan. She placed a hand on her stomach. Maybe she'd eaten one too many muffins for breakfast.

"Since you're talking to me again, does that mean I'm forgiven about not telling you about Christina sooner?" Bridget asked.

"I'm still not happy about the whole thing," she said. "But I don't think you meant any harm, and you did eventually come clean."

Bridget let out a relieved-sounding sigh. "That's good. Are we checking out the other inn today?" She plopped on the bed and slipped on her shoes.

"Whenever you're ready." She glanced at the laptop, which was on the desk. "Playing video games, I see."

"Not exactly." Bridget tied her laces. "I'm creating, not playing."

Grace did a double take and studied the screen closer. "Holy Dooley. You designed that?"

"Yeah. A few final touches and I'll be done." Bridget rose from the bed.

"That's incredible." She sat at the desk, never taking her eyes off the laptop. The graphics were the best she'd ever seen, the detail and color scheme amazing. As impressive as that was, though, appearance wasn't everything.

"Show it to me," she said, wondering if the story compared to the visuals.

"Really?" Bridget asked, sounding excited.

Before she could respond, Bridget kneeled beside her. "It's called *Shipwreck* and geared toward kids." She clicked through the game as she spoke. "It's about an orphan who gets stranded on an island. He encounters all sorts of obstacles and has to figure out how to survive on his own. I wanted to create something that showed kids how strong they are and that they can handle anything that comes their way."

It wasn't lost on her that the game featured an orphan. Maybe Bridget designed video games as a way of healing her past.

"So, it's more than just entertainment," she said, impressed with what she was seeing. "You're helping children learn autonomy and resilience." She looked at Bridget. "This is incredible work."

"You really like it?" Bridget asked with a hopeful expression.

"I love it. I thought you said you were applying for a computer-programmer position."

Bridget stood and sat on the edge of the desk. "I am. Why?"

"After seeing this…" She waved a hand at the computer screen. "You need to be a developer."

"I don't even have a bachelor's degree."

"Who cares!" She threw her arms into the air. "Has Christina seen this?"

"No. I showed her another one I did, and she seemed to like it."

"I know Christina…unfortunately." She swallowed the bitter taste in her mouth. "And her only redeeming quality is that she's a successful businesswoman who can spot talent. Present this, and ask for a game-developer position."

Bridget's eyes widened. "I can't do that. First, there aren't any openings, and second, I'm not qualified."

She felt her jaw drop. "You have no idea how good you are, do you? Remember, I worked for Worth Entertainment. I saw what they produced, and this…" she pointed at the screen, "beats them all."

"I dunno." Bridget rubbed her chin. "The only corporate experience I have is being Christina's assistant."

She exhaled sharply. "Fetching that woman coffee at Sacred Grounds is a total waste of your talent. You're setting your sights too low. You have to ask for what you want in life. Otherwise, you'll just get passed over."

Bridget snorted. "I thought I was setting my sights too high."

"Look at me," she said. "When Melanie announced she was opening an office in Maui and needed someone to run it, I flat-out told her I was the best person for the job."

Bridget's head jerked toward her, eyes intense. "You're moving to Maui?"

"Well, no. I didn't say it was the perfect example. I didn't get the job."

Bridget seemed to relax and looked relieved. Grace liked the idea that Bridget might want her to stick around. Did that mean she desired something more than friendship? She dismissed that thought the moment it popped into her head. Bridget had been clear about her goals, and a romantic relationship was at the bottom of her list.

"Are you disappointed?" Bridget asked.

"Totally bummed. It would have been a huge promotion, and I could have gotten away from Penelope." She felt a dark cloud settle over her head at the mention of her boss. She rose from her seat, not wanting to think about what awaited her back in LA. "Anyway, should we check out Mitsi's inn now?"

"Lead the way," Bridget said, with another one of those heart-stopping smiles.

Once they were on the road, Grace said, "This is what I was thinking. Considering this is Christina and Beryl, it's best to go with classy but simple." She hated to admit it, but knowing the clients personally did come in handy.

"What'd you have in mind?"

"The nicest restaurant in town is the Candlelight Café. The food is excellent, and there's an amazing view of the snow-covered valley."

"It needs to be Christmassy, too," Bridget said.

"Trust me." She snorted. "They have decorations and lit trees galore. Oh, and Victorian carolers walk around singing to the patrons."

"Sounds great, but there needs to be more. You know, something special that stands out."

She stopped at a crosswalk to let several people pass. "That's where the creativity comes in. We could do a million things, such as scatter rose petals from the entrance to the table, where more petals spell out *Will You Marry Me*? Or maybe Christina can give Beryl a box of expensive candy and replace one chocolate with the ring. Or my personal favorite is the Christmas cracker." However, she doubted Christina would be fun enough to want to do that.

Bridget's eyebrows drew together. "Crackers?"

"Not the eating kind. You know, those festive table decorations that snap open when pulled apart." She stepped on the gas pedal when the coast was clear.

Bridget bit her bottom lip, appearing oblivious to what she was talking about. She'd probably never seen one before, which made her wonder if Bridget had ever had a real Christmas.

"When they pop open," she said, "little prizes fall out, like candy and notes with jokes."

"Like a piñata?"

"Sort of, but you don't beat the hell out of it. Anyway, I have a contact who makes personalized Christmas crackers. With enough notice she could do a proposal one." She turned into the Bethlehem Inn and parked. "There's just one potentially big problem."

"What's that?" Bridget asked.

"The restaurant is closed Christmas Eve. But maybe with enough monetary incentive, they could be persuaded to open. You never did tell me the budget."

"That's because I don't have one. All Christina said was to spare no expense."

"Well, that's good, because I'm sure it'll cost a small fortune. We might even be able to get the carolers, too."

"I'll email Christina tonight and tell her the ideas and see what she thinks."

"I still can't believe she wants to get married." She shook her head.

"Are you sorry she's asking Beryl and not you?"

"God, no! I don't want Christina. We were a total disaster. I'm just surprised because she was always so dead set against any type of commitment."

"Maybe when you meet the right person, priorities shift." Bridget looked her square in the eye.

Her heartbeat quickened. She had a feeling Bridget wasn't just talking about Christina. Was Bridget rethinking her priorities as well? Before she could ask, Bridget cleared her throat and suggested they go inside before they froze in the car. Funny, because the last thing on her mind was the cold. The look Bridget had given her had warmed her all over.

Once inside, she stifled a groan at the sight of Mitsi. Hopefully, they could make this quick. Give Bridget a tour of their nicest room, secure the reservation, and split. They made their way through the reception area and to the main desk.

Mitsi looked up from a book she was reading and stood. "Grace. What a nice surprise."

"Hello, Mitsi." She smiled tightly. "Do you remember Bridget?"

Mitsi peered at Bridget over her bifocals. "Oh, yes. From the other day."

"Bridget is making reservations for her boss to stay in Mistletoe Mountain over Christmas and was wondering if you'd have availability."

Mitsi batted her hand in the air. "We absolutely do. Honey, it's been like a ghost town around here. We're barely making ends meet."

"Sorry to hear that. I understand businesses have been suffering."

"Half the stores in town have closed down." Mitsi took off her glasses and tossed them aside. "The Gift Box, Twinkle Town, and now The Ice Palace."

Her heart squeezed. "Gus's skating rink?"

Mitsi lowered herself onto a stool. "If his fund-raiser doesn't bring in enough money, he said he'd have to shut it down after the new year."

She remembered him mentioning a fund-raiser but didn't think the entire business depended on its success. The Ice Palace had been a second home for her and Meghan. They'd trained together, experienced ups and downs, and had fallen in love on the ice. Not that she wanted to go back there again, but she hated the thought of it wasting away in cobwebs or, worse, being torn down.

Mitsi leaned across the desk and whispered, "I heard Betsy had her baby. It's beyond me why someone would want to raise a child without a husband."

She narrowed her eyes.

"It's just not the way things should be done." Misti sneered. "Why, the Bible states that no one born out of an unnatural union may enter the assembly of the Lord. Poor little thing doesn't stand a chance."

Her heart beat wildly, and she wrapped her hands around the edge of the desk to keep from decking Mitsi. No matter how much Bridget needed this reservation, Grace couldn't listen to anyone downgrade her sister or nephew. She opened her mouth but then snapped it shut when she heard Bridget's voice.

"Ignorant, hate-filled people like you drive me nuts." Bridget wagged a finger in Mitsi's face. "There's nothing wrong or unnatural about Betsy raising a baby alone. Oliver is lucky to be born into such a loving family. That little boy is blessed and will have the best life possible. The person you should worry about is yourself. Prejudice doesn't sit well with the big guy."

Grace wanted to jump up and down, pump her fist in the air, and give Bridget a big kiss. That was the best thing she'd ever heard. She focused on Mitsi, happy to see her mouth wide open and her eyes the size of two platters.

"I couldn't have said it better myself," she said with a firm nod.

Mitsi closed her mouth and tugged on the hem of her sweater. She put her glasses back on and cleared her throat. "It doesn't seem as though we have any availability after all."

When they were outside, she grabbed Bridget's shoulders. "That was awesome! Did you see the look on her face?"

Bridget smirked. "She was asking for it."

"I wish Betsy and my mom could have heard you."

"Mitsi's just lucky I didn't bring up her lousy web-design skills, too."

"You looked at the town's website?"

Bridget shoved her hands into her pockets and walked to the car beside her. "Not only that, but I did a demo as well."

"That's awesome. I'd love to see it, and I know Dad would, too." She stole quick glances at Bridget. "I'm going to my parents' house tomorrow night for dinner. Betsy and the baby should be out of the hospital by then. Would you like to come? You can show Dad the website."

"Sure. I could do that."

"Great." She smiled, unable to hide her excitement.

Once in the car, she started the engine and turned on the heater. Bridget rubbed her palms together and said, "Guess I blew it. Christina doesn't have a room now."

"Well, maybe I can talk to Betsy. It's just for two nights."

Bridget brightened. "Do you really think she'd go for it? I mean, I'd understand if she wouldn't want your ex at her inn."

"Let me see what I can do," she said and drove away.

Having Christina and Beryl stay at the Candy Cane Cottage was the last thing she ever thought she'd want, but considering it was for Bridget, she had to at least try.

A strong jolt that felt like someone had dropped an anchor in the middle of the bed awakened Bridget. Her heart raced, and she clutched the blanket as she rocked back and forth. When the movement stopped, she pulled the blanket under her chin, feeling like a kid hiding from the boogeyman. That had definitely felt like an earthquake. She fumbled to turn on the lamp and knocked over the ceramic Santa. She'd given up sticking him in the drawer since the housekeeper insisted on displaying him. She sat up and looked at the clock. Three a.m. Her stomach lurched when the bed swayed with an aftershock. It wasn't nearly as long or hard as before, but enough to make her jump out of bed, race across the hall, and knock on Grace's door. Within seconds it swung open. Grace looked adorable with mussed hair and wearing red-and-white-striped flannel pajamas.

"Are you okay?" Grace's voice cracked.

"Just shaken. How about you?"

"Same." Grace motioned for her to come inside. She sat on the bed and patted the space in front of her.

Bridget sat cross-legged, surprised at how relaxed she felt in such an intimate setting. Sitting on a woman's bed in nothing but her PJs would have felt awkward if it were with anyone other than Grace. "Do you think the earthquake was as big as the one the other day?"

"Didn't feel like it. I just hope it didn't cause another avalanche."

Actually, having to stay in Mistletoe Mountain longer wouldn't be the worst thing in the world. She'd get to spend more time with Grace.

"This reminds me of when Betsy and I would have slumber parties." Grace motioned between them. "Did you ever do that with any of the foster families? I mean, did you have kids to play with?"

"Sometimes. Like I said before, though, it never lasted." She had always avoided talking about her past, but she actually wanted to open up. "I'm not sure why, but just when I thought I'd be adopted, the family would change their minds. Usually, it was right before Christmas. Maybe so they wouldn't have to buy extra presents."

Grace's eyes softened. "Is that why you don't like Christmas?"

"Probably. It reminds me of the family I never had. I don't know what I would have done without video games. They were an escape from reality. When I learned how to create them myself, I was really hooked."

"I think your work is brilliant, but maybe one day you'll find your own family."

"I don't think that's in the cards for me." Ever since she could remember, she'd dreamed of working for Worth Entertainment, and a long-term partner had never been part of the plan. That *was* still what she wanted, right?

"How about you?" Bridget asked. "Have your exes soured you on relationships?"

"Not a bit. If anything, they helped me narrow down the type of woman I want."

"I'm sorry for how Christina treated you," she said. "Just because I work for her doesn't mean I condone her behavior."

"Thank you for saying that."

"Can I ask you something?" She bit her lower lip, unsure whether Grace would be open to this particular topic.

"Sure." Grace stretched out her legs.

"Why don't you skate anymore?" The startled look on Grace's face immediately made her regret the question.

"That's not really something I want to talk about." Grace crossed her arms.

"I can understand that, but sometimes talking helps. I felt like a hundred-pound weight had been lifted off my chest when I told you about my past. Maybe it'd be the same for you."

Grace's face tightened. Bridget knew she was pushing her luck, but Betsy's words echoed in her ears. *Grace tends to sweep her past under the rug. It's time she face things head-on.*

"After we ran into Gus," Bridget said, "I googled you and watched the YouTube video of your last performance."

"Great." Grace rolled her eyes dramatically.

"There's nothing to be embarrassed about. I was awestruck at how beautifully you skated."

"Until I fell on my ass." Grace shot out of bed and took a swig of water from a bottle on the desk.

"Is that why you stopped?"

Grace blew out a strong puff of air and rested a hand on her hip. After a lengthy pause, she sat back on the bed, looking rigid. "Partly."

She wasn't going to make this easy. Bridget was going to have to pry the information out of her. "And because of Meghan? I read that she died a month before the Olympic trials."

"Why do you even have to ask? Sounds like you already know everything after you cyber-stalked me."

Ouch. She'd gone too far. She should go back to her room before she upset Grace more.

"I'm sorry I brought it up. I should let you get some sleep." She stood, took two steps, and stopped when she heard Grace's voice.

"No. I'm sorry."

She turned and saw Grace's gloomy expression.

"To me, skating and Meghan go hand in hand. We were always on the ice together." Grace stared into space with a faraway look in her eyes. "During that last performance, all I could think about was how much I missed her. I lost my concentration and blew my chance to make the Olympic team."

Bridget sat back down and wanted to reach out and hold Grace's hand. Instead, she patiently waited for her to continue.

"Losing Meghan was horrible, but it also changed the entire course of my life. We were going to live together, perform whenever possible, and teach classes with Gus at The Ice Palace."

"I've never been in love, so I can only imagine how you felt," she said. "But to never skate again. Don't you miss it?"

"With every cell of my being." Grace locked eyes with her. "I've never admitted that to anyone. As much as I claim to have moved on, I'm terrified."

"Of what?"

"Years ago, I went to the downtown rink in LA intending to get on the ice. I didn't even make it past putting on skates before I ran out in tears. Being there did nothing but bring up painful memories. Everything I loved about the sport was overshadowed by what I had lost."

"If you ever want to try again, I'd be happy to go with you." She was surprised at how much she wanted to help Grace.

"Thank you." Grace looked at her and smiled. "You're a good friend."

The word friend pierced her heart. Is that all they were? Just friends?

CHAPTER FOURTEEN

Under the Mistletoe

Grace pulled into KissMe Mistletoe Farms and parked in front of a big, red barn. She was seventeen the last time she was here. Visiting the farm for mistletoe and apples had always been a family holiday tradition, one she was happy to share with Bridget. When she had invited Bridget on this little spree, she'd purposely omitted the fact that they'd be outside in the orchard, afraid she'd decline because of the cold weather.

Once inside, everything was just as she remembered. The barn was packed with holiday treasures, one-of-a-kind gifts, and barrels full of apples. She spotted Harlan behind the apple-cider stand polishing glasses, unsure he'd recognize her after all these years. They zigzagged through the store and stood in front of the bar. Harlan raised his head, paused for a full five seconds, and then broke out in a humongous smile.

"Why, if it isn't the star of Mistletoe Mountain herself. Little Gracie Dawson."

She smiled. "Hello, Harlan."

"I was telling my granddaughter the other day about how you almost made it to the Olympics."

Normally, her chest would tighten when anyone mentioned ice skating. Today, though, the comment had little effect. Maybe Bridget had been right. Opening up had released some of the tension.

"This is Harlan," she told Bridget. "He owns the farm."

"Nice to meet you," Bridget said.

"You as well." Harlan pointed a finger at Grace. "I bet you're here for your family's yearly order. Your mom makes the best apple turnovers I've ever tasted."

"And you make the best hot cider." She looked at Bridget. "You have to try some."

"You had me at hot." Bridget briskly rubbed her palms together.

Harlan poured two cups and handed one to each of them. She wrapped her fingers around the mug and inhaled deeply, enjoying the spicy scent. She blew into the steam and watched Bridget take a sip, her eyes practically popping out of her head.

"Good, right?" she asked.

Bridget swallowed. "Very. What's in it?"

"A master never reveals his secrets." Harlan tucked his thumbs in his suspenders and jutted his shoulders back. "But I will say this batch comes from apples I picked just yesterday."

"I thought harvest was in the summer." Bridget picked up an apple off the counter and examined it.

"It's year-round," she said. "Fujis are late November and December, so that's probably what we'll get."

"There are some Granny Smith ones, too," Harlan said. "And plenty of mistletoe on the branches. Feel free to grab a basket and head on out there."

"Out where?" Bridget put the apple back and took another sip.

She lowered her chin and batted her eyelashes. "I may have failed to mention that we'll be picking the mistletoe and apples ourselves."

Bridget gasped. "It's like ten degrees. I see apples here. And there." She pointed to various bins. "We won't get frostbite inside."

"It's more like twenty-eight, and that's no fun at all. Plus, we need mistletoe, too."

"That big sign over there clearly says *Mistletoe for Sale*. Everything you need is in this nice, cozy barn." Bridget took another drink.

"I'm not breaking our family tradition because you're afraid of getting cold." Grace snatched a wooden basket. "Are you coming with me?"

Bridget looked at Harlan, who held up his hands as if to say, "Don't ask me for help."

"Fine." Bridget huffed. "Have another cup of this ready for me when we come back. Extra hot, please," she told Harlan.

She linked arms with Bridget and led her outside and into the orchard. It was as though they'd stepped into a Christmas-card photo. Pristine snow coated the ground, and rows of icicle-covered trees were decorated with hundreds of crimson apples, in stark contrast to the bright white. The cloudless sky was the deepest blue she had ever seen. She'd almost forgotten how magical this place could be.

"I loved coming here when I was a kid," she said. "I'd dance around and pretend I was Snow White."

"I bet you were adorable. Did you also fantasize about being kissed by Prince Charming?"

"*Princess*, thank you very much." She rested her hands on her hips. "Even back then I knew I was more attracted to girls than boys." She held out her arms and twirled in a circle. "Isn't it beautiful here?"

Bridget looked at her. "Yes. It's very beautiful."

She stilled, and her face warmed despite the frosty air. The intensity in Bridget's eyes made her wonder if she was referring to her and not the scenery. She wanted to tell Bridget that she was the beautiful one. Her cheeks were rosy, her eyes bright, and she seemed to glow from the inside. Instead, she said, "I hope you're not too cold."

"I'm freezing my ass off." Bridget smirked, which let her know she wasn't too upset.

"Have you ever been apple and mistletoe picking?" She lumbered through the snow with Bridget beside her.

"Nope." Bridget shivered and slipped her hands into her pockets.

"It's easy." She approached one of the trees and wrapped her fingers around the plump fruit. "First, lightly squeeze to make sure it's firm. Then roll the apple upward off the branch and give it a little twist. Don't pull straight down." She demonstrated and placed it in the basket.

Bridget grasped an apple and glanced over her shoulder. "What do you mean roll it up?"

"I'll show you." She moved close to Bridget and took her hand, feeling a tingle where their skin met. Slowly, she guided Bridget until the fruit was free.

"Perfect." She stared into deep, brown eyes and fought the urge to slide her arms around Bridget's waist. She could hardly remember the last time she'd been in the arms of a woman she really cared for.

Bridget peeled her gaze away and bent down. When she stood back up with the apple in her hand, Grace hadn't realized it had fallen to the ground.

She took a step back. She needed to get it together, sure she was the only one feeling the palpable electricity between them. "We… uh…we should get to work. Mom expects plenty of apples," she said and turned away.

Within a short time, they had a basket full of scrumptious-looking fruit and went in search of mistletoe.

"It's easy to spot," she said. "Just look for a clump of green foliage with white berries on the branches."

Bridget scanned the area and pointed. "Over there," she said, sounding excited.

As Bridget quickly made her way through the snow, Grace rushed to catch up, happy to see that she seemed to be enjoying herself. Upon reaching the tree, Bridget tilted her chin upward and glared at a clump of mistletoe overhead.

"What were you saying before about the mistletoe legend?" Bridget asked, never taking her eyes off the branch.

"When a couple kisses underneath mistletoe that means they'll have a happy life together. And when a single woman isn't kissed, she'll remain unattached for another year."

Bridget looked her in the eye. "The year's almost over. Have you been kissed yet?"

Was Bridget offering? Just the thought made her heart race. One part of her wanted to kiss Bridget more than anything, but the other knew that would be disastrous. Why complicate their friendship with physical intimacy when they had no future together? But then again, it was just one little kiss. People do that all the time, even friends. What would be the harm in a peck on the cheek? It's not like they had to do a full-on smooch.

When she didn't respond, Bridget arched an eyebrow.

"No. I haven't," she said, softly.

Bridget took a step forward and closed the distance between them. She placed her hands on Bridget's hips and dropped her gaze to plump lips as red as the apples they'd just picked. When Bridget leaned down, Grace closed her eyes and their mouths met. An icy breeze swirled around them, but all she felt was the warmth of Bridget's skin. As their lips moved in unison, she melted when Bridget lightly ran fingers through her hair. This was no innocent cheek kiss. She'd had plenty of beautiful women in her arms the past ten years, but they hadn't been Bridget. They didn't make her stomach tighten from one kiss. Her heart fell to the ground when Bridget pulled back and broke their connection. If it were up to her, she would have kissed Bridget forever.

"I guess this means you'll find the love of your life now," Bridget said, her voice cracking.

"I suppose so." She brushed her fingertips over her own mouth, still relishing the feel of Bridget's lips on hers.

Bridget sat in the passenger seat as stiff as a statue while Grace drove them to her parents' house. She had no idea what had possessed her to kiss Grace. One minute she'd been admiring how beautiful Grace looked, and the next she was flirting and kissing. And what a kiss it had been. After coming to her senses and pulling back, she had wanted to wrap her arms around Grace and do it again.

Neither one of them had mentioned their little make-out session since it'd happened that afternoon. Afterward, they'd paid for the apples and mistletoe and gone back to the inn, retreating to their respective rooms until it was time to leave. If Grace thought she'd kissed her just to fulfill that silly mistletoe legend, she'd be mistaken. She'd done it because she had wanted nothing more than to be close to Grace.

"Are you okay?"

She flinched at the sound of Grace's voice. "Sure. Why do you ask?"

"You're awfully quiet. Is something on your mind?"

This was her opportunity to bring up the kiss and say…what exactly *would* she say? That she wanted to do it again? And then what? Grace wasn't the casual three-month-long dating type. Plus, once they were together, she was certain she'd get attached, give her heart away, and never want it to end. And then where'd she be? Relationships never last. People change their minds and leave, never to be seen again.

"I think I know what's bothering you," Grace said when she didn't respond. "I know being around my family will probably bring up memories of your past, but think of them as your family, too. My parents really like you, and Betsy can't stop singing your praises."

A warmth settled in the center of her chest at the thought of belonging to the Dawsons, at the thought of belonging to Grace.

They pulled into the driveway of a house glowing in thousands of white lights. On the lawn stood a life-size Santa sitting in a sleigh pulled by reindeer. The tree trunks were illuminated in red and green, and gold lights twinkled in the branches. They got out of the car and made their way to the porch. Grace knocked twice before opening the door. Wonderful scents filled Bridget's nostrils, making her mouth water. She hadn't had a home-cooked meal in forever. Grace hung their coats in a closet by the door. Strolling into the living room, Bridget eyed a humongous Christmas tree, an evergreen wreath over the fireplace, and several lit candles, which gave the room a cozy, golden glow. Admittedly, the house looked inviting. It made her want to curl up on the sofa with Grace and watch a movie. Not a Christmas one, of course. She wasn't getting soft or anything.

"Mom must be in the kitchen," Grace said.

She followed Grace through the dining room and into the kitchen, where they found Carol stirring something in a large pot.

"I didn't hear you come in." Carol tapped the spoon against the side of the pot and placed it in a holder by the stove. She wiped her hands on an apron and gave them both a hug.

"That smells so good," Bridget said, inhaling deeply.

"We're having stew, cornbread, and apple pie for dessert," Carol said with a smile.

"Speaking of apples. We got these this afternoon at Harlan's farm." Grace handed her mother a bag.

"Thank you." Carol placed it on the counter and looked at the mistletoe in Grace's hand. "Could you two hang that for me?"

Grace seemed to tense all over, and the muscles in her jaw tightened. Was she remembering their kiss?

"Don't you want to do that yourself?" Grace threw the mistletoe onto the counter as though it were a hot potato.

"Oh, no." Carol waved a hand in the air. "Anyplace is fine by me." She opened the oven, stuck a fork in the cornbread, and closed it again, seemingly deciding it wasn't ready.

"Did Betsy get released from the hospital today?" Grace asked, never taking her eyes off the mistletoe.

"She's upstairs in the guest room feeding Oliver. We convinced her to stay here for a few days. Knowing Betsy, if she was at the inn, she wouldn't resist working."

"That's great," Grace said. "Where's Dad?"

"In his study."

Grace turned to her. "Would you like to show him the website now?"

"Sure." She wondered if this was nothing but a way to delay hanging mistletoe.

"Don't be too long," Carol said. "Dinner will be ready soon."

Grace led her down a hall and knocked on the door. Drew opened it, his gloomy expression quickly transforming into joy.

"I'm so glad you two could come tonight." He stepped aside for them to enter.

"Oh, good. You have your computer on." Grace motioned to an oak desk. "Is it okay if Bridget shows you the town's website she designed?"

Drew looked at her, surprise evident on his face. "I know we talked about it, but I didn't think you'd actually do it. I'd love to see it. Have a seat." He pulled out his chair.

She navigated to the web program and input her credentials as Drew and Grace looked over her shoulder.

"Son of a gun." Drew whistled through his teeth as she scrolled through the homepage. "That looks amazing!"

"I added a special section for tourists," she said and clicked. "This is where activities, shopping, lodging, and more can be listed."

Grace tapped her shoulder. "Show him The Cookie Jar."

"I looked at a few of the business websites and found that they could use a lot of improvements as well." She opened the bakery homepage. "I'm not done with it yet, but it gives you an idea of what's possible."

"Wow," Drew said, wide-eyed. "That's so much better than what we have now."

"This might help bring in more people," Grace said. "No one will want to visit Mistletoe Mountain if they don't even know what's here."

"There's still a lot of work to be done to get it up and running," Bridget said. "I'd suggest hiring a web designer."

"How about you?" Drew asked.

She looked from Drew's hopeful expression to Grace's expectant green eyes—those eyes that could talk her into anything. Lord knows she didn't have time to take on a second job, but she also didn't want to disappoint the people she'd come to care about.

"I'd be happy to do it." She was actually excited to help boost the town's tourism and maybe save a few failing stores in the process, especially The Cookie Jar.

"That's wonderful." Drew lightly slapped her back. "I'm not sure how much the town can afford to pay, but I'll find out and let you know."

She stood. "No payment necessary. Consider it pro bono." Joy welled in her heart when a bright smile transformed Grace's face. Seeing that was all the payment she needed.

"I thought I heard voices in here." Betsy waltzed into the office.

"How are you feeling?" Grace embraced her sister.

"Tired," she said through a yawn.

"Where's Oliver?" Grace glanced around as though he might come waddling in.

"Sleeping right now. You can take a peek at him if you'd like." Betsy looked at Bridget. "Thank you for your help the other day. I don't know how I would have gotten to the hospital."

"You're welcome," she said. "I was glad to do it."

"Do you want to see the baby with me?" Grace asked her.

She nodded and followed Grace to a bedroom. She couldn't help but smile at Oliver's chubby cheeks and tiny puckered lips. As far as babies went, he was a cutie. She looked at Grace, and her heart squeezed at her affectionate expression.

"You're going to make a great aunt," she whispered.

Grace looked at her and held her gaze, long enough for her to wonder if the adoration in her eyes was for Oliver or her.

After dinner, Grace whisked Betsy into their father's office and closed the door.

"What's going on?" Betsy asked and sat on the sofa.

"I need a big favor." Grace positioned herself beside her sister.

Betsy rested her feet on the coffee table, eyelids halfway closed.

If she was going to do this it needed to be now, before Betsy dozed off. "It's like this." She clasped her hands together. "I showed Bridget the two inns in town, and neither of them will work."

She considered telling Betsy how Bridget had stood up to Mitsi but didn't want to remind her that some people in town looked down on Oliver's birth. "Sooo…I was wondering if you'd consider letting Christina and Beryl stay at the Candy Cane Cottage."

Betsy sat up suddenly, like she'd just had ten cups of coffee. "You want your ex-girlfriend and her mistress to room at my inn?"

"I'm doing it for Bridget, *not* Christina. So what do you think?"

"It's fine by me if it's okay with you. I'm just surprised. You must really care about Bridget to even consider this."

"I do care about her. In fact, we sorta kinda kissed."

"When? How? Where? Tell me everything."

She held up her hands. "Slow down. It was just one kiss."

"When you go from saying you can't ever date Bridget to smooching her, that's a big deal." Betsy turned in her seat and faced her.

"It happened this afternoon, and it wasn't a *let's date* sort of thing. It was…I dunno…spur of the moment. It doesn't mean we're an item."

Betsy's shoulders sagged, disappointment written on her face. "What did Bridget say about it?"

"Well. We didn't actually talk afterward."

"So, what happened?"

"We bought apples and mistletoe and then went back to the inn."

"Wait a second. You two kissed and then both ignored it?"

She wouldn't say ignore. In fact, she'd replayed the moment in her mind at least a hundred times since then. "What's there to say? Bridget has made it clear that she isn't interested in having a relationship with anyone."

"You really need to talk to her to see what she's thinking." Betsy's expression softened. "I know it's scary."

"I'm not scared," she said, feeling suddenly defensive.

"Am I wrong in thinking that Bridget is the first woman you've had a real connection with since Meghan?"

She opened her mouth but then closed it. She couldn't lie to herself or her sister. "What if by some miracle Bridget did want to date, and it doesn't work out?" she asked. "I don't think I could go through that pain again. Losing Meghan almost killed me."

Betsy reached out and held her hand. "And what if it does work out? What if you're passing up a chance at true, lasting happiness?"

She sank into the sofa. What a joke. All her boasting about being healthy and moving on from the past was a lie. She'd finally met someone special, someone who could turn out to be the love of her life, and she wanted to run away and bury her face in the sand.

After their chat, Betsy went to bed, and she found Bridget and her mother looking at the Christmas tree.

"Where have you been?" Carol asked.

"I had to ask Betsy a favor." She looked at Bridget. "It's a go." She displayed two thumbs up.

Bridget cracked a smile. "That's awesome. Thanks for doing that."

"I have no idea what you two are talking about, but I just had the most amazing idea!" Carol's face lit up.

"Uh-oh." Drew walked into the living room carrying a slice of apple pie on a saucer. "When my wife says that, it's usually going to cost me money."

"You shush," she said with a smile. "I know Christmas is still two weeks away, but why don't we have an early one Saturday while you and Bridget are in town?"

"That's a wonderful idea!" Grace had missed so many Christmases over the years. This was the perfect opportunity to make up for that, and now it would be even more special to include Bridget.

"I second that." Drew sat in his recliner.

Bridget took a step back. "I wouldn't want to intrude. You don't have to include me just because I'm here."

"Fiddlesticks," Carol said. "You're practically part of the family now."

Bridget's face softened, and a satisfied smile crossed her face. She looked at Drew and asked, "I guess this means the road won't be clear by Friday?"

"Afraid not. The earthquake last night set us back until at least Monday."

"That's too bad," Grace said, hoping her comment had sounded believable. She did feel sorry for the workers but was excited to have a few extra days with Bridget and her family.

"I better start planning the menu," Carol said. "That's just three days away." She pointed at Drew. "You get in the kitchen before you get crumbs everywhere."

Without hesitation, Drew rose to his feet and followed his wife.

"I really like your family," Bridget said when they were alone.

"I'm lucky to have them." She released a happy sigh and ran her gaze up and down the tree, landing on one particular ornament. "I had just started taking lessons when I saw this in a gift shop in town." She reached out and touched the porcelain figurine of an ice skater. "Mom bought it for me, and we've had it on the tree every year since."

"Is it difficult to see it again?"

"A little, but mostly it's a reminder of happier times."

"Maybe that's what you need to focus on."

"What do you mean?"

"What did you love about skating? How'd it make you feel?"

She contemplated the figurine and said, "Gliding on the ice with the wind in my hair was so freeing. It was like floating on air, and time seemed to stand still. It was my absolute favorite place to be and the happiest time of my life." She looked at Bridget. "And when I'd nail a move I didn't think was possible, I felt like I could accomplish anything in the world."

Bridget lightly squeezed her hand. "That's what you need to remember. And then maybe one day you'll have the strength to experience that feeling again."

Skating had not only been something she had enjoyed, but it had also been part of her heart and soul. She missed it terribly and felt like a piece of herself was missing ever since she'd quit. She'd love nothing more than to get on the ice again, but could she do so without painful memories stopping her cold? Could she actually be happy skating without Meghan by her side?

Peace washed over her when she felt Bridget's palm on her lower back. With Bridget's support, maybe she could indeed rediscover her passion.

CHAPTER FIFTEEN

Peace on Earth

Bridget wasn't surprised that Christina was irritated when she found out it'd be several more days before she returned to work. Despite her boss's upset, she hung up the phone in high spirits about having more time in Mistletoe Mountain with Grace. They'd seen each other every day for a week, and she was concerned that once they returned to Los Angeles, their busy schedules would prevent them from keeping in contact. Or maybe it was just her busy schedule. She sighed, thinking about all the work Christina was undoubtedly piling up on her desk. She really needed to get that promotion. No way did she want to fetch coffee and run personal errands anymore. She sat in the desk chair in her room and wondered if Grace had been right. Maybe she was setting her sights too low by applying to be a computer programmer. Maybe she needed to ask for a game-developer position. Grace had worked at Worth Entertainment, so she knew video games, and she'd certainly been impressed with *Shipwreck*.

Bridget focused on the laptop in front of her, pleased with her progress on the town's website. She'd worked on it all day yesterday and only took a break to have dinner with Grace. Knowing how busy she'd be once she got back to the office, she wanted to get as much done as possible now. She stood and stretched her arms high overhead, movement outside the window catching her attention. She leaned over the desk, ashamed that it was the first time she'd actually looked out since arriving. There was a nice view of the backyard, where she saw Grace reattaching several large red bows on the gazebo. They'd probably come loose during the windstorm last night. Feeling a sudden surge of excitement to do something other than stare at a computer screen, she hurriedly put on her coat, bounded down the stairs, and went out the door.

"Looks like you need some help." She watched as Grace balanced on her tiptoes, straining to reach a hook.

Grace spun around. "You're a lifesaver."

She took a bow out of Grace's hand and hung it.

"You didn't have to make it look so easy." Grace grinned and sat on the top step of the gazebo.

"A few extra inches does have its advantages." She leaned against a column. "I just talked to Christina. Aside from being upset that I'll be out until next week, she loved the idea of the restaurant and the cracker-thing for the proposal."

"Really?" Grace looked surprised. "I thought she'd be too stodgy for the Christmas cracker. Good news about the Candlelight Café. I spoke with them this morning, and they're happy to open for Christmas Eve…for a hefty price."

"Great. The cost shouldn't be a problem. Thanks for your help. I'm sure it isn't easy planning this particular proposal." She still felt bad about not being upfront sooner.

"It's weird, but it doesn't seem that upsetting anymore. Guess I have more important things to concentrate on." Grace leaned back and looked at her. "Are you still working on the website today? I hardly got to see you yesterday."

She was happy that Grace had missed her. "I think I can afford to take the day off." Her spirits soared with the thought of spending the entire day with Grace.

"That's terrific." Grace jumped to her feet. "What would you like to do?"

"I never thought I'd say this." She exhaled a strong puff of air. "But let's go Christmas shopping."

Grace's eyes widened. "The person who hates Christmas wants to buy presents?"

"I never said I *hate* it."

"You most certainly did. Maybe Mistletoe Mountain is growing on you?" Grace grinned impishly.

"I wouldn't go that far," she grumbled. "Your family's get-together is tomorrow night, and I'd like to get them something. Maybe you could help me?"

"That's sweet. I'd be happy to. First, though…" Grace held up a finger. "We need hot chocolate."

"We do?"

"We can't go Christmas shopping without it. You have so much to learn." Grace shook her head and sighed dramatically, but the twinkle in her eye showed she was teasing.

"Something tells me you're a master at holiday etiquette. Show me the way. I'm all yours." She swept her arms out wide.

Grace held her gaze for a long moment before she spoke. "Can I ask you something?"

"Of course." The thoughtful look on Grace's face made her chest tighten, unsure of what she was going to say.

"When we kissed the other day, was that just because of the mistletoe legend?"

The pit of her stomach fell. Talk about getting right to the point and catching her off guard. "I…uhh…well, yes. You know, so you wouldn't be single for another year."

Grace lowered her gaze. "I see. So it was a favor. A mercy kiss," she said quietly.

"Not exactly." *Actually, not at all.* Her heart pounded, and she could practically feel the blood rushing through her.

"No?"

"I mean, yes…it was because of the legend…but…" She shook her head, frantically trying to find the right words.

"It's okay. I understand."

No. Grace didn't understand, because she sucked at expressing her feelings. In her mind, it was completely clear. She'd kissed Grace because she was insanely attracted to her. In fact, Grace was the reason she was rethinking her priorities. Perhaps there was more to life than just work. Maybe it was time she took a chance on love. But she didn't say any of that. Instead, she'd stammered and led Grace to believe an untruth.

"Don't give it a second thought." Grace smiled tightly. "We should get going." She headed to the inn, leaving her standing in the snow kicking herself.

Three hours later, they lumbered down the sidewalk of Main Street each carrying colorful bags filled with presents. Grace had been right. They did need hot chocolate. The tall cup of sweetness was just the thing to make her least pleasurable task more enjoyable. Well, that, and Grace always made everything more fun, even Christmas shopping.

Thankfully, the awkward encounter by the gazebo that morning hadn't put a damper on the day. Several times she'd wanted to bring up the kiss again, but it hadn't seemed like the right time, and she'd surely screw things up even more. Still, it bothered her that Grace thought she'd kissed her out of pity.

"My feet are killing me." She abruptly stopped. "How about a cookie break?" She motioned across the street at The Cookie Jar.

"Say no more." Grace looked both ways before darting through the crosswalk.

The mouthwatering scent of creamy frosting and freshly baked cookies and cakes filled her nostrils when they entered the shop. She wasn't a bit hungry, but she could have easily devoured everything in the place. Carol certainly knew how to make scrumptious desserts.

"What a nice surprise," Carol said from behind the counter. "To what do I owe this pleasure?"

"Can't I visit my mother without having an ulterior motive?" Grace sat on a stool and placed her shopping bags on the floor.

Bridget sat beside her, never taking her eyes off the cookies Carol was decorating.

"So, I guess you two don't want one of these?" Carol made the outline of a tree with green frosting.

"Well, now that you mention it." Grace grinned.

"Take your pick," Carol said with a smile. "On the house."

"Mmm." Grace licked her lips and snatched one.

"Thank you." Bridget took a sweater-shaped cookie covered with strings of colorful lights. She bit off the sleeve and moaned as it melted in her mouth.

"What have you two been up to today?" Carol asked as she placed the treats in a glass display.

"Christmas shopping," Grace said through a mouthful. "And in a bit I thought I'd take Bridget to Peace on Earth." She turned to her and said, "It's a lookout point where locals go to watch the sunset. Would you like to see it?"

"Sure. That sounds nice."

Grace picked up a flyer off the counter and studied it, looking sullen.

"That's Gus's fund-raiser for the ice-skating rink," Carol said. "You have to pass right by there on the way to lookout point. Why don't you stop and see him?"

"I saw him the other day in town." Grace put her cookie down and folded her hands in front of her.

The bleak expression on Grace's face caused an uneasy fluttering in Bridget's stomach. She hated to see her so upset about something that used to bring her such joy. She had watched plenty of YouTube videos of Grace's performances, and she'd do anything to re-light that twinkle in her eyes.

Grace's sense of dread grew as they neared The Ice Palace. What was she thinking, taking Bridget to Peace on Earth when she knew they'd have to drive right by there? Actually, she thought that watching the sunset would be an amazingly romantic thing to do, which was silly, considering Bridget obviously had no desire for romance. Hearing Bridget had kissed her simply as a favor was a stab to the heart. Fear twisted her gut when the skating rink came into view. When she was younger, such a sight had elicited excitement, but now she felt nothing but anxiety. What she should have done was floor the gas pedal and whiz by. Instead, though, for some insane reason, she slowed down.

"We can stop if you want," Bridget said.

She took a sharp right into the parking lot. She didn't intend to go inside but wanted to get a better look at the place that had practically been her home most of her life. When she parked in front of the building, memories rushed back. She visualized herself and Meghan running toward the entrance, giddy to perfect an axel or lutz, which Meghan would call a "flutz" when either of them flubbed it.

Several minutes passed before Bridget asked, "Are you okay?"

"I'm fine. Just feeling melancholy." She gave a half smile. "This is where I found my first two loves."

Bridget turned in her seat to face her. "Losing Meghan was out of your control, but you have a choice when it comes to skating."

This wasn't the first time Bridget had suggested that she skate again. Why would she care either way?

As though reading the question in her eyes, Bridget said, "What moved me most watching the videos of your performances was how happy you seemed. I've never seen anyone look more content and at home as you did on the ice. I hate to see fear make you give up something you loved."

She wanted to protest that she wasn't afraid, but Bridget was right. She was scared of memories, scared of falling, scared of her emotions…and most of all, she was scared to love again. Maybe it was time to face the past, as Betsy was always saying. Just not right now. She put the car in reverse and sped away.

Twenty minutes later, she parked at the overlook and cut off the engine. Not another car was in sight, which was odd, considering this was a typical make-out place for high school kids. Her cheeks heated at the thought of her and Bridget steaming up the windows.

"I didn't think we'd driven that far up." Bridget looked at the sparkling lights of Mistletoe Mountain below. "It's beautiful. I can see why they call it Peace on Earth."

"I thought you might like it." She was glad they'd arrived at just the right time. The sky was streaked in red and orange as the sun inched below the horizon. "Normally, I'd get out for a better view, but I don't want you to freeze."

"Good call." Bridget crossed her arms over her chest.

"In the summer, there are some great hiking trails up here. Maybe you'd like to do that sometime. You know. When it's warmer."

"That sounds great." Bridget smiled.

Joy filled her from within, knowing their relationship wouldn't end when they left Mistletoe Mountain.

Suddenly, Bridget's eye grew wide, and she pointed straight ahead. "Is that what I think it is?"

She followed Bridget's line of sight. "What? I don't see anything."

"Snow!"

A bright smile transformed Bridget's face. She looked ten years younger and more excited than she had ever seen her. Shockingly, Bridget opened the door and bounded outside, seemingly unconcerned that it was twenty degrees. For a moment, she didn't know what all the ruckus was about until she remembered that Bridget had never seen snow fall before. She got out of the car and watched as Bridget held her face up to the sky. It was so cold that flakes stuck to her nose and cheeks.

"It's even prettier than I thought it'd be." Bridget swept her arms out wide. "Listen." She stood completely still.

A few moments later, she whispered. "I don't hear anything."

"Exactly. It's so quiet. It floats to the ground without a sound." Bridget held out a hand and watched snowflakes land on her glove. "They look like dazzling crystals."

She smiled, Bridget's excitement contagious. Despite seeing the stuff every winter, she had never actually looked at a snowflake before. What else had she taken for granted in her life?

"You're amazing," she said.

"So are you." Bridget spoke softly. "There's something I need to tell you. I didn't kiss you because of the mistletoe legend. I kissed you because…" Her gaze dropped to the ground.

She took a step closer and said, "Tell me."

Bridget locked eyes with her. "I kissed you because you're the most beautiful, incredible woman I've ever met. You make me feel things I've never felt before with anyone."

That was the sweetest thing anyone had ever said to her. More than anything, though, she was overjoyed that Bridget hadn't kissed her out of pity.

Her pulse quickened when her eyes dropped to Bridget's lips, which were slightly parted. "Do you want to kiss me again?"

"Yes." Bridget whispered.

She slipped her arms around Bridget's waist and closed her eyes as their mouths met. It was the perfect kiss—tender, soft, and filled with affection. It was as though Bridget was putting her entire heart into their union. Pulling Bridget closer, she felt safe and protected in her embrace. She could have stayed there all night, the cold wind overshadowed by the warmth of Bridget's body against hers.

"Wow," Bridget said when their lips parted.

"Wow is right." She smiled as they rested their foreheads together.

Bridget drew her head back and spoke in a rush. "Would you go out with me?"

The question surprised her. Yes, they'd kissed, but she didn't think Bridget was interested in having a relationship with anyone.

"I want to say yes," she said, hesitantly. "Before, you said you didn't have time to date because work is your priority. What changed?"

Bridget spoke without delay. "Meeting you. I always thought I was fine being alone, but I've never been as happy as I am right now. My career is important to me, but so are you."

Part of her wanted to run for fear of getting hurt. What if she got even more attached, and it didn't work out like the umpteen other relationships she'd had the past ten years? But then again, as Betsy had said, what if Bridget was her perfect match?

As she gazed into emotion-filled, sincere eyes, she knew Bridget was unlike any other woman she'd ever met. It was time she stop letting fear rule her life and allow herself to care about someone again.

"I'd love to go out with you." Grace placed a kiss on Bridget's lips. Suddenly, she felt light all over, like she could float off the ground at any moment and dance among the snowflakes.

CHAPTER SIXTEEN

A Rockin' Date

B ridget stretched her limbs like a lazy cat and smiled. This was the first time she'd ever woken up so happy. Grace had said yes to dating. And not only that, but they'd shared one hell of a kiss. Forget about the arctic temperature outside. Her entire body had practically melted into a puddle from their heated exchange. It wasn't like her to be so forward with a woman. Maybe it was the beauty of the snowfall or the so-called magic of the season, but standing in front of Grace last night had caused her to decide it was time she be vulnerable to the possibilities of love. She just needed to keep reminding herself that Grace wasn't the type to abandon her, like so many families had done in the past. If there was such a thing as happily ever after, surely it would be with Grace.

She yawned and sat up in bed. Normally, on a Saturday she'd have to go into the office, but not today. It felt freeing not to have any responsibilities, aside from arranging Christina's proposal, and that was pretty much set. Strange how one week in Mistletoe Mountain had changed her perspective on life…and love. She felt like a totally different person. She was even excited about the Christmas party at Grace's parents' house tonight. The Dawsons felt more like family than any of her foster parents ever had. She was also eager to give Grace her present. When they were shopping, she'd spotted the perfect thing and had been able to buy it without Grace noticing.

A ring prompted her to look at her cell phone on the nightstand. It wasn't a number she recognized, but she answered anyway.

"Hi. This is Drew."

"Hello. Is everything okay?"

"Fine. But I do have a favor to ask. I know it's last minute, but we're having a city council meeting this afternoon at three, and I'd love it if you could demo the website."

She rubbed her eyes. "I could, but it's not finished yet."

"That's okay. Just display what you showed me. I told a few people about it, and they're really excited."

"Okay. Should I bring the laptop?"

"No need. We'll have everything set up for you. I'm assuming you can access it from any computer with internet?"

"Shouldn't be a problem."

"Thanks so much, Bridget. I'll see you later."

She disconnected, glad she could help Drew and the town. She got up, went to the desk, and turned on the computer, determined to accomplish more on the website before the meeting. A light knock on the door startled her. Hopefully it wasn't Grace. The just-rolled-out-of-bed look wasn't an impression she wanted to make the day after they'd agreed to date. She looked through the peephole and saw a put-together and totally adorable Grace. Quickly running her fingers through tousled hair, she wondered if she had time to change out of the wrinkled gingerbread-man pajamas. Upon the second knock, she relented, cracked the door open, and gazed into a bright, shining face.

"Oh, no. I woke you up." Grace's expression dimmed.

"Not at all. Please, come in." She opened the door wider and closed it after Grace stepped inside. "Sorry I haven't showered yet…or even looked in the mirror." She cringed.

"You look absolutely beautiful to me."

The sincerity in Grace's eyes was all she needed for her concern to fall by the wayside. She hooked her fingers in Grace's belt loops and tugged her closer.

"I'll tell you what's beautiful," she said. "It's those striking green eyes of yours. It's the first thing I noticed about you."

A slight smile played on Grace's lips. "You sure the first thing wasn't what a damsel in distress I was to get my purse back?"

She cocked her head and grinned. "Well, okay. But your eyes were a close second. It's why I risked making a bad impression in the interview."

"I never did properly thank you for doing that, did I?"

Her heart thumped when Grace moved closer, rose on her toes, and placed a lingering kiss on her lips. This dating thing definitely had its perks. They should have done this a long time ago.

Grace leaned her head back, eyes closed. "What a way to start the morning," she said with a satisfied-sounding sigh.

"I could kiss you all morning and all night." Her chest tightened when she realized what she'd just said. "I didn't mean to insinuate that we'd sleep together. Not that I wouldn't want to, of course, but I'm not assuming anything."

Grace's eyes fluttered open. "It's okay. I know what you meant." She lightly squeezed her hand and sat on the edge of the bed. "Since you brought it up, though, maybe we should talk about that."

The concerned look on Grace's face worried her. Hopefully she didn't have reservations about dating. She sat beside Grace and held her breath.

"I want to take things slow," Grace said. "It's scary how drawn I am to you after such a short time."

Phew. Grace hadn't changed her mind. She was just frightened, and Bridget could totally relate.

She laid her hand on top of Grace's. "I agree we shouldn't rush things. I'm scared, too. You're the first person I really want to be with."

Grace's features softened. "I love that we can be open with each other."

She was amazed at how easy it was to talk to Grace. She was the only person Bridget had told about being abandoned, and now she was admitting that she was afraid. Normally, she'd be embarrassed about such things.

"Anyway." Grace rose. "I didn't mean to barge in on you so early, but I was wondering if you wanted to go on our first official date today."

"I'd love to. Did you have something in mind?" So much for working on the website. She'd much rather spend time with Grace.

"Well, we don't have much of a choice, considering we're in Mistletoe Mountain, but I might have an idea." Grace's eyes lit up. "How about we leave around eleven for an early lunch and take it from there."

"Sounds great." She didn't even care that they were probably going to do something Christmassy. "Oh, wait. Your dad asked me to present the website to the city council at three today."

Grace paused. "That's okay. I think we'll have time to do everything. You care if I tag along to the meeting? I'd love to see Mitsi's face when she sees how much better your version is than hers."

"I'd love that. Having you there will give me some support." She wrapped an arm around Grace's waist and walked her to the door.

Heat coursed through Bridget's veins when they pressed their lips together. Within moments, her heartbeat quickened, and her legs turned to mush. Taking things slow wouldn't be easy with kisses like this. When they parted, she was happy to see that Grace's chest rose and fell with rapid breaths. At least she wasn't the only one affected by their embrace.

She leaned against the doorframe and watched Grace disappear into her room. Suddenly, a blissful feeling overcame her. She hadn't realized how stagnant her life had become. She'd merely been surviving and not truly living. Being with Grace was almost too good to be true.

An eerie sense of déjà vu washed over her. She'd felt this before, every time she'd go to live with a new foster family. Everything would seem perfect, and she'd let her guard down thinking she'd finally found her place in the world. It had always seemed too good to be true…and it always was.

Grace scooped up a spoonful of pecan pie with an equal part of whipped cream and held it out to Bridget. "Try this."

Bridget shoved the spoon into her mouth, closed her eyes, and moaned. "That's almost as good as this." She motioned to the cheesecake in front of her. "You have to sample some."

Even though Grace had grown up eating dessert at the Gingerbread Café, she readily accepted the forkful of decadence Bridget gave her. "Mmm. This is sinful."

"We should have come here on our first day in town. The grilled cheese and tomato soup were amazing, too." Bridget took another bite.

"I'm glad you enjoyed it." She admired Bridget from across the table. How could someone so incredible still be single?

Bridget pushed her empty plate aside and leaned back in her chair. "I'm stuffed."

"We better not eat anything else for the rest of the day. No doubt mom will have a huge spread tonight." She sipped hot tea. "I know you don't like the holiday, but I'm really glad you're going with me."

"I'm looking forward to it. Does your family know about us yet?"

She shook her head. "I haven't had a chance to tell them, but don't worry. They'll be delighted."

Bridget wiped her mouth and placed her napkin on the table. "So, what's next? We better get moving to make your dad's meeting."

She looked at her watch. "You're right. Let me just take care of the bill." She searched for the check that the waitress had placed on the table, and when she looked up, she saw it in Bridget's hand.

"It's my treat." Bridget said it in a way that let her know there was no room for argument.

"Thank you. I'll have to find a way to repay you later." She winked, amused to see the blush on Bridget's cheeks.

Fifteen minutes later they strolled through rows of colorful booths in the town square. Homemade candles, soap, wreaths, jewelry, and plenty of yummy treats were for sale. Every Saturday in December, Mistletoe Mountain hosted a festival around the fifty-foot tree. Sadly, not many people were there, which was probably due to the low tourist rate and the avalanche.

"Let me guess," Bridget said. "We're going to enter a snowman-building contest." She eyed a group of people laughing and packing snow onto their creations.

"Nope. Guess again." She hooked her arm through Bridget's, not even caring if anyone in town had an issue with them being close. She'd finally found someone she cared about and wasn't afraid to show it.

"We're making snowflakes." Bridget pointed to people cutting folded paper.

"Not even close." She inhaled deeply and stopped when she saw a fudge stand. "I have to get some for my dad. He loves this stuff."

After purchasing a bag full, she stored it in her backpack. "Any more guesses as to what we'll do?"

"Wreath making?"

"No. Follow me." She took Bridget's hand, enjoying the feel of her soft skin, and led her to a booth.

Bridget drew her eyebrows together and read the sign. "Rock painting? That doesn't sound very festive."

"Oh, but it can be. Just depends on what you paint."

Bridget picked up a flyer and read. "What are kindness rocks?"

"The idea is to create inspirational, uplifting messages and then anonymously leave them around town for people to find. Would you like to try it?"

"Sure. I'll give it a go."

She liked how Bridget always seemed willing to attempt anything new. After each of them picked out a smooth rock, they sat at a table filled with brushes and colorful acrylic paint. Brimming with ideas, she clutched a pencil and sketched on a nearby pad of paper. A few minutes later she noticed Bridget staring into space with a pensive expression.

"It helps if you doodle to get the creative juices flowing," she said.

"It won't help me because I have no idea what to draw."

"Why don't you make something that you'd like to receive? Chances are someone else would benefit from it as well."

Bridget chewed her lower lip and nodded. Within seconds, she got a pencil and began writing. Curious, she snuck peeks, which Bridget intentionally blocked with her hand, along with stern verbal warnings to keep her eyes on her own paper. Hopefully, Bridget would share after she was done. With her own concept fully developed, she started painting, which was the fun part. She'd first heard about rock painting from Betsy. It was akin to art therapy and one of the tools she had used to heal after breaking up with Christina. Now, she just did it for fun and as a way to bring some light and hope into strangers' lives.

Thirty minutes later, she sat back and admired her work. She looked at Bridget and saw her hunched over, still shielding her rock. "How's it going?"

"Just putting on a few final touches." Within moments, Bridget sat back.

"Can I see what you did?"

Bridget hesitated but finally revealed her creation. The background was dark blue, and the word Trust was written in bright crimson letters, along with dozens of white dots that looked like falling snow. Her heart cracked in two thinking how Bridget's past had probably given her deep-seated trust issues. Not only had her parents abandoned her, but every foster family had as well. Bridget didn't need to worry about that with her. She wasn't going anywhere.

She reached out and touched Bridget's arm. "I love it."

"That was actually fun." Bridget sounded surprised. "Now show me yours."

She held it out for her to see. It had the phrase Let Go on it, along with a pair of skates underneath and tiny wreaths in each corner. Bridget studied the rock and nodded thoughtfully. When their eyes met and held for a moment, electricity coursed through her. How could one look affect her so much? She had loved Meghan, but this was different. She and Bridget had a spark, a connection she had never experienced with anyone before.

Bridget hid her rock by the Christmas tree, and Grace placed hers on a nearby bench. Upon Bridget's suggestion, they stood back and waited to see who might discover them. It didn't take long before a boy around six years old picked up Bridget's painted rock, showed his mother, and then jumped up and down like he'd just located a pirate's hidden treasure. A few minutes later an elderly woman sat on the bench and saw Grace's message. She clutched it in her hand and smiled. Within a few seconds she was on her feet and placed the rock under a nearby tree.

"Why didn't she keep it?" Bridget asked.

"Because she understands that kindness rocks are about receiving a message and then passing it onto someone else." She smiled, thinking she probably wasn't the only one who needed to let go of something.

They meandered through the fair a while longer until it was time to go to the city-council meeting. When they entered the conference room, everyone was already seated around a rectangular table. Bridget visibly tensed when all eyes turned toward them.

She placed her palm on Bridget's lower back and whispered, "You've got this. They'll love what you've done."

Drew stood. "This is Bridget, and you all know my daughter, Grace."

She gave everyone but Mitsi a smile and froze when she saw Gus. She'd forgotten he was a city-council member. Her sudden urge to leave was quickly overcome by guilt. What would Meghan think about her shunning her father, someone who had done so much for them both. No doubt she'd be disappointed in her.

She sat beside Gus. "It's nice to see you again."

"You, too," he said.

The huge smile on Gus's face made her feel even worse. She'd been in Mistletoe Mountain a week and hadn't made an effort to see him, and when she did run into him, she couldn't get away fast enough.

Within minutes, Bridget had the website displayed on a large screen at the front of the room. Everyone oohed and ahhed as she showcased different sections. Well, everyone except Mitsi, who looked like she'd just eaten a sour grape.

"I'd suggest overhauling some of the business websites, too," Bridget said. "For instance, a lot could be done with The Ice Palace, Gus."

"Like what?" he asked, sounding excited.

"It could be interactive. Maybe an online skating game that kids could play."

"You can do that?"

"Sure. And you might think about doing instruction videos. I mean, you trained two world-class skaters." Bridget motioned toward her. "Your talent should be more far-reaching than Mistletoe Mountain."

"I love that idea," Gus said.

"Also, I didn't see anything about your fund-raiser on the website. Isn't that coming up?"

"Christmas Eve. If it doesn't do well, I may not be able to stay open after the new year." Gus cringed.

She studied Gus's distraught-looking expression, wishing she could do something to help him.

CHAPTER SEVENTEEN

Two Perfect Presents

Bridget stood by the fireplace at the Candy Cane Cottage, waiting for Grace to come downstairs. She glanced at the bag of gifts by her feet, hoping the Dawsons liked what she'd picked out for them. A creaking sound prompted her to turn, her breath catching in her throat. Grace looked gorgeous in a sea-green sweater the exact color of her eyes, black jeans that hugged her hips perfectly, and sexy brown knee-high boots. She'd also applied a little lipstick and blush, and had a slight wave to her hair. It took all she had not to rush into her arms.

"You look amazing," she said.

"Thank you." Grace smiled shyly and walked across the room. "You're as beautiful as always."

She had found a black sweater and tan pants when they were shopping. She knew they were going to a holiday party, but she'd wanted to wear something nicer than a snowman sweatshirt. "Are you ready to go?"

"Not quite." Grace snaked her arms around her waist and kissed her. "Now I'm ready," she said with a dreamy expression.

Twenty minutes later, they walked into Grace's parents' house. They shed their coats and scarves and went into the living room, which looked like a scene out of a cheesy Christmas movie. Bright white lights were everywhere, decorations galore, and a muted holiday movie playing on the TV. Usually, she'd scoff at such a display, but today it gave her a cozy, fuzzy feeling that was quite pleasant.

"Hey, you two." Betsy sat in a rocker giving Oliver a bottle.

"Look at my beautiful nephew." Grace beamed.

She wondered if her own mother had ever looked at her with the same adoration as in Betsy's eyes. Had she regretted giving her away? Or maybe she'd been overjoyed to be free of the responsibility.

When Grace put an arm around her and rested her head on her shoulder, Betsy looked strange.

"What's going on?" she asked, eyes darting back and forth.

Grace furrowed her brow. "What do you mean?"

She took Grace's hand. "I think she's talking about us."

"Oh. Right." Grace's lips parted into a wide smile.

Betsy took the empty bottle out of Oliver's mouth, placed him over her shoulder, and tapped his back. "Are you two...you know... together?"

Grace, still smiling, enthusiastically nodded.

"That's wonderful! I'm so happy for you both."

"What's wonderful?" Carol asked, entering the room with Drew by her side.

"Bridget and I are—"

"Is that fudge I smell?" Drew tilted his nose to the ceiling and sniffed.

Grace pulled a bag out of her backpack and handed it to her father. "Festival fudge just for you."

He opened it and took a big whiff. "I always knew you were my favorite."

"Hey," Betsy said. "I'm the one who gave you your first grandchild."

"You're both my favorite." He bit into a piece, his eyes practically rolling back in his head.

Carol put a hand on her hip. "Now what were you saying before your father interrupted?"

Grace looked at Bridget and gave her an affectionate smile. "Bridget and I are dating."

Carol's face was as bright as the Christmas tree. "That's wonderful," she said, right before initiating a three-way hug.

"Wait. What did I miss?" Drew asked through a mouthful.

"Didn't you hear what your daughter just said?" Carol took his arm. "Come into the kitchen and I'll explain it."

"Before I forget, the road should be open Monday." Drew nabbed another piece of candy out of the bag.

"That's good news. I suppose," Grace said, not sounding a bit happy.

Bridget felt an uneasy fluttering in the pit of her stomach. She knew they couldn't stay in Mistletoe Mountain forever but wished they had more time together. Here, they got to see each other every day. When they got back to LA, things would be different.

"Good news for the town, but I'm sure going to miss seeing you two every day." Carol frowned.

"We'll come back and visit," Grace said.

Bridget liked that Grace had said *we* and not *I*. Call her crazy, but she'd love to return to the year-round Christmas village as long as it was with Grace.

"I'll hold you to that." Carol led Drew away and spoke over her shoulder. "Dinner will be ready in about half an hour."

"Does your mom need any help?" Bridget asked.

Both Grace and Betsy chuckled.

"She doesn't allow anyone in the kitchen," Grace said. "We'll have plenty to do when it's time to clean up."

Betsy rose from her seat. "I better put this little guy down. He's almost out."

"I can do that." Grace looked hopefully at her sister.

"Great. I need to wash up and change anyway." Betsy handed Oliver to Grace and kissed his forehead before walking out.

Grace slightly swayed back and forth with the baby in her arms, his eyelids halfway closed. She'd make a wonderful mother one day if she chose to have kids. For herself, Bridget had never considered it before. She couldn't deny, though, how nice it felt to stand next to Grace and Oliver. Like they were a family.

"I'll put Oliver in his crib and be right back." Grace disappeared down the hall.

Bridget unpacked the bag of presents they'd brought and placed them under the tree. When she stood upright, she was face-to-face with a red-velvet stocking with her name on it, hanging by the fireplace. A hard lump formed in her throat. She reached out and touched the writing, which looked like it had been done with a glitter pen. She had never had a Christmas stocking before, but there it was, along with everyone else's.

"I see you found your stocking."

She turned at the sound of Grace's voice.

"What's wrong?" Grace asked, no doubt seeing the emotion on her face.

"Nothing," she said, her voice strained. "It's just...this is the first one I've ever had."

"I didn't mean to upset you." Grace pulled Bridget into her arms.

"You didn't. I'm touched by the gesture. Thank you."

"You're welcome, sweetheart." Grace lightly stroked her cheek.

She had never been anyone's sweetheart before. It felt nice to be connected to someone, and not just anyone, but a woman as wonderful as Grace.

"Why didn't you tell me about you and Bridget before?" Betsy stood by the sink and scrubbed a plate before handing it to Grace.

"It just happened last night." She rinsed the dish under running water. "I know I had reservations before, but she's nothing like Christina or anyone else I've dated."

"So it doesn't bother you that she's never had a long-term relationship?"

She paused, a towel in hand, and considered the question. "Actually, no. It doesn't. I feel like we're both committed to making this work."

Betsy smirked and bumped shoulders with her. "Maybe one day I'll be the maid of honor at your wedding."

It was much too soon to even think about that, but oddly enough, it didn't seem like such a crazy idea. She could easily imagine her and Bridget tying the knot and spending the rest of their lives together. Call her a hopeless romantic, but she'd always thought she'd know in her heart when she'd found the right person, and it certainly felt like that person was Bridget.

"I *am* going to be maid of honor, right?" Betsy asked when she didn't respond.

"Of course, but don't rush us. We just had our first date."

Betsy reached for a saucepan and dunked it in the soapy water.

A few moments later, Grace said, "I'm thinking about skating again."

Betsy gasped. "Seriously? That's amazing. What changed your mind?"

"Bridget." She placed silverware in a drawer and looked at her sister. "Once I talked about my fears instead of pushing them down, they didn't seem so powerful anymore."

"I knew Bridget was good for you." Betsy gave her a knowing look. "Mom still has your old skates if you want to use them."

She felt a jolt of excitement about feeling the ice beneath her feet. Her performance at the national championship had been the last time she'd been in a skating rink. The disastrous event had shattered her heart and soul. Maybe it was time to return to her roots, her true home, and make herself whole again.

"Are you girls almost done with the dishes?" Carol poked her head into the kitchen. "It's time to open presents. Where are Drew and Bridget?"

"Dad has her in his office looking at the website," Grace said.

Betsy released the stopper in the sink. "I just need to check on Oliver, and then I'm ready."

"He's fine," Carol said. "I was just in there, and he's sleeping like a…well, like a baby."

Drew and Bridget walked into the kitchen. Although they'd only been apart for no more than thirty minutes, her heart skipped a beat when she saw Bridget's beautiful face.

"Everyone into the living room," Carol said and led the way.

Situated on the sofa were Drew and Carol, while Bridget rested in the rocker, with Grace on the floor at her feet. Betsy played Santa and passed out the presents until each of them had several.

Carol examined the name tag on one of her gifts and looked at Bridget. "You didn't have to get me anything…but I'm glad you did." She giggled.

"I hope you like it," Bridget said.

Carol ripped the paper and immediately broke out in a smile when she saw the red apron decorated with green wreaths and holiday lights. "I love it." She held it up for everyone to see. "I'm wearing this at the bakery. Thank you."

"Look here." Drew snapped a photo with his phone.

Grace looked at Bridget and winked, glad that she looked relieved. It was sweet how concerned she was about pleasing everyone.

"Oliver is next." Betsy clutched a gift bag from Bridget and Grace. Plunging her hand inside, she pulled out a newborn elf onesie, along with a matching hat. "Oh my God. That's adorable!"

Carol placed her palm on her chest. "My heavens. Oliver will look precious in that."

"I almost want to wake him up now so he can put it on." Drew took a photo.

It seemed as though Carol was about to agree right before Betsy gave them both a stern warning to let the baby sleep.

Grace turned to Bridget. "Open yours from me."

"How about we do it together?" Bridget handed her a gift.

Within seconds, wrapping paper was scattered on the floor. She lifted the lid off the small box, shocked to see what Bridget had given her. Bridget looked just as surprised. They each held up a chain with a Chinese symbol pendant. It was a different symbol but the same necklace. Out of all the things in Mistletoe Mountain they could have bought for each other, they'd chosen the same gift. Or maybe not so amazing, considering how in sync they were.

She turned her pendant over and saw the word *strength*. She gazed up at Bridget and said, "This is exactly what I need."

Bridget's expression filled with emotion when she looked at the back of hers, seeing that her symbol meant *family*. "Thank you," she said, quietly.

In that moment, Grace couldn't have been happier. Everything she loved was right here in this house, including Bridget.

CHAPTER EIGHTEEN

Awakenings

It was almost midnight when they got back to the Candy Cane Cottage after a night at the Dawsons'. This was easily the best day of Bridget's life. First, a date with Grace, and then an evening with the nicest family she'd ever met. She had never felt more wanted and cared for. She pushed aside the nagging sensation that something would happen to take it all away and decided to enjoy the moment.

They walked hand in hand down the hall and stopped in front of Grace's room.

"Are you tired?" Bridget asked, leaning against the doorframe.

"I'm not a bit sleepy. How about you?"

"I feel wired."

Grace's eyes gleamed. "Would you like some hot chocolate?"

"I'd love that." She didn't want this perfect day to end.

"I'll meet you back in your room." Grace bounded down the stairs.

She rushed inside, hung up a few sweaters that were scattered on the floor, and organized papers on the desk. Studying her reflection in the mirror, she fluffed her hair and straightened her clothes. Strangely, she felt nervous, which was ridiculous considering this wasn't the first time they'd been alone in the room together. For some reason, though, things felt different. She did a quick visual sweep of the area, wondering where they'd sit. One person in the chair and another on the bed seemed too distant, but both on the bed might lead to something more. She shook her head. She was overthinking things. Grace had made it clear she wanted to take things slow, so the chance of anything happening tonight was nonexistent. She opened the door when she heard a knock.

"Hot chocolate with lots of marshmallows." Grace handed her a mug.

"That looks yummy."

Grace took off her boots and stretched out on the bed with her back against the headboard. There was no question she wanted Bridget beside her since she'd left plenty of room. She sat and held the cup between her palms.

"I love the necklace you gave me." Grace touched the pendant around her neck.

"I hope it reminds you of how strong you are and that you can accomplish anything. I love mine, too."

"I wanted you to know that you'll always have a family with me." Grace locked eyes with her.

The comment went straight to her heart. After twenty-five years of not feeling good enough, she had finally found someplace where she belonged.

All at once they placed their mugs on the side tables and pressed their lips together. The gentle kiss quickly turned a lot steamier when their tongues touched and swirled around like a perfectly choreographed dance. Grace's hands found their way under her shirt and caressed her back. Tingles shot up and down her spine, and goose bumps appeared on her arms. If she reacted like that when Grace touched her back, what would it feel like in more sensitive places? Just the thought made her head swirl. When the kiss deepened, she felt an ache between her legs, and she'd swear she was already wet.

"Wait." She spoke against Grace's lips.

Grace pulled back, chest heaving and eyes wide. "Did I do something wrong?"

She took a moment to catch her breath. "God, no."

"Then what is it?" Worry flashed in Grace's eyes.

She hated to admit how turned on she was from just one kiss, but she didn't know any other way to slow things down. "You're making me really hot."

Grace appeared amused. "And that's a problem, why?"

"I thought we decided not to rush into anything."

"Oh. Right."

"Unless..."

"Yes?"

"Unless we change our minds about that." She had wholeheartedly agreed when Grace had mentioned taking things slow, but now it seemed like the stupidest thing ever.

"I think that's an excellent idea," Grace said with a mischievous grin.

Bridget jumped out of bed, dimmed the lights, and lit two pumpkin-spice candles on the dresser. If they had been at her apartment, she would have burned incense and worn something sexier, wanting everything to be perfect. Her pulse quickened as Grace removed her sweater, revealing a beautiful sight—pale, soft-looking skin, inviting cleavage, and full breasts covered in pink lace and satin. She went to the bed, never taking her eyes off Grace, and sat beside her.

"You are so beautiful." She placed gentle kisses on Grace's bare shoulder and across her chest, then unhooked her bra, allowing it to fall away. She caressed Grace's breast and lightly stroked, feeling the hardness beneath her fingertips. Wanting the sensation of Grace's skin against hers, she pulled her shirt over her head and covered Grace's mouth with her own. Bodies pressed together, they lay side by side. Her flesh tingled everywhere Grace touched until her entire body sizzled.

"I want to feel you." Grace whispered as she unzipped Bridget's pants and took them off.

Lazily, Grace crept her fingers up Bridget's inner thigh. She spread her legs wider, hoping Grace would take the cue and touch her where she needed it most. Heat coursed through her, and her hips rocked when Grace slipped inside her, stroking in and out.

"Open your eyes."

The sound of Grace's voice was muffled from the blood rushing through Bridget. Realizing what Grace had said, she opened her eyes. Immediately, she was captivated by the affection radiating from Grace's face. She was absolutely breathtaking. Gazing into emerald eyes, she felt emotion swell within her. Sex had never felt like this before. This was a deeper, more intimate bond than she'd ever experienced. Still inside her, Grace's thumb found her most sensitive spot. Within moments, she squeezed her eyes shut and threw her head back when waves of bliss radiated through her. She'd never come that quickly before.

Wanting to bring the same pleasure to Grace, she rained kisses down Grace's body and removed her pants, a musky scent filling her nostrils. Quiet moans escaped Grace's lips when she licked the length of her and easily slipped two fingers inside, delighting in the softness. When she lightly stroked Grace's clit with the tip of her tongue, she felt spasms against her fingers as Grace shuddered. Grace reached down, pulled her into her arms, and kissed her deeply.

It was strange how Bridget hadn't hesitated to give herself to Grace. Her first time with someone always felt awkward and terribly vulnerable. Being with Grace had felt like the safest, most natural thing in the world.

Grace buttoned her pants and pulled on her sweater. She looked adoringly at the gorgeous woman sleeping in bed. What an amazing night it had been. She had relished every moment of their closeness. Bridget had been the perfect lover, attentive and passionate. She fought the urge to strip her clothes off, crawl back under the covers, and wrap herself around Bridget. Instead, she slowly opened the door, wanting to get coffee and muffins to serve breakfast in bed.

Before Grace reached the stairs, she stopped abruptly when she saw Betsy. "What are you doing here?" Hopefully, Betsy hadn't seen her coming out of Bridget's bedroom.

"I own the joint. Remember?"

"Where's Oliver?"

"At Mom and Dad's. I have a few things to take care of here." Betsy cocked her head. "You okay? You look a little frazzled."

She ran fingers through her hair. "I'm fine. Just heading downstairs to grab some breakfast."

Betsy arched an eyebrow. "It's eleven o'clock. You haven't had breakfast yet?"

"I…uh…I slept in." Her face heated. She hurried past her sister, eager to escape before she asked anymore questions.

"Wait!"

She cringed and turned around, resting one hand on her hip and trying to look nonchalant. "What?"

Betsy gasped. "You slept with Bridget."

"Shhh." She waved her hand in the air. She didn't want Betsy's big mouth waking Bridget up. They were only a few feet away from her door.

"Don't even try to deny it," Betsy said. "You're all glowy and have sex-hair. Plus, you're wearing yesterday's clothes."

She touched her face. Was she really glowing? And sex-hair? Was that even a thing?

"All right," she whispered, knowing the jig was up. "Bridget and I were together last night, and before you say anything, we were going to take things slow, but…well…one thing led to another."

Betsy pulled her into a hug, which wasn't the reaction she was expecting. She thought for sure she'd get a big-sister speech about moving too fast.

"I'm happy for you," Betsy said, looking like she was about to cry.

"You're getting emotional because I got lucky?"

"No, silly. After the last ten years of dating the wrong women, I know you wouldn't sleep with someone again unless you were sure it was the real thing."

She went teary-eyed as well. Betsy was right. Bridget was her one and only.

Twenty minutes later, she balanced a tray with one hand and opened Bridget's bedroom door with the other. She was surprised to see Bridget dressed and gazing out the window with a pensive expression.

"Aw. You're up. I wanted to surprise you." She placed the tray on the desk.

"What's all this?"

"Breakfast. I thought we could use some nourishment after last night."

She moved closer, prompting Bridget to cross her arms. A sickening sensation formed in the pit of Grace's stomach. Something was definitely off. This wasn't the same Bridget from last night. She was distant, cold, and looked downright angry. Was she upset they'd slept together? She'd be devastated if Bridget regretted what they'd done, because in her mind it had been perfect.

"What's wrong?" she asked, her insides trembling.

"Nothing." Bridget turned away and gazed out the window.

"Are you sorry we slept together?" Every muscle in her body tightened, and she braced for the worst.

Bridget looked her in the eye. "No. Are you?"

"Of course not. Last night was incredible. I loved being close to you."

Bridget exhaled sharply and uncrossed her arms. "I'm such an idiot. When I woke up and you were gone, I thought for sure you had second thoughts about us. I felt…"

"Abandoned?" And probably rejected and unwanted, too. "You mean the world to me, Bridget. I'm not going anywhere."

Bridget wrapped her arms around her. "I'm sorry. It was a knee-jerk reaction. It won't happen again."

"It's okay. I understand." She looked up into beautiful brown eyes. "How about some breakfast?"

"Later." Bridget took her hand and led her to the bed, where they spent the next few hours wrapped in each other's arms.

The physical sensations were mind-blowing, but what she adored most was their connection. The energy that flowed between them was palpable. She had loved Meghan, but this felt different. Bridget was a kindred spirit.

After eating muffins and drinking cold coffee in bed, she rested her head on Bridget's shoulder. "Dad said the road will be open tomorrow."

"It's going to be hard to get back to the real world." Bridget sighed.

"I'll miss seeing you every day."

"Me, too. Get ready to be asked out on lots of dates."

"And maybe some sleepovers?"

"Definitely." Bridget kissed the top of her head. "What would you like to do on our last day here?"

She sat up and took a deep breath. "I want to go ice skating."

"Really?" A mixture of surprise and excitement flashed across Bridget's face. "Are you sure you don't want to wait until we go back to LA at a rink that doesn't hold so many memories?"

"That's exactly why I want to do it here. If I can skate at The Ice Palace, then I'll know I've really healed the past."

Bridget grinned. "Do you want me to go with you?"

"I'd love that."

"Anything for my girl," Bridget said and gave her a heart-stopping kiss.

Later that afternoon, they pulled up to The Ice Palace. Only a few cars were in the lot, which was unheard of for a Sunday. Gus wasn't kidding when he had said business was slow. Weekends used to be their busiest time. She parked and stared straight ahead at the building.

"I'll be right there with you," Bridget lightly squeezed her hand. "Well, not *right* there. I mean, I've never skated before."

"It's okay." She looked at Bridget, thankful for the support. "Having you nearby is enough."

She got out and retrieved skates from the backseat. They'd made a quick stop at her parents' house to pick up the pair she'd worn at the national championship. Hand in hand they walked to the entrance. Two teenagers bolted past them on the sidewalk, mumbling something about the place being closed. Her stomach tightened. Had Gus already shut everything down? Maybe things were even worse than he'd said. When they reached the doors and saw a sign that read *Closed for a Private Party*, disappointment washed over her. They could come back in the morning before leaving, but it'd taken her forever to muster up the courage to do this. She was ready to skate right now.

"That totally sucks." She frowned.

Bridget grinned and pulled the door open.

"What are you doing?" She tugged on Bridget's arm.

"It's okay." Bridget waltzed across the threshold.

"We can't go in there. It's reserved."

Still grinning, Bridget held out her hand, probably expecting her to grab it. Just because she knew Gus and had trained here, she didn't have the right to crash a party.

"Do you trust me?" Bridget asked.

Without a doubt, she trusted Bridget completely—with her body and, most important, with her heart. She still didn't think this was a good idea, but she grasped Bridget's hand and followed her inside. The rink looked exactly the same, except that it had been decorated for Christmas with a giant tree in the center and white lights and garland everywhere.

"Grace, I'm so glad you're here." Gus approached them from behind. "I couldn't have been happier when Bridget called to reserve the space for you."

She turned to Bridget. "You're the private party?"

Bridget shrugged, looking bashful. "I didn't think you'd want an audience. This is a big moment for you."

Her insides melted at the thoughtful gesture. "Why didn't you tell me?"

"I didn't want you to feel pressured just because we had a reservation."

"You're so sweet." She slid an arm around Bridget's waist.

"Are those what I think they are?" Gus pointed to her skates.

"The very same ones. They should be sharpened, since the last time I used them was at the championship. Hopefully, they still fit. I don't think my feet are any bigger, even though other parts of me are." She patted her stomach.

"You look fantastic." Bridget gave her a squeeze.

Gus smiled and motioned toward Bridget. "I'm glad you found someone special."

"Thanks. Special is right." She smiled at Bridget.

Bridget's cheeks turned rosy, probably because of all the attention.

"Well, I'll be in my office if you need anything," Gus said. "The rink is yours."

Bridget leaned down and whispered in her ear. "When you're out there, remember what you loved about the sport. Not what you lost."

She nodded. Bridget was right. She'd spent the last ten years lamenting the demise of her career, her future, and Meghan. It was time to move on.

Once her skates were on, she paused at the entrance of the rink. She glanced back at Bridget, who had given her space. She knew this was something Grace needed to do on her own. She fingered the Strength necklace and smiled. Wearing it was like having Bridget with her every step of the way. She placed both feet on the ice and held onto the railing with one hand. Surprisingly, she wasn't nervous. In fact, she felt excited.

In one quick motion she pushed off with her right foot, left, and glided. Her spirits soared immediately. She'd almost forgotten what it was like to feel the air on her face and hear the blades slicing across the ice. It seemed ridiculous that she'd waited this long to skate again. After a few loops around the rink, she did a figure eight and, when she felt confident enough, even executed a jump. They were simple moves, but she was amazed at how well she'd accomplished them. The longer she skated, the more the scattered pieces of her soul fell into place. For the first time in a very long while, she felt whole again.

CHAPTER NINETEEN

The Real World

Grace opened the fridge in her apartment and frowned. A carton of expired milk, four slices of cheese, and leftover lasagna that needed to go down the garbage disposal. Grocery shopping was a must after work. What she wouldn't give for one of Betsy's muffins. She smiled, thinking how much Bridget had enjoyed them as well. Eyeing her phone on the counter, she was tempted to call Bridget. They'd seen each other yesterday, when she'd dropped Bridget off at her apartment, but it felt like days since they'd spoken. She picked up the phone and put it back down, not wanting to be clingy.

Resting her hip against the kitchen counter, she sipped coffee and gaped at her pathetic-looking Christmas tree in the living room. The normally vibrant needles were dry, brown-tipped, and most were scattered on the hardwood floor. No water for almost two weeks would do that to a tree. She hated to throw it out, but there was no saving it. Maybe she could get a new one tonight after hitting up the grocery store.

Her heart leaped when her phone rang, and she saw who it was. "Good morning."

"Do you think Betsy would fedex me a muffin?" Bridget asked.

"I was just thinking that myself." She laughed. "How are you this morning? Did it feel good to sleep in your own bed?"

"It did…but I missed having you beside me."

Joy filled her like sunshine, knowing she wasn't the only one feeling the loss of their connection. "Me, too. I thought about you all night."

"Did you now?" Bridget asked in a playful tone. "What were you thinking?"

"How much I wanted to be in your arms, feel the softness of your skin, and gaze into those beautiful brown eyes."

Bridget sighed. "How am I supposed to get ready for work after hearing that?"

"Ugh. Work. I'm not looking forward to seeing Penelope." She shook her head. "Are you going to talk to Christina about the promotion today?"

"I thought I'd wait until after Christmas."

She heard the uncertainty in Bridget's voice and wished she could give her a shot of courage to stand up to her boss. "You should march into her office and show her *Shipwreck*. Trust me. Once Christina knows how talented you are, you won't be fetching coffee anymore."

"You really think so?"

"Definitely." She put her cup in the sink and went to her bedroom.

"Shoot. I didn't realize how late it was," Bridget said, probably looking at the clock. "I haven't even showered yet."

"I'm dragging this morning, too." She opened her closet door, not looking forward to wearing dress clothes after being in jeans and sweatshirts.

"I was wondering…do you want to get together tonight? If you're busy or it's too soon then—"

"I'd love to." Happiness coursed through her. "Would you like to go with me to get a new tree? Mine died from a lack of attention. Or is that too Christmassy for you?"

Bridget chuckled. "Pretty sure I can handle it. Nothing could be more Christmassy than Mistletoe Mountain."

She took a gray pants suit off the hanger and laid it on the bed. "You better watch out. Before you know it, you'll be humming holiday tunes and stringing lights everywhere."

"I wouldn't mind hanging up some mistletoe," Bridget said with a smile in her voice.

Her face heated as she thought about their first kiss. What she wouldn't give to have Bridget in front of her right now. "Is it tonight yet?" She plopped on the bed.

"Not soon enough." Bridget exhaled sharply. "Guess I should go get ready now."

"Me, too." She didn't want to hang up. "The only thing that'll get me through the day is knowing I'll see you later."

After disconnecting, she dressed and drove to Tie the Knot. She stopped in the lobby and eyed the Christmas tree she'd single-handedly erected. Smiling to herself, she recalled meeting Bridget. She hadn't wanted to admit it at the time, but she'd been enamored with her from the start. Hard to believe that had only been a couple of weeks ago. She felt like they'd known each other forever.

"Welcome back."

Grace turned at the sound of Melanie's voice. "It's great to be back." She lied.

"How did the proposal plans go?"

"Good. Bridget seems pleased with everything."

"Excellent." Melanie nodded. "I appreciate you stepping up. I know this was a difficult assignment for you."

"It was at first, but in the end it turned out better than I thought it would."

"Keep up the good work."

She watched Melanie disappear down the hall, wishing she reported directly to her instead of Penelope. If only she had gotten the Maui promotion, but then again, she wouldn't have wanted to leave Bridget. In the end, things had turned out for the best.

Grace passed by the reception desk and stopped.

Paulina looked up from her computer. "Hey, girl. I missed seeing you around here." She leaned over and whispered, "So, how'd things go with Ms. Hottie?"

"Ms. Who?" she asked, but knew exactly what Paulina meant.

"Bridget. Did she keep you warm on those cold, snowy nights?"

"Of course not. She's a client." Hopefully that had sounded convincing. Paulina was a huge gossip, and it'd be all over the office that she had slept with a client. "What'd I miss here?"

"You know who has been on a rampage." Paulina looked around as though to make sure no one was listening. "I can't say why, but I'd steer clear of Penelope today if I were you."

She tensed. That would be impossible in such a small company. "What's going on?"

Paulina pursed her lips so hard they turned white as snow. "I'll get fired if I say anything."

Now Grace was really curious. If Paulina wouldn't talk, it must be something big. Knowing Penelope, she was upset that she had been gone so long, but it wasn't like she'd had a choice. She couldn't drive through a mountain of snow. She made a beeline for her office and found herself face-to-face with Penelope when she turned the corner.

"Oh. You're back," Penelope said.

She didn't know why she'd sounded so surprised. She had sent an email over the weekend letting her know when she'd return.

"Did you enjoy your impromptu vacation?" Penelope rested a hand on her hip.

She took a moment to reel in her anger. "It wasn't a vacation. I was stranded and working on a proposal."

"Well, I hope you're ready to get back to work, because the assignments have been piling up."

Grace forced a smile. "Great. What have you got for me?"

"Actually, I need you to shadow me for a while."

"I don't understand." Her smile faded.

"You'll be my assistant."

"But...we have interns for that. Are they occupied with other tasks?" She wasn't sure what was happening.

"No."

"Then why would I be your assistant?"

Penelope ignored the question. "I emailed you a rundown of what needs to be done. Let me know if you have any questions." And with that she was gone.

Her jaw clenched. Nothing was wrong with being an assistant, but she was an executive planner. Was she being demoted? If her boss were any sort of sensible person, she would have gone straight to her office to discuss matters. But Penelope was anything if not unreasonable.

❖

Bridget sat across from Christina's desk and watched her review the proposal plans. Thankfully, Grace had documented every detail, so all she had to do was print it out and hand it to her boss.

"Who's my contact at the restaurant?" Christina asked.

"Raul. His name and number are on the bottom of the page."

"We'll have the entire place to ourselves?" Christina glanced at her.

"Yes." She opened the photos on her cell phone and turned it toward Christina. "This is what the restaurant looks like." She scrolled through pictures. "It's beautiful with lots of holiday decorations."

"What about the Christmas cracker?"

"It'll be on the table when you arrive. Unless you want—"

"No. That's fine." Christina waved her off. "Do you have photos of the inn where we're staying?"

She opened the directory on her phone. She'd made sure beforehand to put any pictures of Grace in a different folder. The last thing she needed was for Christina to see her ex flash across the screen.

"I think Beryl will love it," she said. "You can't get much more Christmassy than the Candy Cane Cottage." She swiped across the screen.

"You did a good job," Christina said and sat back in her chair.

"Thanks." The rare compliment surprised her.

"It must have been miserable being stuck in such a small town for so long. What did you do?"

She glanced around the room, focusing on anything but her boss. It was as though eye contact would reveal that she had been galivanting around town with Grace. "Well, aside from making the proposal plans, I had to buy clothes, since I hadn't planned to be there more than one day. Be sure to pack a coat when you go. It's freezing."

"I heard there's a mistletoe farm. Did you check it out?"

She clenched her jaw and nodded. What would Christina say if she knew Bridget had kissed Grace under the mistletoe? "It's a nice getaway. There's also a lookout called Peace on Earth. I can add that to the list if you'd like."

"Please do." Christina faced her computer, which was probably a hint that they were done.

"I'll do that right after lunch." She stood. It was already two p.m., and she was starving. She'd been slammed with work the moment she'd walked into the office that morning.

"Bring me back some coffee." Christina spoke to her computer screen and opened an email.

She stiffened all over. She was well aware that she was Christina's assistant, but Grace was right. She was far too talented to waste her life fetching coffee and doing other mindless duties. It was time she stop underestimating herself and speak up.

Slowly, Christina turned and glared at her. "Is there something else?"

She cleared her throat. "I was wondering if you'd given any thought to promoting me to computer programmer."

Christina folded her hands across the desk. "We were going to discuss that after the new year."

"If you have a moment, I'd really like to show you the new video game I created." She looked down at Christina, glad that she was standing. In a way, it made her feel as though she were in control.

Christina arched an eyebrow and smirked. She couldn't tell if she was angry or amused. After a long pause she said, "I'll give you five minutes."

She rushed around the desk and took control of the computer. Within seconds, she connected to the cloud and opened *Shipwreck*. She'd prepared to do a demo, but Christina grabbed the mouse. Maybe it was better if she viewed it on her own, so Bridget stepped back. She was tempted several times to interject comments, but the serious look on her boss's face stopped her.

A full fifteen minutes passed before Christina spoke. "Have you showed this to anyone else?"

"No." Well, yes, but now wasn't the time to mention Grace.

"I want you to present this at the developers' meeting tomorrow." Christina continued to click through the game.

"You mean…what do you mean?" The only time she'd ever been invited was to take notes.

"I might like to add this to our line of Q1 products." Christina wrote something on her desk calendar.

Her breath caught in her throat. She'd never imagined that Worth Entertainment would actually want to sell it.

"And that computer-programmer position." Christina met her gaze. "We'll discuss it after the meeting."

Bridget felt fifty pounds lighter and like she was practically floating on air. She'd never been so excited about the future before. Her career was finally taking off, and she was about to see the woman who had captured her heart. She never would have imagined that she'd meet someone who would make her so happy. This was the first time she'd allowed herself to trust, the first time she'd fallen in love.

She paused at Grace's front door. Was it crazy to think that she loved Grace? Didn't it take months for that particular emotion to develop? She raised her arm and knocked. Her heart squeezed when the door opened and she saw the bright, beautiful face before her. In that moment, she knew exactly what she felt and that no time limit existed when it came to love.

Grace threw her arms around her neck. "It's so good to see you."

"You, too." She closed her eyes and enjoyed the sensation of having Grace pressed against her.

Grace led her inside. "Can I get you something to drink?"

"All I want is this." She pulled Grace closer and kissed her. Within moments, her head spun. How she'd missed those soft lips. Had it only been a day since they'd last seen each other?

"Any more of those and we'll never leave," Grace said with a dreamy expression.

She brushed a strand of hair away from Grace's face, catching sight of the Christmas tree in the corner of the living room. "That is one sad-looking tree."

Grace glanced over her shoulder and frowned. "I know. Hopefully, we can find another Fraser fir."

"Your favorite, right?"

Grace smiled at her. "You remembered."

"Of course." She glanced around the apartment. "I like your place. It's cozy."

"I'll give you a tour later, but first I want to hear about your day." Grace led her to the sofa, where they sat close together.

"I took your advice and showed Christina *Shipwreck*." She was excited to share the news.

"Did she like it?"

"She wants me to show it at a developer's meeting tomorrow and might even want to market it next year." She smiled widely.

Grace gasped and placed a hand over her heart. "Oh my God. That's wonderful!"

"I have you to thank. Your belief in me made all the difference. It gave me the confidence to take a chance."

"I'm so proud of you." Grace gave her a quick hug. "What about the promotion?"

"Christina said we'd talk about it after the meeting."

"This calls for a celebration." Grace jumped up, went into the kitchen, and came back with a bottle of apple cider and two cups.

"Sorry I don't have anything stronger." She poured, handed one drink to her, and held up the other. "Here's to your future."

"*Our* future together." They clinked glasses and sipped. "How was your day?"

Grace's shoulders slumped. "Not so great."

"What happened?"

"I'll tell you later. I don't want to ruin your exciting news."

"You're not ruining anything. I want to know." She put her cup on the coffee table.

Grace sighed and set her drink beside hers. "It's Penelope. For some reason she's upset with me. I've been demoted."

"What do you mean?"

"I'm her assistant for the foreseeable future. You should see the list of tasks she gave me. It's what the interns do, not what should be asked of an executive with the company."

"She can do that?" Anger swelled within her. She hated the way Penelope was treating Grace.

"She's my boss. She can do whatever she wants."

"Maybe you should talk to Melanie."

"I can't. I've already gone over Penelope's head too many times. I just have to grin and bear it."

She took Grace's hand. "This doesn't sound like the first time your boss has been an issue. Have you thought about looking for another job?"

"I have, but I really love the work, and there aren't that many proposal-planning companies out there."

Her heart sank at Grace's sad look. "I'm so sorry you have to deal with this."

"I'll be fine." Grace forced a smile. "I don't want to put a damper on our night. Let's get the tree and pick up some takeout."

A few hours later, a nice-looking Fraser fir stood in the middle of Grace's living room. With holiday music playing in the background, they took ornaments off the dead tree and placed them on the new one.

"This is the first tree I've ever decorated." Bridget hung a figurine of a kid playing the drum and regretted the comment when sadness filled Grace's eyes. The last thing she wanted was anyone feeling sorry for her.

"Can we spend Christmas together?" Grace asked. "I'll show you what a real holiday should be like."

"I'd love that." Joy swelled in Bridget's heart. This was the first time she'd ever been excited about this time of the year.

"I have to work Christmas Eve," Grace said. "But we're closing at three."

"Same here, except I'll probably be there until five. Or maybe I can slip out earlier since Christina is going to Mistletoe Mountain that day."

"Did she like the proposal plans?" Grace rose on her toes and tried to grab the star off the top on the old tree.

Bridget easily reached and got it for her. "She did. I even got a compliment. All thanks to you."

"Good." Grace motioned to the star. "Can you put that up? I won't be able to reach it."

"The second time we met you tried to get me to decorate." She placed the topper on the new tree. "Even though I thought you were nuts, I couldn't help but notice how cute you were."

"I thought you were gorgeous. Nervous, but gorgeous." Grace hooked a shiny, red ball on a branch. "Do you believe in fate?"

She considered the question. "I think we all have free will, so I'm not sure about predestination. How about you?"

"I believe certain events in life are supposed to happen, and it's up to us how we respond. Take you and me, for instance. I think we were meant to meet." Grace wrapped tinsel around the tree and handed the excess to her. "If I hadn't had an event at Sacred Grounds and left my business card there and you hadn't gone that same day and seen it, you probably wouldn't have hired Tie the Knot."

"That's true, but it could just be a coincidence."

"I don't believe in coincidences." Grace adjusted the tinsel, spacing it out evenly. "The universe was bringing us together."

She tugged Grace into her arms. "Well, thank you, universe, for the best Christmas present ever." She pulled something out of her back pocket and held it over their heads.

Grace's face lit up. "You got mistletoe!"

"I bought it at the tree lot when you weren't looking."

"We certainly can't let it go to waste." Grace pressed her lips against hers in a kiss that left her pulse racing.

"You know," Grace said, resting her head against her chest. "You're welcome to stay the night."

"There's no place I'd rather be," she said and held Grace tighter.

CHAPTER TWENTY

A Ticket to Paradise

Grace sat in her office and crossed off yet another task Penelope had given her. Copies. She'd made twenty sets of a fifty-page document. She should be meeting with clients and using her creativity to come up with unique proposals, not trying to figure out how to clear a paper jam. An intern had offered to do the job, but she had declined, knowing Penelope would accuse her of being lazy. Only one thing could brighten her mood. She texted Bridget.

How's your day going?

In less than a minute Bridget responded.

Great. I'm preparing to demo Shipwreck *to the developers this afternoon.*

That's awesome. They'll be blown away. And probably jealous they didn't design it.

Thanks. ☺ *How's things with you?*

She paused, not wanting to be a complainer. But then again, she couldn't lie to Bridget.

I've had better days.

Want me to come over there and kick Penelope's ass for you?

She grinned.

I want you to come over here and kiss me.

An even better idea! I gotta run. I need to do a few things before the meeting.

Good luck.

She sat back in her chair, thoughts of Bridget flooding her mind. They'd had a wonderful time decorating the tree, talking, and spending a passionate night together. When they'd first met, Bridget didn't seem to be what she was looking for in a partner. How wrong she'd been. Bridget was not only everything she wanted, but much more. Excitement rushed through her as she thought about all the wonderful years ahead of them, having adventures and growing even closer.

With her love life in order, she now had to figure out what to do about her job. She couldn't continue working under Penelope and didn't see any chance of her boss leaving any time soon. She reached for the keyboard and googled proposal-planning companies in Los Angeles. There were only four results, including Tie the Knot. Melanie would be hurt if she defected to the competition, but she had to do what was best for herself.

"Hi, Grace. Do you have a minute?"

She looked up to see Melanie standing in the doorway. Quickly, she closed the browser before Melanie could see what she was doing. "Yes. Of course."

Melanie stepped inside and closed the door. A chill ran down Grace's spine. This was the first closed-door meeting they'd had in her office. Was she about to be scolded for something...or fired? She needed to find a new job before she left this one. She rested her elbows on the desk, trying to look relaxed, as Melanie sat in one of the guest chairs.

"What can I do for you?" she asked.

"Lynn needs to take a leave of absence for health reasons."

"Oh, no. I hope it's nothing serious."

"Me, too. She had to turn down the Maui position to concentrate on healing."

"I'm sorry to hear that." Her heart sank. Lynn must have gotten a grim diagnosis to change her mind about relocating. She'd wanted the job just as much as Grace had.

"That's the bad news," Melanie said. "And now for the good news. I'd like you to run the Maui office. There's a twenty-five percent salary increase, manager title, and paid relocation expenses."

She felt her eyes go wide. "Seriously?"

The corners of Melanie's eyes crinkled when she smiled. "Seriously. I hope you don't feel like you're second choice. It was a close race between you and Lynn, and the fact that she has seniority played a lot into the decision."

"I understand," she said, still not sure this was real. She'd thought she was about to get fired, not promoted.

"I'll need an answer by Monday. Considering how much I know you wanted this, I'm hoping it'll be a yes." Melanie stood. "Don't hesitate to let me know if you have any questions before then. And congratulations."

She rose and shook Melanie's hand. "Thank you. I really appreciate this opportunity."

Melanie displayed a friendly smile and walked out. She sank into her chair, amazed she'd actually gotten the job. It was a chance to run her own office and get away from Penelope, not to mention the pay raise and living in paradise. Suddenly, her chest tightened, and she tensed all over. Bridget. She couldn't leave her. They'd just started dating. Disappointment kicked her in the gut. She'd be passing up an opportunity of a lifetime. If she didn't take the job, she'd be stuck looking for a new one, one where she wouldn't be running her own office and probably not even in the proposal-planning field. She'd have to go back to the corporate world, which was the last thing she wanted to do. She slammed her eyes shut. This was a no-win situation.

Picking up her cell phone, she called the person who would have the best advice.

"Hi. It's good to hear from you," Betsy said into the receiver.

"Hey. How are you and Oliver doing?"

"We're great. He's such a sweetheart."

"I miss him already." She grinned, picturing her beautiful nephew.

"What's up with you?"

"I just had a meeting with Melanie. She offered me the Maui position."

"Wow. I thought that went to someone else."

"She's unable to take it for personal reasons."

"Should I be happy or upset?"

"I don't know." She sighed. "I mean, this is a dream job, but I don't want to leave Bridget. Long-distance relationships never work."

"What did Bridget say about it?"

"I haven't told her yet. I literally just got the offer."

"Ah. So you called your big sis for advice. Okay. Listen. You need to discuss this with her. Who knows? Maybe she'd want to go with you. You two should make the decision together, since it affects your relationship."

She nodded. "You're right. Sometimes I tend to awfulize things."

"Personally, I think you two should forget about Hawaii and move to Mistletoe Mountain." She detected a hint of humor in Betsy's tone but was certain she wasn't entirely kidding.

"Riiiight. I'm sure that option will be on the table. Thanks for your help. You always put me on the right track. Kiss Oliver for me, and I'll let you know how things turn out."

She hung up and texted Bridget, asking if they could get together tonight. They'd just seen each other that morning when Bridget left her apartment, but she really wanted to discuss this sooner rather than later. Her stomach growled, letting her know it was past lunch time. Normally, she ate at her desk, but the thought of getting some fresh air and escaping Penelope for an hour was too enticing. She grabbed her phone and headed out. Paulina stopped her in the reception area before she could get out the front door.

"Congratulations!" Paulina's face lit up.

"For what?" Grace wasn't sure she was allowed to talk about the promotion yet or if it was confidential.

Paulina's expression dropped. "I saw Melanie in your office, and she said she was going to tell you this morning."

She leaned over the desk and whispered, "Do you mean Maui?"

Paulina placed a hand over her heart, looking enormously relieved. "Thank goodness I didn't spill the beans."

"Does everyone know about it?"

"Of course. When Lynn, the poor dear, turned it down, we all knew you were next in line. Why do you think Penelope has been so hard on you?"

She narrowed her gaze. "Why would Penelope care? She doesn't want to move."

"Jealousy. Pure and simple. That woman has felt threatened by you since day one. She knows how highly Melanie regards you, and now she's worried you'll make the Maui office more successful than this one."

Her phone dinged. "Excuse me a minute," she told Paulina and read Bridget's text.

Sorry, but I can't get together tonight. I have to work late. Lots to catch up on.

A frown tugged at her lips. She understood but was disappointed they wouldn't get to talk. They needed to have this conversation in person, not over the phone.

No problem. Don't work too hard.

"There you are." Penelope approached her from behind. "I need you to type these notes for my meeting this afternoon." She jabbed a stack of handwritten papers at her.

Heat crawled up her neck. She wished she could march into Melanie's office right now and accept the offer, but she couldn't do that without talking to Bridget first.

"I'll do it right after lunch," she said.

"My meeting is at three." A deep crease formed across Penelope's forehead.

"It'll be ready. Put the papers on my desk." She whirled around and marched out the front door, wishing she were on a plane to Maui right now with Bridget beside her.

That night, she drove downtown to the ice rink on a whim. She felt an insatiable desire to do something that would fill her heart with joy and maybe take her mind off Maui. Although this was the first time she'd skated since Mistletoe Mountain, she didn't feel nervous. Instead, she strapped on her skates and stepped onto the ice without hesitation. Since it was Wednesday, not many people were there, so she had most of the rink to herself.

Following a few laps, she felt confident enough to try an axel. It wasn't perfect, but at least she'd landed the jump and hadn't ended up on her ass. It felt so good to skate again. She vowed right then to do it as often as possible and pushed aside any regret she had about abandoning something she loved for so long.

Thirty minutes later, she skidded to a stop and leaned against the railing, breathless. Ten years ago, she was in much better shape. It was amazing what a few extra pounds could do, plus she was using muscles she hadn't exercised in a while.

"Excuse me."

She turned when she heard a woman's voice.

"I hate to bother you," she said. "But are you Grace Dawson, the figure skater?"

Inwardly, she winced. She hated being recognized. It always led to the question of why she'd quit the sport. For a moment, she considered lying, but when she looked into the big blue eyes of an adorable little girl standing beside the woman, she said, "I am."

"Oh my gosh. I'm a huge fan." The woman gushed. "I wanted to be a skater just like you." She put a hand on the girl's shoulder. "I'm Crystal, and this is my daughter, Lexi."

Grace smiled at the girl. "Hi, Lexi. It's nice to meet you."

"I saw you on the computer." Lexi's eyes grew even larger than her mother's.

"She means YouTube," Crystal said.

"Lexi...as in *Ice Castles*?" She was going out on a limb but thought maybe the name was inspired by the popular 1970s movie about an ice skater.

Crystal's cheeks turned bright pink. "You nailed it."

"I love that movie, too." She chuckled. She knelt to be eye level with the little girl. "Do you like to skate?"

Lexi nodded so enthusiastically her blond curls bobbed up and down. "I fall sometimes. Mom holds my hand."

"It just takes practice," she said, smiling to herself at how cute the little girl was. "How old are you?"

Lexi held up five fingers.

"That's the age I was when I started skating. If you love it and you're having fun, then you could be on the computer one day, too, if that's what you want."

Lexi's expression brightened, and she looked up at her mother.

"Do you teach classes?" Crystal asked.

She stood. "No, but Gus from The Ice Palace in Mistletoe Mountain is amazing. He was my coach. It's a bit of a drive, but well worth it if Lexi has an interest."

"I'll keep that in mind."

"If you'd like, I could give her a few pointers right now."

"Really? That would be incredible." She looked at her daughter. "Would you like Ms. Grace to skate with you?"

Her heart melted when Lexi grabbed her hand without hesitation. Taking that as permission, they glided onto the ice. It surprised her how good she was at instructing Lexi. She'd never been around kids much, but all she had to do was mimic Gus.

He'd been patient, kind, and supportive. Compared to other coaches, he'd probably been a softie. He'd worked her and Meghan hard, but he was a big believer in the fact that if a child wasn't enjoying herself, then she should do something else. Gus had been the best. She really wanted to do something to help save his ice-skating rink, and maybe...just maybe...she had an idea how to do so.

CHAPTER TWENTY-ONE

A Big Mouth

This was the first time Bridget had been in Christina's office when she wasn't taking dictation or getting a coffee order. Instead, she sat in Christina's chair at her computer. They were tweaking *Shipwreck* together, with Bridget at the helm. When she'd done a demo the other day at the developers' meeting, the reaction had been overwhelmingly positive, with only a few suggested changes. She was thrilled when she'd easily executed every recommendation Christina made. She was proving to her boss, and herself, that she was capable of being more than just an assistant.

"I think that's it," Christina said, peering over her shoulder at the screen. "Excellent work."

She wanted to jump up and down but needed to maintain some professionalism. After closing the program, she rose from the seat.

"Give this to marketing and tell them to write a press release." Christina handed her a piece of paper. "This is the list of video games we're promoting in the first quarter." She sat in her chair.

Bridget studied the information, stunned to see *Shipwreck* among programs created by the top designers at Worth Entertainment. These were people she'd admired growing up, and now she was one of them.

"I can't believe it." Her gaze jumped to Christina, embarrassed she'd said that aloud.

"You have a bright future ahead of you, Bridget. I just wish you had said something sooner."

"Me, too," she said, remembering all the dry-cleaning runs and personal tasks she'd done the past year. The only one she didn't regret was planning the proposal.

"And that computer-programmer position." Christina looked directly at her. "It's yours."

Bridget's heart lurched. "That's terrific!"

"I'll need you to stay on as my assistant until I find a replacement, but that shouldn't take long. HR is posting the opening today."

"I really appreciate this opportunity, Christina. Thank you."

Back at her desk, thoughts of Grace filled her mind. She missed her terribly and couldn't wait to tell her about the promotion. Since she had been swamped at work, they hadn't seen each other in several days. She picked up the phone and the hit speed dial but got Grace's voice mail.

"Hi. It's me." I was wondering if you wanted a hot Friday-night date tonight. I'm sorry I've been so busy. Okay. Let me know. I miss you. A lot. Bye."

She hung up and looked at the clock, noting it was noon. Maybe she could make a quick stop by Grace's office and see if she had time for lunch. She didn't want to wait until tonight to see her, so she clutched her bag and rushed out the door.

Twenty minutes later, she stood in front of the receptionist desk at Tie the Knot and read the nameplate. *Paulina Smith*. It was the same woman who had been there before.

"Hi," Bridget said. "Could you let Grace Dawson know that Bridget Cartwright is here to see her?"

Paulina paused right before her face lit up. "I remember you. You're the client that got stranded with Grace. That avalanche was just awful."

"It was quite the adventure."

Paulina picked up the handset and dialed. "Bridget is here to see you." Pause. "Sure thing. I'll let her know." She hung up. "Grace said it'll be about fifteen minutes."

She looked at her watch. They wouldn't have time for lunch, but at least they'd get a few moments together.

"I hope Grace took good care of you on that snowy mountain."

"Um. Yes, ma'am. She did." She hoped her expression hadn't given anything away. It was unlikely Grace had told anyone at work that they were an item.

"We're sure going to miss her around here." Paulina shook her head and made some tsk-tsk noises.

"Miss who?"

"Grace is going to head up the office in Maui."

The pit of her stomach fell. "I don't understand."

"We're opening a new location. I'd kill to go to Hawaii. You know, my husband won't even take me there on vacation. He says—"

"Grace is moving?"

"Of course." Paulina chuckled. "That'd be one long commute."

Bridget felt numb all over, and her head spun. Paulina's lips were moving, and sound was coming out, but she didn't hear one word. She rubbed her forehead and said, "I forgot I have a meeting. Tell Grace…uhh…that I'll talk to her later."

She bolted out the door, her heart beating wildly. Quickly, she got into her car and sped away. This didn't make any sense at all. Grace was leaving Los Angeles? When did she plan to tell her? Was she going to text her from the airport? A wave of nausea hit her in the gut so hard that she pulled to the side of the road and rolled down the window in case she got sick.

It was the exact feeling she'd had every time a foster family rejected her. She'd get blindsided, just like this, and shipped back to the children's home without any explanation. How foolish she had been to let her guard down and trust again. What a joke to think she'd finally found a home. Grace was no different than everyone else who'd abandoned her.

❖

Grace was getting worried. It was seven p.m. and still no word from Bridget. First, she'd abruptly left Tie the Knot earlier that day, and now she wasn't responding to any messages or texts. Busy or not, it was unlike her. Grace sat on her couch and bit the nail on her little finger, unsure what to do. She hated to show up at Bridget's apartment when they didn't have concrete plans, but she had a weird feeling something was terribly wrong. Maybe she'd been in an accident. She grabbed her backpack and fled her apartment.

Thirty minutes later she knocked on Bridget's door, praying that she'd answer. When there was no response, she pressed her ear to the wood, thinking she'd heard sounds from the other side. She knocked again. *Please be in there. Please be okay.*

She fell forward when the door swung open. She stumbled and caught her balance. Thank God, Bridget was safe...or was she? The rims of her eyes were red, and she had a serious, sad expression.

"Are you okay?" she reached out to touch Bridget's arm, but she jerked back.

"What are you doing here?" Bridget spoke in a monotone.

"I was worried. You haven't returned any of my messages."

"I'm fine." Bridget folded her arms across her chest.

"You don't seem fine. Did something happen at work?"

Bridget's jaw line pulsed, and, following a lengthy pause, she turned and walked into the living room. Taking that as an invitation to enter, she closed the door. She wanted to wrap her arms around Bridget and hold her close, but Bridget's rigid stance and cold demeanor stopped her.

"You're really scaring me," she said. "You can tell me whatever it is. It's what couples do. They share the good and bad."

Bridget swung around, fire in her eyes. "Really? That's what couples do? They share things with each other?"

"Y-Yes." She wasn't sure where Bridget's sudden anger was coming from.

"So when were you going to tell me you're moving to Maui?"

She pulled her head back. "Where'd you hear that?"

"Your receptionist told me."

Paulina. Big-mouth Paulina.

"Can we sit down?" She motioned to the couch, but Bridget didn't make a move. "I got the offer a few days ago, but I wanted to discuss it with you in person."

"Good for you. Congratulations." Bridget's tone oozed sarcasm.

"I haven't accepted it yet."

"Yet?" Bridget lifted an eyebrow.

She fell into the couch and shook her head. "This is all screwed up. Would you sit for a minute so I can explain?"

Bridget hesitated before taking a seat, as far away from her as possible, and hugged a throw pillow.

She turned and faced her. "I wanted us to make this decision together. It's an incredible opportunity, but I also don't want to leave you. Would you consider going with me? I know it's a big move, but it could be an adventure. How about it? You and me in paradise."

"I got promoted today. I'm not going to leave when my career is just now taking off. What would I do in Hawaii? Sell seashells by the seashore?"

"You got the computer-programmer job? That's wonderful." She resisted the desire to give Bridget a hug. "You're right. I can't ask you to abandon everything you've worked for the past year. I won't accept the position."

"Absolutely not," Bridget said, defiantly. "I want you to take it. You should go."

She studied Bridget. The distant look in her eyes reminded her of when they'd first met. It was like Bridget had reverted to a time when she'd erected invisible walls to protect herself. She was desperate to break through to her, afraid of what would happen if she didn't.

"You're more important to me than a job," she said. "I don't need Maui. I need you."

Bridget shook her head. "You'll regret it if you don't go. Maybe not at first, but eventually you'll blame me for passing up this opportunity."

"You don't know that." She didn't appreciate Bridget forecasting how she'd feel. "It sounds like you're trying to get rid of me."

"Look," Bridget said, staring at the ceiling. "This was bound to happen. It's better now rather than later, when we're in even deeper."

"I'm already in deep." Her throat tightened with the realization that Bridget was about to break up with her. "Am I the only one that feels that way?"

All the color drained from Bridget's face. "I don't think we should see each other anymore."

Her heart ached, and she found it difficult to breathe. "You don't mean that."

"What we had in Mistletoe Mountain was a fantasy. The reality is that we can't have a relationship with an ocean between us."

"This can't be happening." Surely she hadn't found the love of her life only to lose her a few days later. The universe wouldn't be that cruel.

"I'm sorry." Bridget stood, went to the door, and opened it.

She felt foolish sitting on the sofa, wanting to beg Bridget to change her mind, when clearly she was getting thrown out. She rose on shaky limbs and walked across the living room. She resisted the urge to dive into Bridget's arms and tell her how much she loved her, knowing it wouldn't be well received when she was so upset.

"I'll give you some space right now, and we can talk later." She walked out the door.

This wasn't over. What they felt for each other wasn't imaginary. It was the truest, most genuine thing she had ever experienced. Bridget was just hurt right now. She would fix this tomorrow. Things always looked brighter in the morning.

CHAPTER TWENTY-TWO

The Night Before Christmas

Grace merged onto the 10 Freeway, glad traffic was light. At this rate, she'd make it to Mistletoe Mountain in no time. Not in the mood for holiday music, she drove in silence, which was a first, especially on Christmas Eve. If it had been up to her, she'd still be in bed with the covers pulled over her head, which was pretty much where she'd been all weekend. Apparently, Bridget had been serious about breaking up. They'd spoken briefly on the phone Saturday, which had been nothing but a repeat of the night before. How had everything gone sour so quickly? One minute they were blissfully happy together and the next Bridget was ending their relationship. They were supposed to spend Christmas together. Hell, she'd thought they'd spend the rest of their lives together.

If it weren't for Gus, she would have turned the car around and slept through Christmas. She'd had the bright idea of skating at his fund-raiser tonight and couldn't back out now. He'd spent the weekend emailing announcements and had even contacted news organizations. From the increase in ticket sales, people were eager to witness her first performance in ten years. Hopefully, it'd bring enough money to keep the rink open, and with some luck she wouldn't face-plant on the ice.

She saw an incoming call and connected her headset.

"Hey. How are you holding up?" Betsy asked.

"Okay, I guess." She'd called Betsy right after Bridget dumped her. She didn't know what she'd do without her big sister and best friend. "I haven't told Mom and Dad about me and Bridget yet."

"Me either. They're just excited you're coming. What'd you decide about Maui?"

"I asked Melanie if I could give her an answer after Christmas." She tightened her grip on the steering wheel. "I'm not sure what to do."

She didn't want to accept the job if she and Bridget got back together. Then again, that might not happen even if she stayed in Los Angeles. Not only was she heartbroken, but she was angry that Bridget had given up so easily. It was as though she didn't care enough to fight for their relationship.

"I'm going straight to the rink when I get into town," she said, wanting to change the subject. "I need to practice before tonight." She'd skated only once over the weekend, too depressed to do anything more.

An hour later, she pulled up to The Ice Palace. She gathered her skates and went inside. Gus had said he'd be closed today so the event organizers could decorate, so she found it odd that the rink was dark, with not a soul in sight. It wasn't noon yet, but it still seemed as though people should be milling about getting everything ready.

She made her way to Gus's office, where she found him at the desk talking on the phone. His face lit up, and he motioned her inside. She stepped through the doorway and saw hundreds of framed photographs on the wall of skaters Gus had trained. Her heart swelled with affection when she spotted one of her and Meghan when they were about fifteen.

She clearly recalled the day it was taken. Exhausted and sweaty, they had just finished practice and were sitting on a bench together, removing their skates. Gus had yelled "smile," which had caused them both to look up, right before he took the photo. The expression on Meghan's face was priceless. She'd chastised her father afterward for taking what she'd said was the worst snapshot of her in the world.

"That's my favorite picture of her."

She turned at the sound of Gus's voice. She hadn't even noticed he'd finished his call.

"That look on her face was so Meggie," Gus said with a sad smile. "She'd probably hate that I hung it up."

She placed a hand on Gus's arm. "I'm sure she wouldn't mind. Especially since it's your favorite."

"I'm really glad you're here." Gus gave her a one-armed hug. "And I can't thank you enough for performing tonight. You're saving the rink." His eyes sparkled, the sadness from moments ago gone.

"You're welcome. I just wish I could do more."

"You already have. That was Crystal on the phone."

Grace cocked her head. "Who's Crystal?"

"She said she met you at the skating rink in LA." Gus cast her a puzzled look.

"Oh. Right. I forgot. What did she want?"

"She knows a network of parents who need a coach for their kids, and they asked me to train them. They're going to bring a busload here every Saturday. And Crystal said she'd spread the word to others, too."

Hope fluttered inside her. "That's wonderful. I'm really glad things are looking up." Thankfully, she hadn't shunned Crystal when she'd recognized her.

"So where is everybody?" she asked. "The place looks deserted."

"The event planners will be here this afternoon. That's plenty of time to set up, and I knew you wanted to get some practice in." Gus looked over her shoulder. "Where's Bridget? Is she coming?"

Her chest tightened. No. Bridget wasn't coming. In fact, Grace would probably never see her again. She swallowed a hard lump in her throat and said, "We broke up." And that's when it happened. It was like the floodgates had opened. Until then, she hadn't shed a tear. In her heart, she'd hoped Bridget would have realized what a terrible mistake she'd made, but it'd been four days now and not a word from her.

"Oh, my." Gus guided her to his chair and handed her a box of Kleenex.

She sat and blew her nose. "I'm sorry. I don't know what came over me."

"No need to apologize." He haphazardly patted her shoulder. "What happened? You two seemed so close."

"We were." She wiped her eyes and sniffed. "I got a job offer in Maui, and Bridget didn't even want to talk about it. All she did was kick me out of her apartment."

"That's terrible." Disapproval gleamed in his eyes. "Are you okay to perform tonight?"

"Absolutely." She straightened, resentment simmering in her gut. Here she was bawling over someone who clearly didn't care enough to even try to work things out. Enough. She wasn't going to let Bridget stand in the way of her skating or her life. She decided right then that she'd accept the promotion and pack her bags for Hawaii.

Bridget couldn't remember a time when she'd felt so low. It'd taken all her strength just to get out of bed and drag herself to work. She'd thought about calling in sick, but with Christina on her way to Mistletoe Mountain, someone needed to man the office. She felt terrible for breaking up with Grace, but what she'd said was true. Better to end things now rather than later. Still, though, it hurt something awful.

She placed her bag on the floor by her desk, surprised to see a light on in Christina's office. She crept forward, peeked through the doorway, and saw Christina sitting in her chair.

"What are you doing here?" She marched inside.

"Just needed to check a few things before Beryl and I leave."

"Ah. I was afraid you had changed your mind about the proposal."

"Not a chance. I can't wait for tonight." Christina smiled widely. "This time tomorrow, I'll be engaged to the woman of my dreams."

She'd never seen Christina look so happy, including the time the company had bypassed their quarterly sales goal by twenty percent.

"Are you okay?" Christina asked. "You haven't seemed yourself lately."

"I'm fine. Just women problems."

"I didn't know you were seeing anyone." Christina shut down her computer and motioned for her to sit in one of the guest chairs.

"We didn't date very long and broke up a few days ago." She sat.

"She wasn't the right one for you then." Christina looked directly at her. "Trust me. You'll know when you meet that special someone."

The hairs on the back of her neck stood up when a shiver went through her. Grace *was* special. More amazing than anyone she had ever known.

"Before I met Beryl, I was a different person. When it came to dating, I let fear run my life."

"In what way?" She was surprised Christina was talking about something so personal.

"I was afraid of commitment. I sabotaged more relationships than I can count, and I'm sure hurt a lot of people in the process, which I'm not proud of."

"Why was it different with Beryl?"

A slight smile played on Christina's lips. "Being with Beryl is like coming home. I've never felt that way before. God. I sound like a sap."

"No. You sound like you're in love."

"Hang in there, Bridget. You'll meet your Beryl one day." Christina stood and slung a bag over her shoulder. "I better get going. Merry Christmas." She pranced out of the office with a bounce in her step.

She sat back in the chair and wrapped her arms around herself. She was no different than Christina. She was acting out of fear, too. She'd already found her Beryl, and she was totally screwing it up. She had always considered herself a strong person, but she was nothing but a scared little kid. Burying her face in her hands, she shook her head and recalled the hurt look on Grace's face the other night. It was doubtful Grace would ever forgive her, but she had to at least try.

She rushed to her desk and dialed Grace's number, but the call went directly to voice mail. Not wanting to leave a rambling, incoherent message, she disconnected. Grace had said she was working on Christmas Eve, so maybe Paulina would be able to reach her. She called Tie the Knot.

"Hi, Paulina. This is Bridget Cartwright. Can I speak to Grace?"

"Hello, Bridget. Grace isn't working today. She's in Mistletoe Mountain."

"She is?"

"She's performing at a fund-raiser there tonight. Grace used to be a professional ice skater."

"Thanks for letting me know."

She disconnected, her heart swelling with pride. Grace was helping Gus save The Ice Palace. She'd come so far from the woman who'd been frightened to go near the ice. She looked at her watch and groaned. This was going to be the longest day ever. Whether or not Grace wanted to see her, in seven long hours she'd be on her way to Mistletoe Mountain.

❖

Grace's pulse raced, she felt light-headed, and her blood pressure was probably astronomical. It was quite possible she'd have a heart attack before even stepping foot in the rink. What had she gotten herself into? Only a week ago, she'd skated again for the first time in ten years. What made her think she could do an entire performance? There was a big difference between skating for herself and doing it for hundreds of people, not to mention news crews. She could see the headlines now: *Washed-Up Former Skater Goes Belly-Up*. It would take months before she could show her face in public again.

Her stomach dropped when she heard her name over the loud speaker. Gus came up beside her and placed a hand on her lower back. The last thing she wanted to do was disappoint him, or herself.

"It's time," he said.

She touched the Strength charm around her neck. She'd debated wearing it, considering it'd been a gift from Bridget, but she hoped it'd give her courage. She wiped sweaty palms on her thighs, took a deep breath, and glided to the middle of the rink. She struck a pose, and the sound of violins filled the air. The next five minutes were a blur. Lost in the music, she executed moves, spins, and jumps as though on automatic pilot. Frequently, she'd hear applause, which let her know she'd done something right. Most of the time, though, she blocked everything out. It was just her and the ice.

In what seemed like seconds, her routine was over, and the applause, whoops, and hollers were deafening. She smiled when she saw everyone on their feet. She'd done it. Her comeback had been a success. She made a few laps around the rink, waving at her admirers and mentally thanking them for their warm reception. Knowing where her parents and Betsy were seated, she made eye contact with them, her heart light at their beaming faces. All that was missing was Bridget. She pushed the disappointment aside. Nothing was going to spoil this perfect moment.

An hour later, after all the spectators and most of the skaters had left, Gus pulled her aside.

"I need you to come to my office." Concern knitted his brow.

"Is something wrong?" she asked, curious about his serious expression.

Without another word, he took her elbow and led her to his office. He opened the door, and she felt her eyes go wide to see Bridget standing in front of her. She cursed the flutter in her chest at the sight of the beautiful woman, not wanting anything about Bridget to make her flutter.

"I'm sure you two have a lot to talk about." Gus slipped out and closed the door behind him.

"What are you doing here?" she asked.

"I missed your performance," Bridget said. "By the time I got here it was sold out. I did hear all the applause, though, so I'm sure you were amazing."

The tremor in Bridget's voice gave her an ounce of satisfaction. She *should* be nervous. In fact, Bridget should be downright scared after the way she'd treated her.

"That doesn't explain what you're doing here."

"Right." Bridget chewed her lower lip. "I came to apologize. I'm sorry for the other night. I reacted badly."

"Yeah. You did."

"I don't want to break up. You're the best thing that's ever happened to me, Grace." Emotion filled Bridget's eyes.

This was exactly what she had hoped to hear, but she was still angry and not willing to let Bridget get off that easy. "You threw me out of your apartment without even trying to work things out."

"I was scared."

"Of what?"

Bridget looked her square in the eye. "When Paulina told me you were moving, it brought up all those old, hurtful feelings of being abandoned when I was a kid. I thought you were done with me and moving on."

Her annoyance slowly melted away. "I wasn't leaving you. I never would have done that. All I wanted to do was talk about it."

"I realize that now. Can you forgive me?"

She wanted nothing more than to dive into Bridget's arms and never let go, but something held her back. "How do I know you won't break up with me again the next time we're faced with a challenge?"

Bridget reached out and took her hand. "I promise I won't ever push you away. If you want to accept the promotion, then I'll gladly go to Maui. Being with you is more important than anything else."

The sincerity in Bridget's eyes made her heart swell. "You mean that? You'd move to Hawaii with me?"

"I'm in love with you, Grace. I've never felt this way about anyone and never will again."

"I love you, too." She threw her arms around Bridget's neck.

As she held Bridget tight, she caught sight of the photo of Meghan on the wall. Maybe fate wasn't the only thing that had brought them together. She had the distinct feeling that her first love had led her to her greatest love.

CHAPTER TWENTY-THREE

Epilogue

One Year Later

Bridget hit the snooze button, rolled over, and wrapped her arms around Grace. If it were up to her, this was where they'd stay the rest of the day. There was nothing better than snuggling with the woman she loved.

"The alarm already? Feels like we just went to sleep." Grace nuzzled her face into the crook of Bridget's neck.

"I know." She groaned. "Maybe we could—"

"Today is Christmas Eve!" Grace sat up, looking suddenly awake. "I've been waiting for this day for so long, and it's finally here."

She smiled and brushed a strand of hair from Grace's forehead. "What's so special about today?"

Grace gnawed on the corner of her lip. "That...uhh...that means tomorrow is Christmas."

She peered at Grace, whose eyes were looking everywhere but at her. "Is there something you're not telling me?"

"Of course not." Grace playfully slapped her arm. "I'm just excited."

She narrowed her gaze, not convinced she was getting the entire truth. But then again, Grace did love Christmas. She hated to admit it, but there was something special about the holiday. She'd actually enjoyed helping Grace decorate their apartment with garland, a snow village, a huge Fraser fir, and, of course, mistletoe. Mostly, though, she liked how happy it all made Grace.

"You're adorable." She gave Grace a quick peck on the mouth.

"Oh, no. That won't do." Grace positioned herself on top of her.

She loved being close enough to see the variations of emerald colors in Grace's eyes. Tingles coursed through her when Grace pressed their lips together, softly at first, and then with an intensity that left her heart racing. She had never known a kiss could be so stirring, so loving, until she'd met Grace.

Silently, she cursed the alarm clock when it rang again. She reached over and fumbled to find the switch. Unsuccessful, she pulled on the cord and yanked it out of the socket.

Grace hovered over her and grinned. "That's one way to shut it up." Gently, she ran a finger across her lips and sighed. "Guess we should get up."

"Yeah. I have that long commute into the office."

"All the way into the living room. You sure you like working from home?"

"Are you kidding? It's great. I can wear my jammies all day."

If anyone had told her she'd be living in Mistletoe Mountain with her girlfriend and working as a developer for Worth Entertainment, she'd think they were insane. Grace had turned down the Maui position and resigned from Tie the Knot, realizing that all she wanted was right here in the village. She hadn't hesitated to follow Grace and was willing to leave her job to do so. When *Shipwreck* became Worth Entertainment's best-selling game last year, Christina had agreed to let her work remotely and promoted her from computer programmer to designer.

After showering, she opened her nightstand and took out the necklace Grace had given her for Christmas last year. She ran a fingertip over the word Family. She had finally found her place in the world. She'd never felt like she had a real home until Grace and the Dawsons came into her life. She attached the necklace, as she did every day, and went into the kitchen.

Twenty minutes later, she had a croissant and thermos filled with coffee for Grace. Considering how late it was, she'd probably have to eat on the run.

"Nothing smells better than freshly brewed coffee." Grace walked into the kitchen, unscrewed the thermos, and took a sip. "Remember I'm picking you up at five today to go by the mistletoe farm before they close. I promised we'd take apples to Betsy tonight. Her cook wants to make turnovers."

"Got it." She handed Grace the croissant in a napkin.

"Thanks for this." Grace held up the coffee in one hand and the pastry in the other. "Have a good day, and don't work too hard." She gave her a kiss on the cheek and left.

She felt slightly guilty she hadn't been truthful about being off work today. Instead, she had a ton of errands to do before five— none of which Grace needed to know about.

Grace shifted into drive and drove away. This was going to be the most amazing day ever. She didn't know how she'd get through the next few hours until she could go to Betsy's inn and set everything up. She'd almost blown it with Bridget this morning but had done a decent job of covering up. It was doubtful Bridget had any inkling that she was planning to propose tonight.

She drove down Main Street, happy to see the sidewalks packed with people and stores thriving, a great improvement from last year. The majority of credit belonged to Bridget, since she'd joined the town's city council as media director. She'd put an incredible amount of time into beefing up tourism, all while holding down a full-time job at Worth Entertainment.

She pulled up to The Ice Palace and parked. Last year, she'd sold her condo in LA and bought half of the skating rink, partnering with Gus. Tie the Knot was a great job, but it had never been her passion. Once she'd started skating again, she knew she wanted to coach kids in the sport she loved so much.

When she entered the building, Marni and Jennifer rushed toward her. The six-year-olds were best friends and two of the most talented kids Grace had ever taught.

"Good morning, girls. You're here early." She smiled, thinking how much they reminded her of Meghan and her at that age.

"We wanted to practice before class starts," Marni said.

"That's great, but don't tire yourselves out." It was important to her that her students not overdo it, which was always a possibility with these two. They were determined to follow in her footsteps, except maybe they'd actually make it to the Olympics. What had happened at the nationals still stung, but if she had taken another path in life, she never would have met Bridget.

"Guess who's coming tonight," Jennifer said, eyes wide.

"Who?" she asked.

"Santa!" the girls said in unison.

She conked herself over the head. Focused on the proposal, she'd actually forgotten that tomorrow was Christmas.

"He's bringing me pink ice skates," Marni said.

"And I'm getting purple ones." Jennifer nodded, her expression completely serious.

"That's wonderful. I'll see you girls when class starts."

She made her way to Gus's office and saw him hunched over his desk, punching numbers into an adding machine. She had attempted to help him modernize the accounting system, but Excel spreadsheets weren't for him. Besides, whatever he was doing was working, and she would much rather focus on coaching than operations.

"Mornin', Gus." She stood in front of his desk.

He held up one finger, eyes focused on whatever he was doing. A few moments later he looked at her. "We have officially doubled our income from this time last year."

"That's wonderful!" She was grateful that The Ice Palace hadn't gone out of business and was instead thriving.

"All thanks to you. Every kid within a hundred-mile radius wants you as their coach, and those online-instruction videos you did are selling like hotcakes."

"I'm so glad to hear that." She smiled. "I just stopped by to remind you I'm taking off early today."

Gus sat back in his chair. "Doing anything special?"

"You could say that."

"From the gleam in your eye, I'd say it has something to do with Bridget."

"I might have some good news to share soon." She smiled even wider. "If I don't see you after my second class, have a Merry Christmas, Gus."

She went into the dressing room to change and put on her skates. She loved teaching, but she had a feeling the morning would go by slower than the line at the DMV.

That afternoon, she walked into the Candy Cane Cottage, wonderful smells luring her into the kitchen. Oliver was in a highchair, stuffing a handful of spaghetti into his mouth, while Betsy and her parents sat at the table, each with a plateful. She chuckled at the red sauce smeared across his face. Cleaning him up would no doubt be a chore. She snapped a few photos of him to show Bridget later, who loved Oliver just as much as she did.

"Don't bother putting those on Facebook," Betsy said. "Mom's already posted at least twenty of them."

"Can I help it if my grandbaby is precious," Carol said through a mouthful.

Grace went to Oliver, intending to give him a kiss on the cheek, but reconsidered and opted for the top of his head.

"Are you hungry?" Betsy asked. "There's plenty on the stove."

She laid a hand across her stomach. "I'm too excited and nervous to eat."

"I remember when I proposed to your mother." Drew put his fork down. "It was at Peace on Earth. I was afraid I'd drop the ring off the cliff I was so nervous."

Carol reached out and touched Drew's arm. "It was so romantic."

Maybe what she had planned wasn't special enough. She'd thought about the overlook and mistletoe farm, but she didn't want anyone else around. The gazebo seemed like the perfect location. It was private, and with Betsy and her parents' help, she'd transform it into a breathtaking place with hundreds of candles, a forest of pink camellias, and, of course, mistletoe. Bridget and she would have a scrumptious dinner prepared by Betsy's cook, and after dessert, she'd pop the question.

"How are you getting Bridget over here tonight?" Betsy shoved a forkful of spaghetti into her mouth.

"I told her I promised to bring you apples from the farm." She could have said they were going to the inn for dinner, but she wanted to revisit the tree where they'd had their first kiss.

"I can't believe my little sister is getting engaged." Betsy shook her head.

"We're happy for you, sweetie," Drew said with a wink.

Carol stood and wrapped her arms around her. "I can't wait to help you plan the wedding."

"Bridget hasn't even said yes yet."

"Oh, she will." Carol nodded.

For the first time since she had decided to propose, doubt crept into her mind. She and Bridget had been happy together, and Bridget had shown no signs of fearing commitment, but maybe it was too soon. They'd been together only a year. Maybe she should be doing this next Christmas Eve. She'd be absolutely crushed if Bridget turned her down.

It was six o'clock by the time Grace and Bridget arrived at the KissMe Mistletoe Farm. They only had an hour before closing, but that was plenty of time to pick apples before going to the inn.

"Were you busy at work today?" Grace clutched a basket and followed Bridget outside, cold air swirling around them. Renting a heat lamp for tonight had been a great idea, considering they were eating outside in the gazebo. Grace wanted chill bumps on Bridget's arms from her kisses, not the freezing temperature.

"Not too much," Bridget said, trudging through the snow.

They stopped in front of a tree and took several apples, placing them in the basket.

"Remember what happened over there?" She pointed.

"How could I forget?" Bridget grinned. "That's where we had our first kiss."

"I think we should recreate the moment."

"You won't hear any arguments from me." Bridget linked arms with her as they made their way through the grove.

A few moments later, she stopped when she spotted something on the ground. It was a painted rock with the word Grateful written on it. She picked it up and showed it to Bridget.

"That's beautiful." Bridget touched the surface.

"I'd love to keep it as a reminder of how lucky we are to have each other, but that's not how it works." She placed it back on the ground for someone else to find.

After walking a bit farther, Bridget stopped. "Hey, look. Another one." She bent down and picked it up.

"Joy," Grace said, reading the bright-red word on a yellow background. "This makes me want to paint rocks. It's been so long since we've done it."

"Me, too," Bridget said and put it back in the snow.

"Hey. I see another one over there." She rushed and retrieved a pink-colored rock with the word Love surrounded by a heart. Rock painting was popular in Mistletoe Mountain, but this was the first time she'd found three in a row.

She felt guilty for what she was about to say. "We should keep these. It's like they're meant for us." She was sure the universe was sending them a gift on the day she was going to propose.

"I think you're right." Bridget nodded. "We can get the other two on our way out, but right now we have a mistletoe appointment."

When they reached the tree, she put the bucket down and slid her arms around Bridget's waist. She did a double take, spotting something out of the corner of her eye. A fourth painted rock was the only thing that could make her remove herself from Bridget's embrace.

"I can't believe this." She bent down and picked it up. When she saw the sentiment, she realized that the rocks they'd found— particularly this one—were obviously not meant for them.

"What's on it?" Bridget asked.

"Just about the sweetest thing ever. It says, 'Will You Marry Me?'"

"Huh. What a strange thing to write on a rock. I think you should keep it."

She drew her eyebrows together. "We can't do that. It's for someone else."

"Maybe it's for you." Bridget reached into her back pocket and pulled out a small box.

Her heart raced. That looked like the perfect size for an engagement ring.

"Grace, will you marry me?" Bridget opened the lid with a shaky hand, displaying a beautiful diamond ring.

She gasped, her insides quivering. "Is this for real?"

Bridget released a nervous-sounding laugh. "Is that a yes?"

She threw her arms around Bridget's neck. "It's absolutely yes!"

Bridget lifted her off the ground and twirled her around. "I was afraid the rocks would make you suspicious."

"You did those?"

"I'm *grateful* for the *joy* and *love* you've brought into my life." Bridget slipped the ring on Grace's finger.

Despite the chilly air, her insides warmed. She guided Bridget underneath a clump of mistletoe and kissed her. The mistletoe legend was surely true, because she had no doubt she and Bridget would have a long, happy life together.

The End

About the Author

Lisa Moreau is an award-winning Bold Strokes Books author who loves creating lighthearted, happily-ever-after romances. With a degree in journalism from Midwestern State University in Texas, the completion of many creative writing courses, and a shelf full of writing and editing books, Lisa never ceases to learn her craft.

When Lisa isn't writing or editing, she's reading fiction or new-age books, meditating, spending time in nature, or hanging out in a bookstore. Lisa lives in Los Angeles with her partner, Judi, and their betta fish, Rusty.

Lisa can be reached at www.LisaMoreauWriter.com.

Books Available from Bold Strokes Books

A Fairer Tomorrow by Kathleen Knowles. For Maddie Weeks and Gerry Stern, the Second World War brought them together, but the end of the war might rip them apart. (978-1-63555-874-6)

Holiday Hearts by Diana Day-Admire and Lyn Cole. Opposites attract during Christmastime chaos in Kansas City. (978-1-63679-128-9)

Changing Majors by Ana Hartnett Reichardt. Beyond a love, beyond a coming-out, Bailey Sullivan discovers what lies beyond the shame and self-doubt imposed on her by traditional Southern ideals. (978-1-63679-081-7)

Fresh Grave in Grand Canyon by Lee Patton. The age-old Grand Canyon becomes more and more ominous as a group of volunteers fight to survive alone in nature and uncover a murderer among them. (978-1-63679-047-3)

Highland Whirl by Anna Larner. Opposites attract in the Scottish Highlands, when feisty Alice Campbell falls for city-girl-about-town Roxanne Barns. (978-1-63555-892-0)

Humbug by Amanda Radley. With the corporate Christmas party in jeopardy, CEO Rosalind Caldwell hires Christmas Girl Ellie Pearce as her personal assistant. The only problem is, Ellie isn't a PA, has never planned a party, and develops a ridiculous crush on her totally intimidating new boss. (978-1-63555-965-1)

On the Rocks by Georgia Beers. Schoolteacher Vanessa Martini makes no apologies for her dating checklist, and newly single mom Grace Chapman ticks all Vanessa's Do Not Date boxes. Of course, they're never going to fall in love. (978-1-63555-989-7)

Song of Serenity by Brey Willows. Arguing with the muse of music and justice is complicated, falling in love with her even more so. (978-1-63679-015-2)

The Christmas Proposal by Lisa Moreau. Stranded together in a Christmas village on a snowy mountain, Grace and Bridget face their past and question their dreams for the future. (978-1-63555-648-3)

The Infinite Summer by Morgan Lee Miller. While spending the summer with her dad in a small beach town, Remi Brenner falls for Harper Hebert and accidentally finds herself tangled up in an intense restaurant rivalry between her famous stepmom and her first love. (978-1-63555-969-9)

Wisdom by Jesse J. Thoma. When Sophia and Reggie are chosen for the governor's new community design team and tasked with tackling substance abuse and mental health issues, battle lines are drawn even as sparks fly. (978-1-63555-886-9)

A Convenient Arrangement by Aurora Rey and Jaime Clevenger. Cuffing season has come for lesbians, and for Jess Archer and Cody Dawson, their convenient arrangement becomes anything but. (978-1-63555-818-0)

An Alaskan Wedding by Nance Sparks. The last thing either Andrea or Riley expects is to bump into the one who broke her heart fifteen years ago, but when they meet at the welcome party, their feelings come rushing back. (978-1-63679-053-4)

Beulah Lodge by Cathy Dunnell. It's 1874, and newly engaged Ruth Mallowes is set on marriage and life as a missionary…until she falls in love with the housemaid at Beulah Lodge. (978-1-63679-007-7)

Gia's Gems by Toni Logan. When Lindsey Speyer discovers that popular travel columnist Gia Williams is a complete fake and threatens to expose her, blackmail has never been so sexy. (978-1-63555-917-0)

Holiday Wishes & Mistletoe Kisses by M. Ullrich. Four holidays, four couples, four chances to make their wishes come true. (978-1-63555-760-2)

Love By Proxy by Dena Blake. Tess has a secret crush on her best friend, Sophie, so the last thing she wants is to help Sophie fall in love with someone else, but how can she stand in the way of her happiness? (978-1-63555-973-6)

Loyalty, Love, & Vermouth by Eric Peterson. A comic valentine to a gay man's family of choice, including the ones with cold noses and four paws. (978-1-63555-997-2)

Marry Me by Melissa Brayden. Allison Hale attempts to plan the wedding of the century to a man who could save her family's business, if only she wasn't falling for her wedding planner, Megan Kinkaid. (978-1-63555-932-3)

Pathway to Love by Radclyffe. Courtney Valentine is looking for a woman exactly like Ben—smart, sexy, and not in the market for anything serious. All she has to do is convince Ben that sex-without-strings is the perfect pathway to pleasure. (978-1-63679-110-4)

Sweet Surprise by Jenny Frame. Flora and Mac never thought they'd ever see each other again, but when Mac opens up her barber shop right next to Flora's sweet shop, their connection comes roaring back. (978-1-63679-001-5)

The Edge of Yesterday by CJ Birch. Easton Gray is sent from the future to save humanity from technological disaster. When she's forced to target the woman she's falling in love with, can Easton do what's needed to save humanity? (978-1-63679-025-1)

The Scout and the Scoundrel by Barbara Ann Wright. With unexpected danger surrounding them, Zara and Roni are stuck between duty and survival, with little room for exploring their feelings, especially love. (978-1-63555-978-1)

Bury Me in Shadows by Greg Herren. College student Jake Chapman is forced to spend the summer at his dying grandmother's home and soon finds danger from long-buried family secrets. (978-1-63555-993-4)

Can't Leave Love by Kimberly Cooper Griffin. Sophia and Pru have no intention of falling in love, but sometimes love happens when and where you least expect it. (978-1-636790041-1)

Free Fall at Angel Creek by Julie Tizard. Detective Dee Rawlings and aircraft accident investigator Dr. River Dawson use conflicting methods to find answers when a plane goes missing, while overcoming surprising threats, and discovering an unlikely chance at love. (978-1-63555-884-5)

Love's Compromise by Cass Sellars. For Piper Holthaus and Brook Myers, will professional dreams and past baggage stop two hearts from realizing they are meant for each other? (978-1-63555-942-2)

Not All a Dream by Sophia Kell Hagin. Hester has lost the woman she loved and the world has descended into relentless dark and cold. But giving up will have to wait when she stumbles upon people who help her survive. (978-1-63679-067-1)

Protecting the Lady by Amanda Radley. If Eve Webb had known she'd be protecting royalty, she'd never have taken the job as bodyguard, but as the threat to Lady Katherine's life draws closer, she'll do whatever it takes to save her, and may just lose her heart in the process. (978-1-63679-003-9)

The Secrets of Willowra by Kadyan. A family saga of three women, their homestead called Willowra in the Australian outback, and the secrets that link them all. (978-1-63679-064-0)

Trial by Fire by Carsen Taite. When prosecutor Lennox Roy and public defender Wren Bishop become fierce adversaries in a headline-grabbing arson case, their attraction ignites a passion that leads them both to question their assumptions about the law, the truth, and each other. (978-1-63555-860-9)

Turbulent Waves by Ali Vali. Kai Merlin and Vivien Palmer plan their future together as hostile forces make their own plans to destroy what they have, as well as all those they love. (978-1-63679-011-4)

Unbreakable by Cari Hunter. When Dr. Grace Kendal is forced at gunpoint to help an injured woman, she is dragged into a nightmare where nothing is quite as it seems, and their lives aren't the only ones on the line. (978-1-63555-961-3)

Veterinary Surgeon by Nancy Wheelton. When dangerous drugs are stolen from the veterinary clinic, Mitch investigates and Kay becomes a suspect. As pride and professions clash, love seems impossible. (978-1-63679-043-5)

A Different Man by Andrew L. Huerta. This diverse collection of stories chronicling the challenges of gay life at various ages shines a light on the progress made and the progress still to come. (978-1-63555-977-4)

All That Remains by Sheri Lewis Wohl. Johnnie and Shantel might have to risk their lives—and their love—to stop a werewolf intent on killing. (978-1-63555-949-1)

Beginner's Bet by Fiona Riley. Phenom luxury Realtor Ellison Gamble has everything, except a family to share it with, so when a mix-up brings youthful Katie Crawford into her life, she bets the house on love. (978-1-63555-733-6)

Dangerous Without You by Lexus Grey. Throughout their senior year in high school, Aspen, Remington, Denna, and Raleigh face challenges in life and romance that they never expect. (978-1-63555-947-7)

Desiring More by Raven Sky. In this collection of steamy stories, a rich variety of lovers find themselves desiring more, more from a lover, more from themselves, and more from life. (978-1-63679-037-4)

Jordan's Kiss by Nanisi Barrett D'Arnuck. After losing everything in a fire, Jordan Phelps joins a small lounge band and meets pianist Morgan Sparks, who lights another blaze, this time in Jordan's heart. (978-1-63555-980-4)

Late City Summer by Jeanette Bears. Forced together for her wedding, Emily Stanton and Kate Alessi navigate their lingering passion for one another against the backdrop of New York City and World War II, and a summer romance they left behind. (978-1-63555-968-2)

Love and Lotus Blossoms by Anne Shade. On her path to self-acceptance and true passion, Janesse will risk everything—and possibly everyone—she loves. (978-1-63555-985-9)

Love in the Limelight by Ashley Moore. Marion Hargreaves, the finest actress of her generation, and Jessica Carmichael, the world's biggest pop star, rediscover each other twenty years after an ill-fated affair. (978-1-63679-051-0)

Suspecting Her by Mary P. Burns. Complications ensue when Erin O'Connor falls for top real estate saleswoman Catherine Williams while investigating racism in the real estate industry; the fallout could end their chance at happiness. (978-1-63555-960-6)

Two Winters by Lauren Emily Whalen. A modern YA retelling of Shakespeare's *The Winter's Tale* about birth, death, Catholic school, improv comedy, and the healing nature of time. (978-1-63679-019-0)

Busy Ain't the Half of It by Frederick Smith and Chaz Lamar Cruz. Elijah and Justin seek happily-ever-afters in LA, but are they too busy to notice happiness when it's there? (978-1-63555-944-6)

Calumet by Ali Vali. Jaxon Lavigne and Iris Long had a forbidden small-town romance that didn't last, and the consequences of that love will be uncovered fifteen years later at their high school reunion. (978-1-63555-900-2)

Her Countess to Cherish by Jane Walsh. London Society's material girl realizes there is more to life than diamonds when she falls in love with a non-binary bluestocking. (978-1-63555-902-6)

Hot Days, Heated Nights by Renee Roman. When Cole and Lee meet, instant attraction quickly flares into uncontrollable passion, but their connection might be short lived as Lee's identity is tied to her life in the city. (978-1-63555-888-3)

Never Be the Same by MA Binfield. Casey meets Olivia and sparks fly in this opposites attract romance that proves love can be found in the unlikeliest places. (978-1-63555-938-5)

Quiet Village by Eden Darry. Something not quite human is stalking Collie and her niece, and she'll be forced to work with undercover reporter Emily Lassiter if they want to get out of Hyam alive. (978-1-63555-898-2)

Shaken or Stirred by Georgia Beers. Bar owner Julia Martini and home health aide Savannah McNally attempt to weather the storms brought on by a mysterious blogger trashing the bar, family feuds they knew nothing about, and way too much advice from way too many relatives. (978-1-63555-928-6)

The Fiend in the Fog by Jess Faraday. Can four people on different trajectories work together to save the vulnerable residents of East London from the terrifying fiend in the fog before it's too late? (978-1-63555-514-1)

The Marriage Masquerade by Toni Logan. A no strings attached marriage scheme to inherit a Maui B&B uncovers unexpected attractions and a dark family secret. (978-1-63555-914-9)